WITHDRAWN
FROM THE COLLECTION OF
SACRAMENTO PUBLIC LIBRARY

Unruly

By Ronnie Douglas

Unruly
Undaunted

Unruly

Ronnie Douglas

wm
WILLIAM MORROW
An Imprint of HarperCollins*Publishers*

This book is a work of fiction. The characters, incidents, and dialogue are drawn from the author's imagination and are not to be construed as real. Any resemblance to actual events or persons, living or dead, is entirely coincidental.

UNRULY. Copyright © 2016 by Melissa Marr. All rights reserved. Printed in the United States of America. No part of this book may be used or reproduced in any manner whatsoever without written permission except in the case of brief quotations embodied in critical articles and reviews. For information address HarperCollins Publishers, 195 Broadway, New York, NY 10007.

HarperCollins books may be purchased for educational, business, or sales promotional use. For information please e-mail the Special Markets Department at SPsales@harpercollins.com.

FIRST EDITION

Library of Congress Cataloging-in-Publication Data has been applied for.

ISBN 978-0-06-238962-6

16 17 18 19 20 DIX/RRD 10 9 8 7 6 5 4 3 2 1

Unruly

Chapter 1

ALAMO STOOD IN THE MIDDLE OF A SEA OF BOXES THAT filled his new house. He was no stranger to moving. Growing up, he'd been rousted from his bed more times than he could count to move to a new place in the middle of the night. His mother would let the back rent build up as far as she could, and then they'd skip out. Mix in a few turns in foster care over the years when she was arrested, and he'd become something of a pro at traveling light and moving quickly. This time, though, he was moving everything he'd accumulated over several years of stability. He had absolutely no desire to put it to rights in a new place.

Truth be told, this new house was the nicest place he'd

ever lived. It wasn't *home*, though. Home was a modest-sized apartment in Durham, North Carolina. Home was having his sister Zoe in the house, badly imitating his Spanish cusswords and singing like a cat in a surly mood—and he missed it.

He'd lost that right when he'd lost his temper. He knew it, but that didn't make it any less frustrating. He'd done the right thing, and there wasn't a minute of it that he regretted. The man deserved every punch, but that was neither here nor there. Truth didn't change facts, and the facts were that Alamo was a big man, and his long-gone father wasn't as white as his mama had been. Race shouldn't matter, but sometimes having darker skin still did, especially in a city where drug traffic was as common as it was in Durham. The police tended to blame it on one segment of the population, those with darker skin. He was a large man with darker skin. To add to that, once the police saw the motorcycle club patches on his jacket, Alamo was far too likely to end up in jail if he stayed in North Carolina.

This time they had a reason of sorts. He had put that *pendejo* in the hospital. And an uptown white boy in his expensive clothes could afford the sort of lawyers who twisted truth until it looked nothing like reality. Alamo knew it, had known it before he'd taken the first swing. Sometimes, though, a man had to stand up for a woman regardless of the cost. Zoe's friend had no one else to stand up for her, so Alamo did what needed doing. It was that simple.

"You can't just do that!" Zoe snapped at him when he'd

walked into the little apartment they shared. "I might not be a kid, but I still don't need my brother in the lockup."

"He hurt Ana."

"You are not the law, Alejandro. You wear that jacket"—she pointed at the vest with the Southern Wolves patches prominently displayed—"and you forget that you're not above the law."

"Lobita," he started.

"Don't you 'little wolf' me, mister!" His sister's hands landed on their customary position on her hips. She was a tiny little thing, but she had the attitude of a dozen girls. "If you end up in jail, I'll . . . I'll find someone big enough to kick your ass. Then where will you be, eh?"

Alamo bowed his head, as much to hide his smile as to let her know he was listening to her chastisement.

"You call Nicky, you hear me? You find out where you can move because you're not staying here. That boy . . . he has friends. I don't want this to get worse."

"Lobita . . ."

"No! You call your Wolves, and you move. *We talked about it for next year, anyhow. Clean start." Zoe took a shaky breath, let it out, and looked at him. "Ana says thank you and that she's okay. She's . . . sorry."*

"Don't need to be sorry. She did nothing wrong, Zoe. You make sure she gets that." His hands fisted despite his intention to keep calm, and the already bloodied knuckles smarted.

Alamo might not have had a father most of his life, but

he knew what a man was supposed to be like just the same. Growing up, he'd just studied what his mother's long list of lovers did. Whatever they did, he did the opposite. That was all the guidance he'd needed. That *was why Alamo went after the buttoned-up man-boy who'd gotten Ana drunk and taken what wasn't his right to take.*

"Call Nicky," Zoe said, and then she turned away. "And put ointment on those cuts."

She was right. Being the stand-in parent for Zoe had always been harder because she *was* right more often than not. Her excesses of common sense made her awfully hard to handle. Of course it also meant that it was less worrisome to leave her behind with Ana. She'd be okay; he knew that. Both of the Díaz siblings were survivors.

So far there hadn't been any charges filed, and the jackass who hurt Ana claimed never to have seen Alamo's face. He *did* see Alamo's jacket, though, and it was best for everyone if there was no reason for the police to be looking too closely at the Wolves. The local chapter president, Nicky, agreed with Zoe, so he'd made a call to another chapter. Within forty-eight hours, Alamo's things had been boxed, and he was in Tennessee. Between a move and a stay in jail, moving was a better choice—but that still didn't mean Alamo was happy with it.

He looked around the cluttered house. Boxes and furniture sat in a jumble, but he needed to get out. Being here, being alone with his thoughts, wasn't going to do anything but make him think about the mess he'd gotten mixed up in. He didn't regret it. He didn't think he was wrong to defend Ana. That didn't mean the consequences were easy to take.

He walked outside, pulled the door shut behind him, and headed to the bar that the Tennessee chapter frequented. Getting to know his new brothers was the best thing he could do now. The Southern Wolves were the only family he had other than Zoe, and while Zoe would visit, she was still in North Carolina while she finished up her college degree.

By the time he pulled his Harley into the parking lot of Wolves & Whiskey, he felt more like himself. All he needed was to stay focused. No distractions. No trouble. No fights unless they were ordered by the club. He had to focus on his job, the Wolves, and not let himself get invested in anyone else's life. He could keep his distance from everyone. That was the one surefire way to keep his temper under control.

No more bad habits. No more mistakes—regardless of how good the reason for them was. Tennessee was going to be the beginning of a new lifestyle, one that would keep him out of trouble and able to build a stable home for his sister once she finished college.

"ELLIE?" NOAH REACHED out, fingers catching a lock of hair and tugging like we were the kids we hadn't been in years.

Noah was turning twenty-four this year, old enough to have more of a plan for his life, old enough to stop running from anything that had even the shadow of commitment to it.

I was only two years younger than him, but sometimes I felt older. He was a mistake I kept making and had been making since not long after I was old enough to get a driver's license. Noah helped me learn, and we'd celebrated with what had turned into a decidedly unhealthy relationship. I wasn't ever going to get my life together if I didn't figure out how to change my bad habits, and Noah Dash was a bad habit. We were never going to be anything but friends who were naked together sometimes.

He was propped up on one arm in his bed, looking like we'd been doing exactly what we had been.

"Do you want a ride to the bar tonight?"

"I thought you didn't want me on your bike where we might be seen," I asked, my voice sounding a little more upset than I wanted to admit. He'd given me a lift to his apartment, but that wasn't quite the same.

"What's between us is between *us*," he said, as if that answer was going to sound less irritating with repetition. It didn't.

I rolled onto my side so I was facing him. "I'm going to drive myself."

"Come on, Ellie, don't be like that."

"Leave it alone." I folded my arms, feeling silly as I did so. It was hard to look stern while we were both naked.

"You know people would misunderstand if you were on my bike regularly." Noah's fingers trailed up my spine. "Showing up at Wolves is like a statement."

"Well, we wouldn't want them to *misunderstand*."

"There's no one else on the bike." Noah sat up and eased closer. "You know that, don't you? I might go on a date or whatever, but that's not anything. I just like a little strange, you know?"

"I know, Noah." I'd known that he wasn't particularly *celibate* before we were together, and that hadn't ever changed. It was his way of making quite clear that he wasn't in a relationship.

I wasn't sure whether I was more embarrassed that I'd wasted years in and out of Noah's bed or that I'd resorted to manipulation to try to get him to see that we *were* having a relationship. Either way, the truth of the matter was that Noah Dash wasn't going to change—and neither was I. I didn't want forever, but I was over being someone's secret. He wouldn't carry me on his Harley more than once in a while because people might think I mattered. God forbid, they might even think I was his old lady. The truth was that I was his best friend and regular bedmate since we were young enough to start exploring. That was it, though.

I used to think it was enough.

I used to think it would change, that he would change.

I even used to think *I* might change.

"Do you think you'll ever let people know about us?"

I asked, even now hoping that he'd tell me I was wrong, even now hoping that there was an answer he could offer that would let us keep this messed-up thing that we'd had. Neither one of us had ever tried dating anyone else. We'd settled for this, and it was no good. Not for me. Not for him.

"What if people *did* know?" I asked, pushing a little harder for the answer I hoped to hear.

Instead he looked as if I'd just told him I loved him. Sheer terror was written on his face. "Ellie . . . come on. People know we're friends. All they don't know is that we do *this*." He gestured between us at the bed. "Why would we need to tell anyone our business?"

That's all this was to him: friends who sometimes had sex. That was the bald truth. We were friends, so we talked, and if we were in a bad way about anything, we knew that we could call at any hour of the day or night. And if we had a need for something other than talk, we had that too. It looked a lot like a relationship, and maybe it was. It wasn't one that worked for me, though. I wasn't ready for kids or a husband or any of that forever stuff, but I was ready to *matter*. I was ready not to be a dirty secret.

And I was ready for someone who *knew* why I was in a lousy mood this week, who cared enough to remember what week it was, who understood why I needed reassurance. I didn't want to have to tell Noah to be kind to me because I needed it a little extra *this week*.

Noah wouldn't change, and I couldn't. What we had

wasn't enough. I was done with that, with *him*, with being the girl who didn't deserve more.

I started to climb out of bed to grab my clothes.

"Where are *you* going?" Noah tugged me back onto the bed and rolled me under him. "I just got you here, El."

"You got me here six years ago, Noah."

"I did, didn't I?" He grinned down at me. "Beautiful Miss Ellen, all naked and in my sheets . . . so why can't I take you to the bar tonight? It's been a while. No one would think anything."

"Just let it go. Please?" I asked, hating that he thought that my worry was being found out. I'd all but asked him to be open about us, and he still couldn't hear what I was telling him.

"I'll take you home later if you still want to get your car." He was curled behind me, holding me to him as he did only when he was too exhausted to remember that friends don't cuddle. He kissed my shoulder and murmured, "I hate when we fight, Ellie. Just think about it."

And then he slept . . . and I slid out of his bed for the last time. I felt like a thief as I tiptoed over to gather my clothes, shoes, and books—but better a thief than a fool. Maybe there wasn't anyone out there who would be happy to be with me. Maybe I was an idiot for caring that Noah didn't want more. I didn't mean to care, but I had enough of my heart in the mix that I couldn't stay, not if I wanted to respect myself at all. The next time I let a man into my bed, he sure as hell wasn't getting into my heart. Keeping sex and love in separate rooms was a safer plan. I didn't love Noah anymore, but I had been lingering on the edge of it far too long. I could love him like a friend, but I couldn't do it *and* sleep with him. I'd rather have love *or* sex because this half-assed mess of neither and both was breaking my heart. No matter what, though, I wouldn't be hidden away by anyone again.

"Never again," I promised myself as I went downstairs.

At the bottom of the steps, I pulled the building door closed behind me. Not for the first time, I was left stranded because of Noah Dash.

Truthfully, I was stranded in more ways than one. Job opportunities meant moving, and because of Noah I hadn't been willing to leave Williamsville. Admittedly, fashion industry jobs weren't thick on the vine in Tennessee—but those that *were* certainly weren't in Williamsville. I was here because of him, though.

My more immediate issue was getting out of his neighborhood. Later, when I was calm, I could think about getting out of town entirely . . . or decide if I really wanted to go. For now I needed a ride.

I could call my mother—who was more a roommate than a parent—but I didn't know that I was in the mood for her counseling me on patience. For reasons I wouldn't even try to fathom, she thought Noah could do no wrong. That left me with calling my friends who didn't know about Noah, calling Noah's cousin, Killer, or calling the bar.

I called the bar.

"What's up, little bit?" Mike asked.

"I need a ride. No questions, and no one who'd tell tales about . . . anything." I walked farther from the building where Noah lived. I felt like a vagabond with my boots, bag, and helmet, but I was afraid I'd wake Noah if I tried to put them on inside.

Mike sighed. "I can call a taxicab. Depending on who's working, they might not tell Miss Bitty."

"Ugh." I sat on the curb and shoved my feet into my boots. "Mama's got everyone in her damn pocket. I swear she'd put a tracking chip in my ass if the veterinarian would do it."

Mike snorted. "Don't go giving her ideas."

It was one of the mysteries of my life. My mother never put any restrictions on me, but she kept awfully close tabs on my comings and goings. There was no way that the local drivers wouldn't tell her where I was.

"I can send the new guy to fetch you," Mike said. "He just walked in. Seems a good sort. Wouldn't tell . . . either of the young'uns."

"That works."

Mike paused and cleared his throat before asking, "Do I need to guess where you are, or do I just assume you're *with* one of the young'uns?"

"Got it in one." That was the thing. People *did* know, maybe not everything, but enough for me to be embarrassed by the fact that Noah treated me like I was a secret.

"Do I need to send a helmet?"

"I have mine," I said, glancing at it, trying not to think of going shopping for it with Noah and Killer. "I just need a ride . . . and if you can avoid mentioning it to Uncle Karl or Echo."

Mike's tone shifted. "You know better than that, Ellen."

I nodded even though he couldn't see me. Everything to do with Noah or Killer was reported to the Wolves' president *and* to the biker who'd raised both boys. It was simply the way of it. Hell, I'd been the one reporting things over the years. Everyone did it. Echo cared about every little detail of their lives. Nothing was considered too insignificant to mention. Killer had coped by devoting himself to Echo, becoming Echo's right hand. Noah had done the opposite—refusing to even be patched into the Wolves.

"What's the new guy's name?" I asked.

"Alamo."

"Okay." Admittedly this was a somewhat silly question. I'd know him when he arrived because he would be wearing club colors, the Wolves' insignia clearly marked on either a black leather vest or jacket. Plus, there weren't any Wolves I didn't know *other* than the new guy, so a biker who arrived with club colors was obviously my ride. That said, I wasn't going to be rude and not know his name.

I disconnected and sat on the curb. I wondered if anyone else realized that this week was the anniversary of my father's death. Noah certainly hadn't, and that told me more than anything else. A man who wasn't there for me wasn't what I needed. A woman didn't *need* a man at all. Mama had been telling me that since my father died . . . but sometimes I wanted one, not just in my sheets but in my life. I wanted someone who cared about me, who remembered to hold me, who treated me like I was special. Instead, I was waiting for a stranger.

Chapter 2

TEARS OF FRUSTRATION WERE STARTING TO STREAK DOWN my cheeks when I heard the gorgeous growl of a Harley headed my way. There weren't a lot of Harleys in Williamsville that weren't ridden by Southern Wolves. It was sort of an unwritten law that if you were going to ride for pleasure but *not* be a Wolf, you rode something else. It was odd to me, but folks seemed to think it was a sign of respect to the club.

Regardless of what I thought of the town logic, the result was that I knew that the sound of a Harley likely meant that I'd know the rider. Noah didn't like drop-by visitors, either. It was just another way to keep me hidden. Well, it *had* been. No more. I wasn't anyone's dirty secret as of the past hour.

"No one respects a woman who doesn't respect herself," I whispered.

Then I stood, wiped the tears from my face, and watched the arrival of my ride home. So far Alamo had my respect. Loud pipes were something I always appreciated. People who didn't ride thought pipes like that were about arrogance or intimidation, but after you'd seen a biker laid up in the hospital because someone had plowed into him, claiming "I didn't see him!" you realized exactly why a Harley roared.

No one was going to miss Alamo. I was fairly sure that his pipes were only just this side of legal. As he cruised up the alley, I took a breath. I wasn't looking for anyone to distract me from what I'd just lost, but if I had been, I'd be glad my gaze fell on the man who'd just ridden up to me on a cherry-red Wide Glide. Alamo was tall; I'd guess he was over six feet. He had on a black leather vest that revealed broad shoulders and muscles that made him look like he should've been on a football field.

"Ellen?" he asked as he stopped beside me. Even with that one word, I heard a pleasant drawl. He'd obviously *not* moved to Tennessee from up north or out west. He was a Southern man.

I nodded, feeling oddly self-conscious. I'd heard that the new guy was from another chapter, but that was all. I hadn't seen him, and no one had described him to me. I didn't expect Mike to tell me that Alamo had almond eyes I could get lost in. Mike was rough and blunt, like most of the club.

"Climb on, darlin'. Bartender says I'm to carry you wherever you want to be."

"Is that so?" I asked. "What if I want to go to Wilmington and see the ocean?"

Alamo looked at me and grinned before replying, "Well then, I'd hope you're going to want to stop for a meal along the way because that's . . . what? Nine or ten hours easy?"

I laughed, pleasantly surprised by Alamo's relaxed attitude. Bikers as a rule were either wired too tight or mellow. Of course I'd seen even the calmest of them turn from chill to ready to throw down in a blink, so I wasn't naïve enough to think that what I was seeing was the all of it. A man as tall and built as Alamo undoubtedly needed to have fighting skills because wannabe badasses would've tried him.

"So the beach is a little too far," I said.

"It is."

"Any other restrictions?" I prompted.

Alamo shook his head. "Barman said you were in need of a ride, no questions and no trouble."

"Mike's good people," I said. "The Wolves don't put up with folks who aren't, though." I looked back in the direction of Noah's apartment, despite everything. Noah *was* a good guy, just not good for me.

Alamo looked at my tear-wet face and added softly, "What say we get going?"

I nodded and took a step toward Alamo. This was it, the start of a life without Noah. For years he'd been tangled up in my life, and I'd been waiting for magic to happen. Sometimes you just gotta cut bait and go. The magic I wanted wasn't going to happen for me or for Noah if neither of us was willing to move on.

"Do you have anywhere you have to be?" I asked impulsively.

"Nothing that won't wait." He shrugged. "What do you need?"

"Have you ever been to Memphis?"

"Not yet."

"I'll treat if you want to go," I offered. "I could go for a little music."

I knew that music wouldn't fix everything that ailed me, but it would go a long way toward making me feel better. My father had played, so I grew up with music until he passed. It used to be a joke that the best way to tweak my mood was with music, but no one tried it anymore—not since Daddy died and I stopped singing. Today, though, I wanted to sing. I wasn't going to make a habit of it, but I could break my silence for a little while.

"I'm in," Alamo said.

"Perfect." I put on my helmet and climbed onto the bike behind Alamo, careful to keep some distance between us. He might be easy on the eyes, but this wasn't a date or an invitation for anything other than a meal. I didn't want either of us to get the wrong idea. He wasn't acting like he had, but the reputation bikers had for casual sex wasn't all lies and exaggerations. Most of them had no trouble getting regular loving, and only a few of them turned down a little strange if it was offered up. I wasn't offering.

"You good?" Alamo asked as I settled my feet on the pegs.

"I will be," I said, surprised that I wasn't lying.

He started the engine, filling the quiet street with the sound of his Harley.

Alamo eased us onto the street and headed out of town, and I let my mind go silent. All that mattered was the feel of the road. Every curve and dip resonated through the machine, and the rush of the wind—even at lower speeds—was tantalizing. There was no metal frame, no cage between us and the world. There was no radio to distract us. It was air and nature. It was speed and elegance. Alamo handled his bike as if it was an extension of his body. There was no doubt in his management of the road, no hesitation in his choosing the right speed for each twist or turn.

An hour or so later, we were tooling down the streets of Memphis.

"Where to?" Alamo asked.

I directed him to BB King's Blues Club; it was a great spot for everything I needed just then: blues, food, and a great atmosphere.

By the time we had placed our order, Alamo got a call. He frowned and said, "I need to grab this."

I nodded, but he was already gone. I wasn't particularly displeased by the timing. I liked that it meant avoiding talking. I'd never been much for small talk.

I sipped my drink and watched a couple of women dance. The beauty of blues bars is that there isn't any sort of computer-generated music. Here it was the traditional stuff—guitar, drums, bass, and voice. This was the sort of music I still sang in the privacy of my house. Whether it was blues, rock, or country, the classics worked for me.

"Come on," a woman said as she shimmied past my table to the tiny dance floor. The band wasn't even on the schedule, and I wondered if they were just musicians passing through who felt like jamming for a few songs. They were all senior citizens, which made me like them even more. They were still jamming at their age and obviously loving it.

"If you're going to dance in your seat, you ought to be willing to dance with us," the woman said with a wide smile.

I glanced in the direction Alamo had gone. He was nowhere in sight, and even if he was, I didn't owe him—and if he thought I looked the fool out on the floor, I didn't much care. I was sick of thinking about what other people thought. "What the hell."

"That's right," the woman said and wriggled up to three other women who seemed to know her.

Two songs later, I was singing out loud as well as dancing. I hadn't realized that the singer had hopped down and was approaching me until he leaned in and put the mic near enough to pick up my voice. I started and stepped back.

He shrugged and finished the song from out there on the floor with us. He looked at me and frowned, and I met his gaze. I'm not sure which of us recognized the other first, but it was he that said, "Little Ellie, all grown up. Well, look at you."

"Mr. Lavon," I said with a smile. "Still looking spry and sounding damn fine."

The band had continued playing as we'd been chatting, and he looked up at them and said, "This here's Roger's little girl, Miss Ellie."

The drummer nodded at me. The other men might've too, but then Lavon asked, "Just sing us one song, little bit. Been a long time since I heard you sing."

I wanted to. I might've even needed to. That didn't mean it was easy. I'd not sung in public in years. People had finally stopped asking me to do so.

"I was sorry to hear about Roger," Lavon said quietly when I didn't reply. "I hope you and your mama been doing well."

The words at the end of the sentence went up in a manner that told a listener they could be either a statement or a question. It was a courtesy I always appreciated, a Southern tendency to ask without outright asking. Today I wasn't willing to dwell much on anything that could bring me down, and thinking about my father always did.

"We've been good," I said, being as truthful as anything I said could be when reducing a decade to a couple of words.

He nodded. "Good to hear . . . I've been down in New Orleans these last years. Moved away right before your daddy passed. I'd have been at the service elsewise. I didn't hear he was gone until a whole lot later."

I nodded. We didn't know each other in a talking way, and I suspect we were both near out of words already. "One song wouldn't be bad," I said softly.

"I could stand for hearing some Nina Simone. I remember you singing her with your daddy when you were just a wee little thing."

Briefly I glanced around the bar. There wasn't anyone here who'd hear me and let the folks back in Williamsville know, and it wasn't like singing was off the table when I'd asked to come here.

"Anyone here play piano?"

"Charlie," Lavon called into the mic, "get yourself up on the stage for Miss Ellie." Then he looked at me expectantly and extended the microphone to me.

I took it, but I didn't climb up on the stage. Here, standing on the floor with a man I'd only ever met when I was with my father, I felt like I could sing. Here, where none of my family of Wolves would hear me, I could let myself get carried away by the music.

So I did.

I closed my eyes and sang the opening lines of "Feeling Good." After I'd finished the first verse, the band came in right where they should.

The waitress who had taken my order when I'd been seated leaned in and said something to Lavon. He nodded at her, and she walked away. I was curious, but I figured if it was any of my concern, I'd find out sooner or later. For now I threw myself a little further into singing.

Even though I hadn't been feeling good when I'd arrived at the bar, I was starting to now that I was singing. Music healed. That was sheer truth.

I was *choosing* to feel good. I was choosing freedom. After today I was free of the way Noah had made me feel, free of the humiliation of hiding our relationship, and this was the beginning of a new life. I was going to change things, and no man was ever going to make me feel like I was something to be ashamed of.

Never again.

I channeled all my feelings into the lyrics, and it felt like a weight was lifting from me. This was what music did. It was why I needed to sing, why I still did when no one was listening.

Today, though, they *were* listening.

Lavon motioned to the stage, but I shook my head.

He pulled up a chair and nodded along with the song, as if it wasn't weird to sing from where we were.

When the song ended, he stood, and I handed him the microphone.

The band started playing "Baby, Please Don't Go." Lavon sang the first few lines to me, and I had to laugh. I danced with him as he sang to me. There was no way around it. He didn't go back onstage, and I didn't go back to my seat. He held the microphone out toward me several times so I could join him. I didn't sing much of the song, but I joined in enough that I was pretty sure we both knew I wasn't done singing just yet.

I danced and sang with a man old enough to be my grandfather, and as it almost always had, music erased any trace of stress for me. My upset over Noah wasn't completely gone, nor was the feeling of loss, but it was easier with every verse. I wasn't weak. I wasn't foolish. I was going to be just fine.

By the time Alamo returned to the table, I was singing the Stones' "Honky Tonk Woman" as a duet with Lavon.

I saw Alamo join the rest of the room clapping their hands in time with Lavon. Then he shook his head in wonder and sat down. It felt good to have him look at me, not that I was planning to do anything about it. I couldn't help preening just a little at being watched appreciatively, though.

I held up my hands in a "what can you do?" gesture and then leaned in to whisper to Lavon, "Just one more song."

He nodded, and when we finished "Honky Tonk Woman," he told the band, "Stones' 'Satisfaction.'"

We segued into the song, and he pointed at the stage.

Giving in, I gestured for him to precede me. He did so, and then he held a hand down to me like any proper Southern man should.

With a nod, I took it and rejoined him. We continued as we had been, taking turns with the lyrics as the mood struck us. There was something pure about singing like this—no grandstanding, no competition. It was about the joy and the music. Mama never understood why I wouldn't sing for money. I knew I *could* do it. We both did. Maybe someday I'd think about it more seriously; so far, though, that wasn't what I wanted. I wanted to focus on my designing for a career, but I wanted this in order to feel transported and free.

I let go of everything but the music.

By the end of the song, I'd all but forgotten the people watching us. Then they started applauding, and I glanced at them.

"Let's hear it for Miss Ellie," Lavon said. He grinned and bowed to me.

"And thank you, sir." I curtsied to him. Then I looked at the rest of the band and curtsied again. When I turned back to face the crowd, I waved and then made a sweeping gesture at the whole band and started to applaud. The listeners joined in. While they were doing so, I hopped down off the stage and walked over to my table.

I hadn't been seated but a couple of moments when the waitress brought our food over and told us that at Lavon's request the bar had comped our meal on account of my singing.

I looked up at Lavon, and he tipped his hat at me.

I blew him a kiss and mouthed, "Thank you."

"You always sing for your supper?" Alamo asked lightly when I turned my attention back to him.

"Been a long time, actually," I admitted. "I needed to sing tonight, though. I won't ask you to keep a secret, but I *will* tell you nobody would believe you if you told them I did it."

"Why's that?"

I shrugged and set to eating my meal. I didn't know him,

and I was already far more at ease with him than made sense. He wasn't making a big deal of it. He eyed me curiously, but that was it.

We ate our lunch without a lot of talk. That was something most people couldn't seem to do. I liked talking, but there were times that the only sound I wanted was music. When the band was decent, I saw no need to take away from it with a lot of words. Lavon's band wasn't going to break any new ground, but they were solid bluesmen.

When they took their break, Lavon stopped by the table, kissed my cheek, and told me, "You give us a shout you want to be up onstage where you ought to be, Miss Ellie. I suspect your daddy's old boss man would like you to do so too. Mr. Echo always did like your voice."

I promised I would, and he left us.

Alamo looked at me. "I feel like I'm missing enough things that I need to ask: Should I expect trouble because of bringing you here?"

A wave of guilt washed over me. He was new in town, and here I was telling him secrets and dragging him halfway across the state. There wasn't any reason to think trouble would be coming from it, though, so I shook my head. "I used to sing all the time, but when my father died—ten years ago now—I stopped. Today I ended things with the guy I've been . . ." I shook my head. I couldn't say *dating* and I wasn't going to say a vulgar word for what we'd been doing. Even if that's all it was to Noah, it had been more to me. "I realized I wasn't in love, and he's never pretended he was. We're friends who made a mistake, and now I'm done."

"A Wolf," Alamo asked. "The guy was a Wolf."

There wasn't a good answer to that, either. Noah was the son of the late club president, Eli Dash, and while Noah might not be flying club colors, he was still an unofficial club member as a result of his father. "More or less."

"Prospect?"

"No," I said carefully. There was no real way around it, so I clarified, "Dash's dad was the president before Echo. Dash is . . . commitment shy."

Alamo nodded, and I could see by the way he looked at me that he understood the words I hadn't expressed as well as those I had. All he said, though, was "So you and Dash split up, and—"

"We weren't ever together," I corrected. "I was his dirty secret. I'm done with that."

"Right." Alamo looked past me, frowning now. "And Echo likes your singing, but you don't sing."

"Echo knows I'll sing if he tells me to. My father was one of Echo's friends. A Wolf for life."

"So let me see if I have this, darlin'. You're the daughter of a Wolf who was regarded enough that Echo still cares about you—"

"Echo cares about *all* the Wolves' families," I interjected. "Echo's . . . there's nobody better for the club or club families."

Alamo nodded. “I’ve heard plenty good about him. Not disparaging him. I wouldn’t be here if I hadn’t heard the right things.” He caught my gaze before adding, “I’m just trying to see what I’ve walked into here.”

I realized that he thought there was going to be fallout. There was no way to avoid saying the things I’d really rather not. I owed him the courtesy of a blunt answer so he knew he wasn’t going to have problems with the Wolves.

“Alamo?” I started. Once he met my gaze, I explained, “Dash doesn’t care. As to the rest . . . Mike sent you to pick me up, and all we did was have lunch. There’s no stepping out going on here.”

He nodded, but I wasn’t sure he completely believed me.

“No one will be *angry* that I sang,” I added. “They might not believe it, but that’s all. Echo knows that I sing at home still. My mama . . . well, let’s just say that she’s pretty sure the Good Lord himself made Echo personally and on a particularly good day. If Echo told her he was able to call God up on his cell phone, Mama would ask him to pass along a few notes. She probably reports exactly what I sing and how often—and how much she’d love it if he’d maybe tell me to do it more.”

Alamo laughed. “Your mother sounds interesting.”

This time I was the one laughing. “Oh, you’ll meet her. Miss Bitty is like the local news when it comes to anything having to do with the Wolves. She’ll be coming round to get the scoop on you.”

We dropped to silence again for a few moments before Alamo said, "You don't owe me an explanation, but thanks all the same."

We were both quiet, but the ease that I'd been feeling had vanished. There was something else here, something I couldn't let happen. There wasn't any trouble coming right now, but I wasn't ready to start being attracted to another man. I hadn't done anything wrong, and I wasn't looking to do anything, but I couldn't deny the spark I felt with Alamo—not if I kept sitting here with him.

"Are you ready to head back?"

For a moment Alamo looked at me like he was studying me, but then he nodded, and that was it. My escape ended. Now all that was left was putting together my life as a truly single woman, instead of one who was only pretending to be single. I could do it. I knew that.

It still hurt.

Chapter 3

ALAMO HADN'T ENTIRELY BELIEVED ELLEN'S THEORY THAT Dash wouldn't care that he'd had lunch with her, but he realized that *she* believed it. He didn't know the guy, but whatever Dash had said or done was enough to convince Ellen that she didn't matter to him. That much had been clear. Whether or not she was right remained to be seen.

A day later, Alamo was at Wolves & Whiskey, sitting at the bar and enjoying a drink. He needed to start work the following week, but until then he wasn't doing much. He'd done enough unpacking to get himself sorted. He had pots and pans, towels and soap, bedlinens and a pillow, and of course his tools, in case the bike needed anything. Food, rest, bath, and bike were all in order. The rest could wait. That left him with time on his hands and no woman to distract him. In most of his life, that would've been a recipe for trouble. He was hoping that wasn't the case now. Seeing Dash stalking across the dingy interior of the bar, however, was leading Alamo to think that trouble was determined to find him.

"I hear you picked Ellie up at my place," Dash said, menace consciously in every bit of his body and voice as he walked up to stand next to Alamo at the bar.

Alamo shrugged and said, "Mike said the girl needed a ride. I picked her up in some alley."

"She was at my place."

Carefully keeping his attention on his beer wasn't quite enough to keep his disdain hidden. He was new here, and he really didn't want to be in a fight. He also really wanted to punch the idiocy right off Dash's face. Instead, all he said was, "Then maybe you ought to be the one driving her home."

"She is off-limits to Wolves," Dash stressed. "Stay away from her."

Alamo stood and turned to face Dash. There was a "favored son" air to him that made it clear that he expected people to obey him, but he wasn't backing that with fists or skills. It was a coincidence of birth that he was the young prince of this chapter. Regardless of *why*, it still should've been reason enough for Alamo to mind his own business, but something about Ellen made him feel protective. There weren't a lot of things that made Alamo want to take a swing at a man without provocation, but leaving a woman in tears was one of them. It meant that he'd disliked Dash before they'd even met. Now? Dash was only adding to the growing distaste Alamo felt. Being talked to as if he was an underling wasn't *ever* particularly good for his temper. If someone had the authority to do so, that would be different. Noah Dash didn't.

They stood, neither speaking, neither backing up. Dash might have started this because he was an entitled prick, but he held his position like he could throw or take a punch. It raised Alamo's regard for him infinitesimally. He grinned, and at his side, his hand curled into a fist.

"Everything okay here?" Killer's voice interrupted the tension, not erasing it, but inserting a pause.

Alamo shifted his gaze to eye the man who had walked up behind Dash. He didn't know many people here yet, but Killer had been present when he'd first reported to Echo. He seemed like good people when they'd talked—and he *did* have the authority to tell Alamo to step back.

"Just clearing things up about Ellie," Dash said, his voice much friendlier. "I don't think the new guy knew she was under my protection."

"Does *Ellie* know she's under your protection?" Killer prompted in the same light tone. "I thought you two were . . ." His words faded.

Dash said nothing, and Killer let out a low whistle.

"We had an argument or something, but she's still Ellie."

Dash looked like he might be frustrated enough to try to throw a punch at both of them. Alamo almost felt sympathy for the guy. Clearly he had no clue what was going on if he wasn't even certain whether they'd had an argument. That sympathy faded just as quickly as it had begun when Dash added, "She'll calm down and come back. She always does."

"Ellie's got a temper on her that would send anyone smart into retreat when she's all het up," Killer told Alamo. Then he grinned in a way that made Dash's hands ball into fists. "She's always been a feisty thing, but there are times that's not a bad thing at all. No guesswork about what Ellie wants or what she thinks."

There was obvious subtext, but Alamo kept his mouth shut. Whatever Ellen did or didn't do with either of these men was *her* business. He'd met her once, and although she was intriguing, she apparently wasn't as single as he'd thought from the sounds of it. Maybe she and Dash were one of those crazy couples who were on and off again like a strobe light. She hadn't seemed like that sort of woman, but Alamo had spent only a couple of hours with her and most of those were either riding in silence or listening to her sing.

Dash, for his part, looked like he'd been chewing glass.

Killer glanced at Alamo. "Dash says she's hands-off, man. That's clear?"

"Crystal."

Killer nodded and turned back to Dash. All grins were gone as he said, "Don't start shit with him for giving the girl a lift home because you fucked up again. You keep treating her like that and she's going to stay gone one of these times. You want to keep her? Man up, cuz. If not . . ." He shrugged. "Just don't start trouble in the house because of a girl who isn't even your old lady. We clear?"

"I'm not a Wolf, *cuz*," Dash said. "You don't get to tell me what to do."

Then he walked away.

Once he was gone, Killer pulled up a stool and motioned to the barmaid that she should get him and Alamo both a drink. Then he said, "Dash isn't a bad guy, but he's shit on sticking to anything. Club or woman. But he and Ellie have been screwing around for years."

"I gave her a ride. That's all," Alamo pointed out.

"Clear over to Memphis," Killer said blandly. "When Ellen sings, people talk. We got a call. Echo likes to know what she's doing."

"She was upset."

"That happens a lot where Dash is concerned," Killer said. "Those of us who know about them don't say anything. He might not be patched in, but he's family . . . so if he says she's off-limits, she is."

Alamo nodded.

Killer motioned to the barmaid. "Plenty of girls to go around, man. Dash certainly doesn't limit himself. He just likes to have Ellen to go back to when he's feeling like he wants a little talking or cuddle or whatever with his fucking. She deserves better, but for some reason, she puts up with him."

The barmaid came over with their drinks. She was a cute little thing, all curves and smiles. "Here you go."

Alamo took his drink from her, but he didn't comment on Ellen. Whatever her deal was with Dash, it wasn't Alamo's business. He wasn't getting involved. His temper was already an issue. That didn't mean, however, that he was going to be a dick to Ellen because of Dash.

Once the rather pretty barmaid walked away, Alamo said, "Just so we're clear: I told Ellen she could call if she needed anything, and I'm not going to take my word back."

Killer nodded. "Keep it platonic. I don't need to deal with property issues between you two. You're new here, and Echo's happy to have you. Says you're worth keeping here. Don't fuck it up. If you do, it becomes my problem, and don't neither of us want that to happen."

"Makes sense," Alamo agreed. He'd heard enough about Killer to know that he was a lot more experienced with violence than someone their age ought to be, but he'd been raised in the club and working for them since he was a kid. He was the current president's son whether or not anyone said so. It didn't take more than a glance to see their resemblance. Alamo had no intention of coming to blows with him, not because he couldn't handle Killer, but because there was no way to win that sort of fight. Losing wasn't appealing, but beating Echo's son was risky too. Doing so might mean Alamo wasn't going to be welcome in the club, and he needed the club.

"I'm not going to start anything," Alamo said.

"Good. That mess in Carolina seem to be following you here?"

Alamo shrugged. "Not so far. It was good of Echo to be willing to take me on."

"Wolves are family," Killer said, as if that policy was easy. It wasn't, but the simplicity of it was that the club was a lifeline to almost all of them at one point or another. The Southern Wolves had one another's backs.

"If it looks like it followed, I can move on," Alamo offered. Protecting the club was a priority, as much as the club protecting the members was.

"No need." Killer flashed teeth. "We got it. Just keep us updated."

Business concluded, Killer motioned the bartender over again. His intimidating expression faded into a warm flirtatious assessment of the young bartender, who preened under his attention. "My boy here is new to our chapter. I need you take him out and show him the town tonight, okay?"

"Anything you say, Killer." She smiled at Killer and then at Alamo. "Best job I've been offered."

Alamo couldn't deny that she was a pretty little slip of a thing, but he was a lot more interested in the beautiful singer he'd met earlier than the sweet girl in front of him. Nonetheless, he saw Killer's move for what it was and went along with it. He smiled at her and asked, "What's your name, darlin'?"

Chapter 4

"TELL ME WHAT YOU WANT ME TO SAY," NOAH SAID WHEN I walked out the front door a couple of days later. "I don't know what I said, but—"

"Nothing." I stepped around him.

"Bullshit." He stayed at my side as I walked to my car. "You ignore my calls. You haven't come by at all . . . So what did I do *this* time to piss you off?"

"Let it go, Noah."

"Is it someone else?" Noah stepped in front of me, forcing me to back up or shove him aside. I backed up. I wasn't ready or willing to touch him even casually. I had self-control in most things, but Noah was a bad habit. Resisting him wasn't easy, even now.

"It's not someone else," I told him, even as the thought of Alamo flitted through my mind. Alamo wasn't *why* I left Noah. I'd not even met him when I walked out on Noah, but I knew that I was noticing Alamo because I was over Noah. There was no way to explain that well, though. Telling him I'd been thinking of another man wasn't going to do anything good for Noah's temper.

"So what then? I don't understand, Ellie."

Noah didn't often admit to having feelings for me, and I wasn't sure that the ones he had would've ever turned into enough. Tonight, though, they were raw in his expression. Whether he could own it or not, he wanted more than this mess we had between us. Leaving him was good for *both* of us.

"I'm not angry," I said. "I promise. I'm just . . . tired."

"Are you sick?"

I laughed. I didn't mean to, but he had been my best friend for too long for me to forget the person he was when we weren't whatever we'd been trying to be. He was dense.

"I'm fine," I said gently. "I'm just not happy."

"So . . . you took a break," he said slowly. "You're not mad, but you're tired and unhappy."

There was something sweeter in him than I got to see these days, but in that instant I saw it again. He didn't understand. Even now that I'd explained it, he couldn't follow what I was saying.

"Don't you ever want . . . I don't know . . . to *matter*? To be in love? To get so drunk on someone that you don't want to get out of bed?"

He stared at me for a moment. The frown that flashed on his face was echoed in his voice as he said, "But you always have fun when we—"

"Never mind." I took a steadying breath. I didn't want to argue. I wasn't trying to talk him into anything. I had decided, and I was terrified that if I tried to explain, he'd talk me into staying. He'd done so often enough as it was. It wasn't something I could let happen again.

Sometimes saying goodbye was exactly what a woman meant—not a trick, not a plea to change. Noah and I weren't ever going to be what I needed or what *he* needed, and discussing it wouldn't change reality. It was sad and it hurt, but that didn't mean it was the wrong choice.

"Let me *go*, Noah."

He looked up and met my eyes. Maybe he understood. Maybe he was willfully obtuse. "Sure. You need to get to class." He smiled a little. "I could give you a ride."

"I'm fine on my own," I said levelly. "Just step aside."

At that, he tensed, and I knew he understood far more than he wanted, but instead of making things easier, he gave me this determined look and said, "Take your space and rest or whatever it is you think you need, but . . . I'm not going anywhere."

I sighed. Where was this determination when I wanted him to take a chance on us? Where was it when I *wasn't* already walking out the door? I wasn't going to go backward—and even if I wanted to, he wasn't offering me something worth going back to. He might not be going anywhere, but he wasn't willing to claim me as his woman or even publicly acknowledge that we were dating and had been for a long time. Noah might believe that what we had in private was enough, but it wasn't. Not for me. Not anymore.

Never again, I reminded myself.

Noah opened my car door, and I slid into the seat without another word. It would almost be easier if I *were* mad at him. Getting ugly was something I could do. Yelling was high on my skills list. Walking away wasn't something I'd ever done. It felt like failure, and I didn't particularly like the feeling.

I swiped at a few stray tears as I drove away from him. It was for the best. He might not see it yet, but if we stayed the way we'd been, I'd end up hating him. Right now I thought I could still find my way back to friendship. It wasn't going to be right away, but I believed it was possible. First, though, I had to manage to stay quit of him.

The next few weeks felt a lot harder than I anticipated. It wasn't that I necessarily thought it would be easy after Noah and I stopped being whatever we were, but I don't think I expected it to be as hard as it was. Stupid little things throughout the day made me think of him, and I kept starting to text him or email him or call him only to realize that I couldn't. We'd been in each other's back pockets for most of our lives, and going from that kind of closeness to total silence was hard.

By the third week, I realized that I really missed my *friend*, not the man I'd been sleeping with, and somehow that made things even less comfortable. There was something a little heartbreaking in the realization that what I wanted back in my life was my *friend*, not my lover. I wanted to find a way to have one without the other, but I wasn't sure we knew how to do that yet or if I could ever have Noah's friendship once I started dating someone else. I wanted to believe that we were adult enough to do that, to go back to where we had been, but we had never been known for bringing out the best in each other.

I was able to distract myself soon enough, however. Not only did the new semester start up, but my old English teacher's granddaughter, Aubrey Evans, moved into Williamsville. Echo was interested in her, and I wasn't foolish enough to ask whether it was because of who Aubrey's grandmother was or because Killer was sweet on her. It didn't matter, though. I simply did as I was told—sent Aubrey out to the bar, kept my eye on her when I saw her on campus, and let her know I was around if she needed anything. It wasn't *just* spying for the club. I liked her too. It had taken all of three minutes for me to like her enough to want to call her a friend.

Nothing I did was unethical. I sent her to apply for a job, and I gave her my phone number. I might have done both *without* knowing Echo wanted her looked after. As it was, it was both a genuine act of concern and obedience to the Wolves. It worked out. If it hadn't, I would've defaulted to club orders. That was simply the way of it.

There was no harm in it.

The harm came from the way that watching Aubrey put me in Alamo's path again. I was at the ice cream shop indulging in some well-deserved dessert therapy when I ran into him. Dairy Delight had a small yard behind the shop, so after buying a cone, most people went through the back door to the benches, tables, and chairs out there.

I stopped in shock at the sight of Alamo. He was sitting on a picnic table outside the shop with a red-and-white cone. It was an oddly adorable look for a leather-vest-wearing, six-foot-plus, muscle-bound biker.

"Strawberry and vanilla?" I asked. The shop had only four flavors: the standard vanilla and chocolate, plus two daily specials.

"Better than *that*." He crinkled his nose at my chocolate and pistachio cone. "You got a problem with strawberry?"

"I like things that are either dark or have a bite." I shrugged and stepped up to the bench. I had a moment of wondering if I ought to be thinking about propriety, but shook it off and sat on the table like I always did if it was cleanish. Alamo's gaze dropped to my bare legs briefly, and I had to hide my smile by licking my cone—which made his gaze shift abruptly.

"Why are you so concerned with Killer's girl?"

I stared at him. I knew damn well that Aubrey wasn't the thought on his mind as his gaze lingered on my legs or on my mouth. He knew her only through the bar, which was a lot less well than I knew her. He *also* had known Killer only a few weeks. Admittedly, they were both people who were easy to care about, but I wasn't so innocent as to mistake a sudden digression for anything more than a distancing tactic.

And I wasn't interested in playing games where I was the loser anymore. I took a leisurely lick of my cone, swirling it as the tip of my tongue carved patterns in the ice cream. Once I had his attention, I smiled and said, "Well, *darlin'*, I've known Killer since we were in nappies. I'd pull a trigger for him. I'd take a slug for him, so don't *ever* suggest that I might have any ill intent toward that boy."

Alamo held his hands up in a gesture of surrender, which was silly looking with a pink-and-white ice cream cone in one hand. "Just asking, darlin'."

"Well, unless you're Killer or Echo, I'm not answering." I smiled to be clear that no sting was intended, but I wasn't going to be interrogated or allow him to do so to pretend he wasn't looking at me like I was the next treat on his mind.

He watched me in silence for a moment before asking, "Are you doing okay?"

"I'm fine," I said firmly. That tactic did a lot more to take the flirt out of me. I didn't want to talk about anything serious, didn't want to be reminded that he'd seen me sad. I wanted to be lighthearted. "Perfectly fine."

"That you are," Alamo said after a moment. He grinned at me and this time he looked at my legs very obviously. "Any man would have to be blind to not notice that fact, darlin' . . . and I suspect blind men would catch on the moment you spoke."

I laughed. "Damn straight!"

We sat there for a comfortable moment before he stood and tossed the rest of his ice cream in the trash bin. "You holler at me if you need a friend."

Biting back the exceptionally inappropriate response that I had, I nodded. What I needed was fun, relaxation, and a good ride. He looked like exactly the right prescription for all of the above, but he tossed the word *friend* around so pointedly that I wasn't about to ask how far his definition of friendship stretched. I wasn't sure I was ready to be there with another man either. Being over Noah wasn't the same as being ready to ride with another man.

So I kept my peace and said goodbye to Alamo. My ice cream cone wasn't anywhere near as satisfying as a good ride and post-ride roll with a gorgeous man could be, but it was a helluva lot less complicated.

Chapter 5

A FEW MONTHS LATER, I WAS A LOT LESS SATISFIED WITH desserts and . . . well, everything in my life. I'd become closer and closer to Aubrey, who had definite plans for every detail of her life—too much so, really. I didn't want to be that ordered, but talking to her made me realize that I had short-changed myself. She hadn't meant to give me a wake-up call, but she had. Now I needed to figure out what to do with that epiphany. It was one thing to realize that you needed to change your life. It was another to figure out *how* to do it. Making any real change seemed huge and overwhelming. Even figuring out where to start seemed like a task I couldn't begin. I wanted to, but I didn't know how.

I went to look at my design notebooks. If I was going to get to a new place, I'd need new designs . . . or maybe just more samples. What I'd love to do was find clothes that reflected the sense of the South, to create pieces that captured not only the romance and the ferocity that Southern women embodied but simultaneously flattered women who weren't afraid to have dessert. Too many styles were about hiding any perceived imperfections or were simply unflattering to women with curves.

Southern women—black, white, and brown—had a "don't cross me" attitude that they could demonstrate while being ladylike and delicate all at once. It was, to my way of thinking, the epitome of what it meant to be a woman. It was what bikers' women were like: graceful and terrifying simultaneously, appreciative of a strong man but not afraid to handle things themselves. If I was going to design clothes, I wanted them to speak of that duality.

I started sketching. I wanted clothes a woman could wear onstage, knowing that all eyes were on her. In my mind's eye, I pictured the small stage at BB King's Blues Club. What would I feel sexy and confident wearing up there? Maybe the key was looking to the classics—just like in a lot of the music I liked.

Over the next week or so, I mentioned my plans to Aubrey a few times, sorting through her closet and trying to get a sense of her style. I offered to lend her a few of the clothes I'd sewn from my new ideas. Her self-esteem was starting to grow, but there was still something tentative in the way she moved and acted. It was as if a stronger woman hid under her skin. I'd see glimpses of her, but then she'd insist on locking that sultry and ballsy side away. Clothes, in my opinion, are modern armor. We don't need them to stop arrows or blades. We just need them to give us courage, like armor once did. If I could reach my ideal, it would be in this area.

Aubrey and I had lunch together several times, and she was fast becoming a good friend. I was still surprised to see her name on my caller ID not an hour after I'd just seen her.

"Miss me already?" I answered, instead of saying hello. "Class *just* ended."

"Are you busy tonight?"

"What happened?"

She lowered her voice to say, "I think Noah sort of hit on me . . . or something."

I almost laughed aloud at how shocked she sounded. I liked Aubrey, but her confusion when guys found her attractive baffled me. Too many women were like that, and I hated that Aubrey was one of them.

"And you're offering him to *me* instead? I'm not sure he's going to go for that idea."

"Ellen!" Her answering laughter let me know that I'd done my job as a friend. Sometimes that was what I valued most in friendships, the parts that weren't obvious. I could handle the obvious ones too, of course, so when she asked me to go to the races and act as a buffer with Noah, I agreed. I wanted to be there for her. I was also hoping that letting

Noah see that I was okay being around as his friend would help us reach the place I wanted us to be. I wanted things to be better. I missed the friendship part of what we'd had. He knew me in a way that I wished we could have back—although admittedly sometimes I wished the same thing about Killer, and it had been years since we were truly close.

I got myself ready, and then I went to dress up Aubrey. She seemed to think my urge to do so was a joke or selfless, just a favor to her. It wasn't. I was trying to design, and she made a great model. We were roughly the same size—although she was a bit bustier than I was.

Aubrey's discomfort meant that I had to go a little slow. The jeans we agreed on were her own, but I lent her a green tank, kicking aqua cowboy boots, and a statement necklace. Seeing her in classic country woman was a great start, but that wasn't unique enough for the feel I wanted. So I added starlet makeup—cherry lips and heavy eyes—as well as a hairstyle that was a bit of a 1940s homage. By the time I was done, she had a sexier Rosie the Riveter thing going on. It wasn't so risqué that she'd be uncomfortable, but it was a bit more "notice me" than she typically sported.

She'd settled in, and I felt as if I could see the stress melt away as we walked. Men and women noticed her, and whether it was conscious or not, on some level she could see their attention and liked it. Then the first real test walked up to us.

"Aubrey?" Noah said.

I stayed back, watching him stare at her. I could see him

tense up at seeing me there with her. He'd seen us talking on campus, seen us having lunch, but that didn't mean he was at ease right now.

Then Aubrey motioned to me. "Do you know Ellen?"

"Ellie," he said, sounding awkward, like he didn't know what to do or say. "It's been . . . a while," he said after a too-long pause.

My temper slipped at the awkwardness we had still between us. I'd thought I was ready to be friends again, but my lingering anger slid into my voice as I said, "Has it? I hadn't noticed."

Noah tensed, and he stared at me for a long enough moment that I thought he was going to say something that put it all on the table. Then he turned to Aubrey and asked, "Is that Ellie's shirt?"

He knew it was. It had been on his floor more than once. He couldn't say that, though, and oddly or not, considering my anger, I was glad he was not letting that secret out. I didn't want to have that conversation here or now. I didn't want Aubrey in the middle of it, especially when I had zero intention of the past mattering now.

"She needed a dress-up doll," Aubrey was telling him. "Apparently I'm going to be going shopping with her too."

He nodded. "She has a great eye for that sort of thing."

This time I was the one tensing. Was this an olive branch? I smiled at him before looking down. I was doubtful that anything would come of it for them, not with the way she lit up every time Killer was mentioned, but I wanted *all* of them happy. Despite everything, Noah and Killer were my oldest friends. Aubrey was fast becoming a new friend, so I leaned in and whispered in her ear, "Not a date, my ass. He's certainly hoping. You could do a lot worse than Dash."

Then I squeezed her hand and left.

Aubrey was well looked after with Noah at her side, and the Wolf *I* wanted to talk to was sitting in the bleachers. The Wolves always sat in the same section. Much like a lot of other things in town, what had been merely habit had evolved into an unwritten law. That was one of the benefits of living in the same town for long stretches of time: you knew the unwritten laws. Only Wolves and those connected to the club sat there. There was no one saying that other townsfolk *couldn't* join them, but even though the club was tolerated—and looked at as almost a volunteer police force sometimes—a crowd of black leather and tattoos was off-putting to most people.

I wasn't most people. Something warmed in me when I saw them. Echo wasn't here, but Billy was, as were most of the younger Wolves. Killer was racing, so I wasn't surprised to see the group of them there. Big Eddie, Hershey, and Skeeter were together, loud and raucous as usual. Alamo was with them, but he was frowning at his phone when I started up the bleachers. The other three lifted beers in greeting. Hershey called out, "Little bit!"

Alamo, however, didn't see me approach.

I wasn't there to see him, but I was going to try to talk to him. Maybe it was like my designing: I just needed to woman up and try harder. He'd never been outright rude, but he seemed like he'd been avoiding me the past couple of months. Tonight, though, there was no way for it to be subtle if he *was* avoiding me. There were a lot of Wolves and their old ladies here. That meant that we were both just part of the crowd.

"How's Miss Bitty?" Big Eddie asked.

"Cantankerous as always."

Skeeter snorted. "I swear the boy's got a crush on your mama, Ellie."

Big Eddie shrugged. It was far from the first time he'd been accused of that. He was a bit over halfway between my age and Mama's, so I wasn't so sure what to think. Mama was young when Daddy died, with a school-aged daughter, and Big Eddie came round to help out a lot. It wasn't anything untoward, but it made for a strange relationship between us. He was young enough to be friends with Killer, but old enough to regard me more like a favored niece or little sister. It had made him increasingly tense with Noah over the years.

"You see Dash?" he asked in a voice a little too edged for my liking.

"He's here on a date with my friend Aubrey," I said as levelly as I could. I looked up and met Big Eddie's gaze and told him, "I have no problem with it."

He shook his head, but didn't reply.

"Red? The one Killer's growling over?" Hershey prompted.

I nodded.

"Dash never was too bright," he muttered.

Alamo had put his phone away at some point and was watching us silently. I wanted to be witty or wise or charming, to make him talk to me, to somehow show him that I was worth his time and trouble. Instead, I was tongue-tied.

"You all right?" he asked quietly once the others were back to focusing on whatever football or basketball or hockey game they'd been discussing.

"Completely," I said truthfully. "Aubrey's good people, and Noah's a great guy."

The look on Alamo's face said everything he wasn't saying. "If you need anything . . ." he offered.

There was a part of me, a blunt and reputedly off-putting side, that wanted to tell Alamo exactly what I *did* want from him, but he hadn't given me any reason to think he'd be receptive. A lot of the Wolves were folks who wouldn't look at me with lust in their eyes if I did a striptease right in front of them. I suspected they would stop me, put a blanket or shirt or something over me, and tell my mama that I needed a talking-to. They either knew my family or had known me since I was a kid. The only Wolves I had dated were those just passing through—and Noah. Admittedly, Killer and I had gone riding once or twice, but I was fairly certain that was as much about Killer trying to prompt Noah to man up as it was anything else.

Of course, as much as I appreciated both the club as a

whole and the men individually, I hadn't been interested in inspiring any lust in most of them either. Alamo was different.

"I doubt you'd want to hear what I need," I told him lightly.

He studied me in that way of his, as if I was a puzzle he couldn't quite solve. I couldn't decide if I liked it or found it obnoxious. I liked that he was looking at me, but I didn't like not knowing what he was thinking.

Then he smiled. "Darlin', you might just be surprised."

I smiled back, hopeful that maybe we were making progress finally, but then Noah and Aubrey showed up. Alamo's friendly smile faded. He nodded at Aubrey, but that was the extent of his greeting.

Noah said nothing to me, but Aubrey motioned me over.

As much as I wanted to stay and talk to Alamo, I'd come with Aubrey as moral support. That was what friends did.

I wasn't there but ten minutes when I saw Alamo leave. I couldn't say whether he was leaving for good or just going for a walk. He wasn't toting anything with him, but he wasn't the sort to carry much in general. He left his helmet on his bike—most of the Wolves did—and there wasn't need for anything else.

The truth was, unfortunately, that Alamo had a habit of vanishing anytime I was alone with him *or* if Noah was around too. As much as I tried not to watch Alamo go or notice the pleased look on Noah's face, I doubted that I was very subtle—a theory that was confirmed a few moments later when Aubrey asked, "Is everything okay?"

"Dash and I grew up together," I said. I wanted to know *why* Dash was smiling at Alamo's departure. Did they have words? Was there something there that I didn't know? Sometimes new Wolves took issue with the way Dash was and was not a Wolf. Maybe Dash was sore that Alamo had been the one to pick me up when I'd left months ago. That seemed unlikely because it had been *months*, but stranger things had happened. Explaining what was wrong would take too long, though, and it would involve sharing secrets, so all I said was, "Sometimes he irritates me."

"Do you want to go? We can—"

"No," I interrupted Aubrey. "I want you to have fun. Enjoy the races. Enjoy *Dash*. He really is a great guy. We just had words last time we talked, and seeing him . . . I forgot how angry I was until I saw him."

Alamo didn't come back. I tried not to let it ruin my mood. I was out with friends and my virtual family. I was enjoying a beautiful Tennessee event with great weather. By all rights, I should've been happy.

My less-than-ideal mood was nothing compared to Killer's, though, after the race when he and Noah and Aubrey had a run-in. Anyone who couldn't see the sparks flying between Killer and Aubrey would have to be blind. I couldn't decide who I felt worse for. Killer and Noah had both been my friends long enough that I wanted to see them happy, and they'd never seemed to genuinely be at odds over a girl. Aubrey had enough going for her that I was certain she didn't need to feel like a chew toy being tugged two ways.

I tried to keep my mouth shut and waited.

Finally Killer turned to me and said, "I'll walk you both to your car then."

Like most of Killer's actions and words, this statement was more order than question. He was so much like Echo that it was a little uncanny sometimes. I felt like he was putting me in the middle of a drama I didn't need, but my silence wasn't helping.

"I can take you home, Aubrey," I offered, hating that I was left navigating a mess. Aubrey clearly wanted Killer, but both of the boys were looking at her. It reminded me far too much of seeing them fight over too many things when we were kids.

Aubrey looked half sick when she glanced at Killer and said, "No."

And for the first time in longer than I could remember, it was Killer I wanted to defend and protect. I'd never seen him look at anyone the way he was looking at Aubrey. He stared at her as if she'd just stomped on his heart. For all of his attitude, he had a softness hidden under the muscles and tattoos.

Gently I nudged his arm. "Come on."

Aubrey shot me a grateful look, but Noah didn't glance

my way. Unexpectedly, Killer nodded at me, and after an awkward moment, we walked away.

I wasn't surprised that Killer didn't look back. I wasn't even surprised by the tight fists he'd curled his hands into. "Are you okay?"

He shot me a look that would've made me step back if I hadn't known him since forever.

"You know what I mean," I clarified.

"She's mine." Killer looked increasingly determined as we walked. "I'm not going to be okay as long as she keeps walking away. There's something there. She knows it, too."

"She isn't like us," I reminded him gently. "The club is our family. She can't see that."

He stared at me, but he didn't comment.

Killer hadn't ever been one for heart-to-hearts. There were a few rare conversations, but as a rule, he wasn't a talker . . . which was why I was caught unprepared when he said, "Are *you* okay?"

I frowned at him. "Why wouldn't I be?"

"Dash."

"We're . . ." I tried to think of the words that weren't lies but weren't admissions. There wasn't a good solution there. "Noah and I are friends. That's all."

Killer quirked his brow. The same look was one everyone had seen on Echo's face enough that it worked *almost* as well when Killer did it. "You two aren't usually split up this long."

I opened my mouth, couldn't find words, and closed it again.

"If you're going to work things out, maybe now's a good time. Red's the sort of woman who could make a man throw everything away. Dash isn't going to be with her, but . . . if you two are—"

"Are you asking me to patch things up with Noah so he's out of your way?" I gaped at Killer. "Seriously? The rest of the world might not realize that you were a *ladykiller* before you decided it was the sort of name that chased off the women, but I haven't forgotten. Don't think I'm going to either." I shoved my arm into his shoulder. "Your game gotten that weak, Ladykiller?"

He gave me the sort of simmering assessment that had resulted in a lot of women forgetting their common sense and said, "Not likely."

I laughed. "Then figure it out, because I'm not getting with Noah ever again, even to help your sorry ass get the girl." I shook my head. "Man, I never thought I'd see the day when the great Ladykiller needed help with a girl. Used to be they were ready to wrestle for a chance in your line. Oh, how the mighty have fallen!"

Killer narrowed his eyes at me, but the corner of his mouth lifted in an almost smile. "Red won't know what hit her. I'm going to find a way. This one's the *one*, Ellie."

I could hear the boy I used to know in his voice. This was my old friend; under the leather and the gun and the fists, this was Zion, the boy he'd been before he started answering to Ladykiller *or* Killer. I smiled at him. "I hope you can figure it out then . . . for both of you. I like her, you know?"

He nodded.

"I still like you, too." I paused and then added in a small voice, "I've missed talking to you."

He nodded again. "Don't know why we stopped talking. Sure, Dash was a dick after you and I . . ." His words faded. "I should've been around, though, not let Dash's issues mess up our friendship."

"Right there with you," I admitted. "I hated that you knew about me and him, but I still had to pretend you didn't."

"You know that *you* were the last time Dash and I were at odds over a girl. The only other time, actually," Killer pointed out. "That time I stepped off. He said you were his, and I stepped away."

"Then tell him to do the same now," I suggested. "If Aubrey means that much . . ."

Killer gave me a slow smile. "Difference between Dash and me is that I want her to *choose* me. I don't want to be the only choice she could make, but the one she wants to make. Stupid, maybe, but there it is."

We had reached my badly dinged and faded Honda Civic, and when we stopped, I looked up at Killer and told him, "It's not stupid at all."

He nodded and motioned toward the car. "Go on. I need to go tend to a few things, and I'm not going to be able to go do any of them until you're in the car and on your way."

I debated pointing out that I'd have been walking to my

car on my own, that I did so all the time, that I was the daughter of a Wolf, so most people wouldn't bother me anyhow. Killer knew all that. The fact was, he'd always had an overprotective streak, and if we were going to be friends again, I'd need to either deal with it or fight with him regularly. I decided I'd *try* to accept it.

"If it's meant to be with her, it will be," I told him.

Killer grinned. "It is. Red's the one. She just needs to admit it."

I shook my head, not in doubt but because I felt a little bit of sympathy for Aubrey. Killer wasn't the sort to let anyone or anything stand in the way of what he wanted. Neither was Noah. That used to be something we *all* had shared, but I'd let myself forget it. I wanted things with Noah to work, but he hadn't. If he had really wanted us to work out, we would've. That was all the proof I needed to realize that we would've never been more than the half relationship we'd had. Once Noah realized that, too, we could resume our friendship. He would realize it eventually. The thought made me smile slightly: I'd have my friend back someday. Of course, then I'd have both him *and* Killer circling me like rabid guard dogs again.

I climbed into the car, thinking about the past and the future. Noah and I weren't meant to be, and we'd been fighting it by pretending that we could be something we weren't. If Aubrey and Killer were *right* together and they both wanted it, they could find a way. That was the magic: fitting and wanting it to work. Noah and I had neither, not in a relationship way. The longer we'd been apart, the more obvious this became to me. When I was around Alamo . . . I felt something unexpected. It was a click, a strike of lightning, that rare zing that marked an incredible possibility. That didn't guarantee anything, but I wanted the chance to find out.

Chapter 6

LIFE WENT BACK TO NORMAL. I WORKED ON MY DESIGNS and tried to keep up with everything else. The familiar routine of it was comforting. I wanted more, but after years of drama with Noah, I'd come to enjoy the peace of the way things had been the past few months.

Okay, I wasn't *entirely* enjoying it. I was frustrated that Alamo hadn't so much as asked me to grab coffee. His gaze lingered often enough that either he was studying me like I was an insect or he liked the look of me, but he did nothing about it. So when I finally ran into him at the parking lot of Wolves & Whiskey bar alone, I stepped in his path.

"How are you?"

He looked at me, expressions on his face changing so

rapidly that I didn't know what to think. After an awkward moment, he said, "I'm good."

"You seem busy."

"Settling in with the club." He shrugged. "Doing a few jobs."

The door opened and a couple of strangers came out of the bar. Alamo tensed as he glanced at them. I wasn't sure if it was simply the tendency of Wolves not to like people walking behind them or if it was being seen with me. I tried to tell myself that not everyone was like Noah. There was no reason I could think of that Alamo wouldn't want to be seen talking to me.

"Are you okay, Ellen?"

"Always."

"Did you need anything?"

I forced a smile and said, "No. I just never seem to be able to catch you unless there's a bunch of people around, so I thought I'd stop you . . . Sometimes it's nice to talk without an audience, you know?"

Alamo looked away from me, gaze fixed on the door of the bar as if he was expecting it to open again. When he glanced back at me, he said, "You let me know if you *do* need anything."

"Right," I muttered. "If you don't mind, just tell Aubrey that I'll call her. You'll save me a few minutes. I was to be here, and I can't stay, so . . . do you mind?"

Apparently, it wasn't just a coincidence that he was never around long when I was. Sure, he offered to be there for me if there was an emergency or a crisis, but offering to be there was just what the Wolves did. Bikers were all about protecting the people that were part of their club. Since Alamo's first encounter with me was a rescue, it wasn't shocking that he was stressing that he would be there for me. He knew that Killer and Noah cared about me, so it was good logic to watch out for me. Maybe it wasn't all politics—and I hoped it wasn't—but it wasn't what I wanted from him, either. His attitude today made it far too clear that he wanted nothing to do with me.

I tried to tell myself that it didn't hurt, that it was nice not to have a plateful of drama. I tried to convince myself that it didn't sting that Alamo rejected me at every turn. I tried to pretend that it was better to know now. I lied. I felt that connection, that potential for electricity, and I wanted it.

He obviously didn't.

"Are you sure everything is okay?" Alamo asked as I started to turn away from him.

I waved over my shoulder without turning back. "A lot to do," I lied.

Then I got in my car and drove away without even glancing at him. It was silly to let myself care that a man wasn't interested in me. I'd spent enough time dealing with that with Noah. I wasn't going to do it again . . . except I couldn't seem to stop thinking about Alamo. I felt like the air around us was humming when I saw him. How could he not feel it, too?

I cranked up the radio and sang the whole way home.

Like always, music was the cure to my mood. I wasn't so foolish as to think that singing would fix the *causes* of my emotions, but it let me siphon them off so I wasn't a wreck because of them.

When I pulled in at my house, I was extra glad that I'd done so. The man sitting on my front porch was the one man I owed the most loyalty in this world. The president of the Southern Wolves was the man who'd protected and sheltered my mother and me for as long as I could remember. His visits weren't always a good omen, but as the daughter of a Wolf, I was still at his command—as were the families of the rest of the Wolves. We could've stepped away from the club when Daddy died, but instead we'd become even closer to the Wolves, especially Echo.

I cut off the engine. The lack of music seemed suddenly loud in that way that sudden absences can be. My tension was lessened slightly as Echo looked my way and gave me a small smile.

"Ellen," he said by way of greeting as I walked toward him.

"Echo," I said as lightly as I could. It was still an effort not to sound like a child about to be chastened when I was alone facing him. Of the three of us who had Echo's attention growing up, Killer was the only one who managed to pull off sassing Echo. Noah and I still looked at the club president like he was a combination of God and Santa Claus.

It wasn't exactly normal to see Echo on my step, but I had always been more niece than anything to him. Maybe it was just that Dash and I were Killer's childhood playmates, or maybe it was that Dash and I lost our dads, but he paid close attention to both of us, too. There weren't a lot of club-related deaths, but things happened. It was inevitable when guns, tempers, and cash were just a part of business. Regardless of the reason, I had a complicated relationship with the man who held the leash on the rest of the Wolves.

"Tell me what you think of the new guy," Echo said when I sat down on the steps in front of him.

"Alamo?"

Echo nodded. Much like his son, Echo didn't usually phrase things as questions but as orders. Usually, however, with us there were pleasantries of a sort. He was a gentleman. Even if his business included drug deals, gambling, and strip clubs, Echo still remembered his manners.

"What do you need to know?" I asked.

He shook his head. "Everything."

"Killer trusts him" was my first answer. There wasn't a higher endorsement I could give. Killer was a great judge of character.

Echo nodded. "You?"

I resisted the urge to just blurt out "Yes!" because this wasn't a question of libido or even affection. Echo was asking my opinion, and it wasn't the sort of thing to take lightly when *he* wanted my opinion. There was obviously something on his mind if he was asking about Alamo.

"He's a good man," I said. "Loyal to the club. Came around asking why I was paying attention to Aubrey"—

I paused and met Echo's eyes before continuing—"and I told him that it wasn't his business, but he was trying to look out for Killer. He offers me help, but isn't . . . asking for . . . anything."

Echo gave me a paternal look before saying mildly, "I know you're not an innocent, Ellen, but thank you for not spelling it out any further."

I fought a blush. "My point is that he's a gentleman. When Noah and I . . . you know, I assume?"

"That you kicked him to the curb? I knew the day Mike sent Alamo to fetch you home." Echo gave me a patient look. "You are the only one outside the club who's spent time with him."

"I'm not exactly outside the club," I muttered.

Echo quirked a brow at me. It was an old argument. I didn't exactly raise my voice at him over it, but it was certainly a subject that we'd discussed in heated tones. "You're not patched in, girl. That's never going to change. Women have their place, and it's *not* in harm's way."

I sighed. "I trust him. He's got good instincts, is aware of his surroundings, pays attention to the little things, and . . . hides it behind a drawl and throwaway smiles. He's kind without looking for anything in return, and he's loyal to Killer."

We sat in silence then, and I waited. Echo wasn't one for a lot of extra words or noise. It was a trait of his that I'd adopted years ago, and I found myself slipping into silence more with him and Killer than anyone else. Most of the bikers were noisy bastards, and my mother managed to *speak* even when she was technically silent. Echo's silence was comforting. The only other biker I'd met who seemed able to just *be* in silence was Alamo.

Finally Echo nodded at me and said, "I always thought one of the boys would snap you up. They both missed out."

"Thank you, but . . . I wasn't what either Killer or Noah needed, and they aren't what I need."

Echo sighed. "I would've liked you to be with one of them. They're good men, and you've grown into a good woman. Roger would've been proud."

My throat tightened a bit at the mention of my father, but I only repeated, "Thank you."

"He wouldn't like that you stopped singing, though. You ought to start singing again, but I suspect it'll happen sooner or later, won't it?" Echo lifted that one brow inquiringly again, and I knew without his having to say it aloud that he knew that I'd been singing in Memphis. "A man who can get you to sing might not be someone Roger would dislike, either."

"It was the anniversary of Daddy's death. I missed him extra, and . . ."

"So you had Alamo carry you to Memphis to sing."

I nodded. Aside from my one afternoon in Memphis, my car was the closest to a public place where I sang. Sometimes I sang at home, but Mama was an unholy terror about it. We'd had the Talk about what a career I could have if I'd "use my God-given talent" one too many time *years* ago.

These days, it was one of the few surefire ways for us to end up in a fight.

"No shame in that, Ellen. Miss Bitty would prefer you to sing here. She misses Roger's singing too." Echo held my gaze, and I suddenly felt like a recalcitrant child again. It wasn't anywhere near the first time he'd made me feel that way.

Usually Uncle Karl and my mama handled discipline, but when Noah, Killer, and I had all three ended up in a brawl with some drunks one Friday night a couple years back, Echo had been the one to take us to task that night—*after* Uncle Karl had read the boys out and Mama had done the same with me. That was the night Echo went into a long, patient, level-voiced explanation about our responsibility to the town. Wolves had an obligation to protect their territory and their subjects. The citizens of Williamsville might not consider themselves subjects of the Wolves and I might not *be* a Wolf, but as far as Echo was concerned, that was how things were. None of us had argued.

And I wasn't arguing today.

"I know she misses him," I told Echo. "I know she likes my singing, too. I just . . . I don't want to sell a record, or even know if I could. I want to design clothes."

Echo gave me the sort of look that made me feel like I was missing the most obvious thing in the world and said, "Is there some rule I don't know about that says you can't do both?"

I grinned, both in relief that he'd spoken lightly and because I liked being teased by him. "There are things you don't know?"

He laughed. "You only get away with that sass because your mama'd lay into me if I growled at you for it like the boys got."

I mock-shuddered, instead of pointing out that I'd never *truly* sass him. "I'd have taken your growls over Mama's groundings any day of the week."

"I don't know any clothes people, but you know I have ties over Memphis way and in Nashville if you decide to sing more often," Echo said blandly.

"Yes, sir."

He laughed again, and I was grateful that I'd been able to cheer him a little bit. He patted my shoulder in what substituted for an affectionate embrace from him and added, "Now I know you're sassing me, missy. You don't 'sir' people."

"If anyone rates a 'sir,' it's you." I felt a little embarrassed at saying it aloud, but there was no shame in admitting the truth. Echo had always made sure Mama and I were provided for, and I knew for certain that there was money that showed up in our bank account because of him. He didn't make a thing about it, either. He simply provided for us when we needed it. Wolves were only supposed to have your back for life, but the club had been there for us a lot longer, even though my father was long gone.

A lot of folks misunderstood bikers. They didn't realize that a motorcycle club was really just a big family, one with a few more crazies than a lot of families owned up to having, but a family all the same. Families looked out for one another. That was just the way of it.

"Do you need me to do anything? For the club? Or . . . ?" I asked. I might not know what all Echo planned and plotted. It was best that way. The one certainty was that I owed Echo my loyalty.

"Not right now," he said. There were no false expressions of gratitude or faux misapprehensions. Echo knew he deserved my loyalty. I suspected, not without reason, that he assumed he deserved *everyone's* loyalty. Most of the time I thought he was right about that.

"If there is . . ." I said, wanting him to know that I could be every bit the dependable Wolf my father would be if he were still alive. A woman couldn't be a Wolf, and I had no desire to change the system. There were plenty who did, who saw all sorts of things wrong with our way of life, but at the end of the day, I was who I was. If I didn't like it, I wouldn't be keeping my roots here at home. If I took issue with the things my biker family did, I wouldn't still be here. And if I didn't like the options for me within the club, well, I wouldn't take up with a Wolf in a serious way. Some women were like that. Aubrey was looking like she was one of them, and *that* was okay. Me? I would give my support where Echo wanted it as a way to pay back a little of what he'd given to us over the years. I wanted him to know that too.

I looked at him and said, "I might not wear colors, but my heart still belongs to this family."

Echo nodded. "I know that."

There was a not-so-small part of me that used to wish he'd court my mother. It was moments like this, when he was smiling at me the way my dad used to, that made me feel that way. He and my mother wouldn't suit each other, and I knew that now that I was older. I also knew that I missed having a father, and as far as I was concerned, there wouldn't be anyone else likely to be able to fill my daddy's shoes.

"You think about what I said about singing, and give Miss Bitty my regards," Echo said, and then he was gone.

I watched him walk back to his Harley. It wasn't often that Echo was out without a shadow, but whether he had bikers at his side or was on his own, Echo walked around like he was invulnerable. He might even believe that he was, but I remembered uglier days. I remembered when my father died. I remembered the conversations I wasn't to overhear—when Killer, Noah, and I hid and eavesdropped. There was a good reason that Killer dogged Echo's steps.

Worst of all, I remember Mama drunk and sobbing, breaking every one of Daddy's records until I called Echo and he came to the house. Big Eddie was with him. He'd stayed on our sofa for weeks that time, looking after us. Back then, I thought it was just on Echo's orders. Now I knew better. Wolves look out for Wolves—and for a Wolf's blood family. No one needs to order them to do it.

But that didn't mean that I had to keep being looked after. That was what Echo was meaning, even if he didn't come right out and say it. He was right, like always. I should reconsider singing for money. I loved it, and maybe I could do it without sacrificing my other passion. Selling a few songs might be a way to make money for Mama and me, money that the club wouldn't need to give us. I felt suddenly guilty that I hadn't thought about that before. It wasn't that I wanted us to be beholden to Echo, but I hadn't wanted to sell my voice. There were dreams that were too real, too important. If I failed at most things, it wouldn't be devastating, but singing was something that I'd held on to as a link to my father. Surrendering that, being rejected for that, would break something inside me, and I didn't know that I'd recover from it.

On the other hand, accepting Echo's offer to make some calls was a lot less appealing than I'd have liked. If I succeeded, I needed it to be on my own merit, on my own terms, not because someone knocked down doors for me. There were things I could accept, had accepted, over the years from the club. I paid them back with the same loyalty I'd expect to have been given by my father. This wasn't about the club, though. It was about me. That meant I needed to do it my way.

Before I could think twice about it, I picked up the phone and called Alamo.

"Are you okay?"

"Is that how you always answer the phone?" I asked lightly.

"You've never called until today." He sounded slightly calmer, but he paused and added, "Are you?"

"I think so," I said, feeling silly now that I had him on the phone. "I want to go over to Memphis . . . and I want you to come with me."

Alamo was silent so long I thought he might have hung up. Softly I asked, "Are you there?"

"I am."

"Okaaaay . . ."

"Maybe Dash should take you," he said.

This time I was the one who went silent. I was torn between defending myself and telling him to fuck off. The one and only time we'd discussed Noah in any real detail was months ago, and that was the day Alamo had seen me tearful.

"If you don't want to—"

"I didn't say that." Alamo sighed. "This is a favor for a friend you're asking for, right?"

"It is." I was feeling more mortified by the minute. "You know what? I'll drive myself. It was stupid to ask you to c—"

"I'll be there in twenty. Thirty tops. Just let me make a call, and then I'll be headed your way." He hung up before I could reply, but that might've been the best thing because I had no idea what I would say. Calling him had been impulsive, but it had seemed like a good idea . . . up until he answered the phone. Now I wasn't sure whether or not I even wanted to wait for him.

Okay, that was a lie. I *wanted* to, but it was a thoroughly ridiculous thing to want. I felt like I was throwing myself at him. He'd all but said I was bothering him, not just by his silence but by bringing up Noah. Sadly, despite those facts, I still wanted to see him. I wanted him to come with me to sing. I wanted him to carry me home afterward . . . and stay for a while.

I was pitiful.

Chapter 7

ALAMO LOOKED DOWN AT THE PHONE IN HIS HAND LIKE it was a viper. Ellen wasn't making anything easy for him. It was hard enough watching her sit there while Dash flirted with Aubrey in front of her, but now she was calling him, asking him to go to Memphis. She hadn't said that she and Dash were on the outs, but they obviously must be fighting if she was asking Alamo instead of Dash to carry her over to Memphis—not that having her on his bike was a hardship. She had exactly the right sort of everything to make him forget good sense: a curvaceous body, bold attitude, and smart mind. Add in that voice of hers, and it was almost too much appeal in one person.

She was also firmly off-limits. It wasn't fair, but life

wasn't supposed to be fair and Alamo wasn't about to start whining about it now. He hadn't bitched about any of the bullshit that was far from fair growing up, so he wasn't going to start whining over being denied a woman—even one as ideal as Ellen.

What it meant practically was that Alamo had to keep his distance from Ellen. He'd been working at it. He'd left the races so he didn't slam his fist into Dash's face. He'd managed to avoid being alone with Ellen almost entirely. He was polite, but he let himself exchange words with her only if there were others around. He wasn't going to get into a clusterfuck with the new Wolves chapter because he couldn't keep his hands off someone else's property—and that was what it meant that Dash had her under his protection. Ellen was *his*. No questions. No exceptions. If Dash wanted to grant an exception, he could, but without his say-so, no Wolf was allowed to touch Ellen. Alamo wasn't the sort to ask permission, and even if he were, Dash sure as hell wasn't going to grant it. That left Alamo in a lousy spot. Every time she talked to him, it was like she was inviting him to risk everything. He couldn't do it.

He also couldn't tell her no—which was a ridiculous situation to be in. Getting into a world of bullshit for giving her a ride wasn't appealing. He'd settled in here, and the trouble from Carolina didn't seem to be following him. The last thing he needed was to have to go back there or have to go somewhere else because he stirred some shit here.

Alamo closed his eyes and smothered a growl.

He picked up his phone. There should be a better option. Asking anyone for permission was not his style. Ignoring the consequences wasn't a possibility today, though, not unless he wanted headaches he *really* didn't have the patience for. That left him very few choices.

He did the only thing he could do: he called Killer.

"I'm carrying Ellen over to Memphis. She wants to sing."

"You volunteer?"

"No. I suggested she call Dash." Alamo tried not to sound as surly as he felt. The last thing he wanted was to pass Ellen over to Dash, even for a second. He'd done it, though. He was playing by the rules despite the fact that Dash was acting as if he could set his own rules. "I don't know if they're fighting or—"

"Christ, Alamo! I'm like to grow a pussy the way you're talking."

"Fuck off." Alamo wasn't sure there was any shame in admitting to thinking about a woman's situation rather than just her body, and truth be told, Killer was the same when it came to Red.

Killer laughed.

"Seriously, I hate that I'm doing this shit, but I'm asking if this violates the rules. I get that she's under Dash's protection. I get that she's hands-off. I also gave her my word that I'd be around if she needed me. Tell me that I'm in the clear here, or call her and tell her that I'm not. Your boy Dash has put me in a situation."

"Not my boy," Killer muttered. "Fucker took my girl out to the races."

"I was there. Left because he was sitting there with Ellen, too."

"You couldn't chase his ass off my girl?"

"Red know she's your girl?"

"We're working on that," Killer grumbled. "I've got your back with this trip, but don't make it a habit and just . . . keep your hands to yourself." He paused, and then he shocked Alamo by saying, "And tell Ellie I'm glad she's singing again. I missed it."

Alamo considered remarking on the fact that Killer was just as soft as he'd accused Alamo of being, but they both knew it already.

After they disconnected, Alamo grabbed his jacket and helmet and headed off to his torture. Having Ellen on his bike again, knowing the whole time that she was off-limits, sounded like a fresh ring of hell.

He pulled up outside her house.

It wasn't Ellen who walked out the door, though. An older woman, presumably Ellen's mother, stepped out. She was beautiful in that way that only strong women can be. Attitude radiated out from every hard-edged muscle, and she wasn't the least bit subtle about her sexuality: jeans that were all but painted on, a halter-type top, and bright-red toenails all screamed "Look at me!" Unlike Ellen, she was rail thin. She had curves, but not the way Ellen did.

Her mother looked like life had carved away anything that might be mistaken for softness.

She paused on the porch, lifted a cigarette to her lips, and looked at him.

Alamo tensed a little, realizing that his assessment had been noted and filed. She wasn't smiling, but she didn't look angry, either. In the custom of so many women, she was weighing and measuring him, deciding if he had worth or was useless.

She didn't light her cigarette. Instead, she descended the stairs and walked out to the street where he was.

"You're the new Wolf," she said by way of greeting. Her entire attitude was one of confidence, as if she were the old lady of one of the oldest club members. If he'd heard right, she very well might've been, except that he'd died years ago. She wasn't wearing a vest like most of the old ladies, but she had the attitude that made quite clear that she deserved—and expected—respect.

"Yes, ma'am," he said. "Alejandro Díaz. Most folks call me Alamo."

"Miss Bitty," she said as she peered up at him. "You're not all white. Most of the Wolves here are. I got no issue with you, but some folks will."

He grinned. "Ellen gets her subtlety from you, then."

Miss Bitty looked him up and down. "I got no problem with your skin—the color or the muscles it's covering up. You're easy on the eyes, Alejandro. You're okay in a scuffle?"

"Yes, ma'am."

"If you're spending time with Ellen, you keep her safe. I find that she gets hurt on your watch, and I'll be making a call to Echo. Understand?"

He met Miss Bitty's fierce gaze and said, "I have a sister. I raised her most of our life. I understand completely."

Miss Bitty stared back at him, studying him as if she was a juror holding his fate in her hands. He wanted to tell her this wasn't a date, but for a moment he wanted her to give her approval more. Logic won over impulse, and he said, "I'm just here as a friend. Ellen wanted a lift."

"Dash know you're here?"

Alamo shook his head. Miss Bitty didn't mince words at all. "Killer does. I have his permission to be here *as Ellen's friend.*"

"He's a good boy." Miss Bitty glanced back at the house. Then as abruptly as all the rest of her remarks, she said, "Ellen's singing is all from her daddy. Hell of a voice my Roger had. Ellie's better, though she won't do squat with it."

"I got my never-fading tan from some guy my mother slept with, and my hatred of drugs from the way she couldn't keep quit of them." Alamo met Miss Bitty's gaze. "Anything else I can tell you?"

She looked down, taking him in from boot to jacket before meeting his eyes again. "Already asked Echo about you, pup. You might be a friend; you might be something else. Right now, I have no trouble with you. You're following club rules, and Echo speaks well of you. Killer does, too. Fact is that you took my Ellie to sing. Not just anyone could get her to do that."

He debated telling her that he was there to do the same again, but volunteering much of anything to this woman seemed unwise. All he did was nod—and hope Ellen showed up soon. Searching for a way to buy a little time, he reached into his pocket and found a lighter. Silently he held it up.

Miss Bitty nodded, and he flicked the lighter while she leaned forward and lit her cigarette. After she inhaled, she said, "Since you're minding your tongue so careful, I'm going to guess she's going singing again."

As casually as he could, he told her, "Ellen didn't say where we were going, just asked for a ride." It wasn't a lie, not precisely.

The older woman let out a cigarette- and whiskey-edged laugh and turned away. He wasn't sure whether he was to follow her or not. She was as unsettling as the guys had said she was. He couldn't fault her for the way she was. He was protective of Zoe, and when he dropped a warning on whatever boy she brought around, he wasn't nearly as *subtle* as Miss Bitty was being.

Chapter 8

I GLARED AT MY CLOSET AGAIN. I WANTED TO DRESS UP, BUT Alamo should've already been here. I didn't have much time to primp—and it wasn't like this was a date anyhow. I pulled on a prettier blouse all the same. I wasn't lacking in the bust, but this shirt emphasized what I had to best advantage. Then I grabbed my leather jacket. It was weathered, sturdy, and unadorned.

Unlike my mother, I had no right to wear club colors. The only way a woman could wear a Southern Wolves patch was if she was someone's "old lady." Then she'd get a "property of" patch too. Being a Wolf's daughter or niece or ex wasn't enough. I was all *three* of those, but I wasn't anyone's old lady. Aubrey had been willing to give up on Killer in order not to wear those patches. I didn't understand it, but like Killer and Dash, I had grown up within the heart of the club.

The difference was that Dash could easily be a Wolf. I, however, was a woman, and woman weren't allowed to be Wolves. Wolves also couldn't ride anything other than Harleys or Triumphs. Like most 1% clubs, there were rules that were pretty set in stone.

The Southern Wolves were unusual in that they also allowed bikers who weren't Caucasian. It seemed odd sometimes that the Southern Wolves were progressive on this, but I figured it was because they were a newer club. A lot of the other clubs had histories that stretched back to the eras when racism was far more tolerated. Then again, the other reason could be simply that the founder of the Southern Wolves had done a lot of time, and his cellie was a ranked member of a gang out of Chicago. When the guys who had your back were Latino, it wasn't likely you were going to get out of prison and forget that. Maybe a lot of people didn't believe it, but there was definitely a code. Honor among thieves was a throwaway phrase for how it worked, but it was *truth*, too. When someone had your back, you remembered it. When someone did you a solid, you repaid it. When they did you wrong, you repaid that, too. It was pretty straightforward, and even though I wasn't ever going to be a Wolf, I lived by that same credo.

I wasn't shopping for a Wolf of my own, but I sure as hell wasn't dismayed if one worth noticing happened to look my way. I'd been riding with Killer years ago, and until a few months ago, I'd ridden with Noah in secret. Somehow, though, neither of them made me half as excited—or nervous—as Alamo did. There was something about him that made me feel nigh on crazy. It made me want to fuss with my clothes and try to be whatever it was that made him look back at me with that same sort of *want* in his eyes . . . even just a little of it.

I glanced out the window, only to see him standing there with my mother. He looked even better than usual, sporting his club vest that bared most of his arms. He was bigger than Killer and Noah, but just as fit. For a moment, I stared in awe—and disappointment. It was a cruel twist to have a man built like that waiting for me and know I wasn't going to be able to enjoy him.

Then reality hit: regardless of how fine he was, my mother was there with him. I wouldn't wish her undivided interrogation on most people.

"Shit!"

I grabbed my helmet and scurried downstairs as fast as I could. Unlike most of the Wolves, Alamo hadn't had the dubious pleasure of my mother's undivided attention before. God love her, but that woman was terrifying even if you *did* know her.

With as calm a smile as I could manage, I jerked open the front door—just as she was reaching for it.

Her grin was knowing. "Worried, Ellie?"

"You're a bit much sometimes, Mama." I leaned in and

kissed her cheek. "But you know I wouldn't trade you in for all the gold lost at sea."

"So you say," she teased. "What about all the lost blues songs?"

I pretended to think. "Nah. I'll just write new ones and keep you."

For a moment she stared at me in silence. Then she reached out to cup my cheek. I could smell the mix of menthol cigarettes with her vanilla and lavender perfume. It was a scent that was uniquely her and always had been. "You could write amazing things if you wanted."

"Maybe I will," I said softly. "Or maybe I'll just sing a little."

"When you're ready . . . I'd love to hear them."

I nodded.

"Your daddy would be so proud of you already, Ellie, but knowing you're singing again . . ." She teared up. "I know he's up there smiling at us."

"Or saying, 'It's about damn time,'" I added.

"That too." She blinked away tears, which mostly just meant that they clung to her mascara-heavy lashes. Then she patted my cheek and lowered her hand. "Go on with Alejandro. He's not running despite meeting me, so he's got balls at least."

Alejandro? I glanced back at Alamo, who had walked back toward his Harley. He looked a little perplexed, but Mama did that to a person when she was in a mood. I looked back at her. "Did you threaten him?"

She patted my cheek again and stepped around me. When she turned back, she grinned. Then the door closed on me as I stared at her.

I shook my head and walked out to Alamo.

"She's a bit intense," I said.

He shrugged. "Family is supposed to protect family. She was just making it clear that you were to be treated like you should."

"How's that?"

He slung his leg over the bike before answering. "With respect. Kept safe."

I climbed on the bike behind him, not sure what to say. It wasn't that I wanted to be disrespected or hurt, but I got the impression that Alamo was already keeping me so far away from him that Mama's warnings were far from necessary.

We exchanged no other words. He turned on the bike, and after he checked to be sure my helmet was on, he eased out into the street. There was something like teasing at the start of a ride. The engine wasn't nearly as unrestrained as it could be, and the initial slips and slides into and out of traffic weren't as fast as they could be. Everything was still low-key.

And I kept my distance from Alamo. He wasn't mine, and from the way he treated me, he had no interest in *being* mine. There were moments I thought he might—glances that proved that he was aware that I was female, hints of heat in his eyes, and a slow rolling drawl as he spoke. Today, though, the man steering the massive motorcycle underneath me was as distant as he could be while sharing a small space. My knees were against him, but I stayed back as far as I could.

He kept the speed moderate, and the only hint I had that he was in possession of the passion I knew he had simmering inside was when we were stopped at a light and some asshole and his buddies pulled up alongside us in an overpriced sedan. The passenger had his window down, and he was all but leaning out.

He grinned, staring like I was something cheap and easy. When the sleaze made what I guessed was to be a sexy come-on face at me, Alamo let out an honest-to-goodness growl.

The sleaze ignored him and said, "Damn, girl! Why you wasting your time with—"

"Mind your fucking manners," Alamo snapped.

"You want to start something?" the sleaze taunted.

Alamo put the kickstand down, and for the first time I got a glimpse of the man that I'd heard about. Up until that moment, I'd seen only the sweet biker who, while distant more often than I'd like, was infallibly gentle. This was another face of Alamo.

"Four of us. One of you," the man taunted from his car. He stared at Alamo, and I wanted to point out that Wolves weren't unaccustomed to brawls. The buttoned-up man in the sedan didn't strike me as a fighter; neither did the others I could see in the car.

"Let's just go," I murmured, my hand coming down on

Alamo's biceps. The touch of his bare skin under my fingers was electrifying, so much so that I didn't pull away.

Alamo glanced at my hand, but he didn't reply.

"They're not worth it," I added.

"Slide off."

I listened. Maybe it was being raised around Wolves. Maybe it was a biological need to obey that tone in his voice. Either way, I dismounted the bike and stepped to the side.

The light turned green, and cars went around us. The sedan didn't move. Alamo didn't look away from them, not even for the cars zipping by us.

"Open the door," he ordered.

Unlike me, the men didn't obey him. The window rolled up and the locks came down. From the look on the front passenger's face, I could tell it was the driver who was responsible for both.

The men were all clean-cut, khaki-wearing, and didn't look like the sort to even pay attention to a woman on the back of a Harley—at least not so as to be obvious about it. Guys like them looked, and more than a few made stupid remarks when they saw me on my own. It didn't happen often. Once it was obvious that I was frequently in the company of bikers, most men discovered manners, but when they thought they could be asses with impunity, they were.

The door started to open. Presumably the nitwit in the passenger seat had unlocked it.

Alamo stepped closer and reached for the door handle.

All I could do was try to take in what details I could. I looked closer at the car. Dark blue. Newer. No visible dings or scratches. No defining traits I could see on the two passengers in sight.

Someone inside—not the passenger in the front seat—was yelling, "Go! Jesus, just *go*."

As the sedan sped away, I noticed North Carolina plates. I suspected Alamo saw them too. For a moment Alamo stared after them, and then he walked back over to the bike as if nothing had happened.

"Someone you know?" I asked.

"Not that I recall." He shook his head. "Are you okay?"

"I'm fine."

"Good." He threw his leg over the Harley, shrugged, and said, "They had no business looking at you like *that*."

I couldn't help it. I leaned forward and kissed his cheek. He drew in a sharp breath and froze. If he were any other man, I'd think his reaction was interest, but from the way he'd been so far, I was doubtful. Maybe he was trying to be polite. Maybe he thought I was throwing myself at him. I wasn't sure there was any way to ask that, and he wasn't offering any clues.

We stayed like that, him motionless and silent on the bike and me standing in the street behind him. The light turned yellow, and cars rolled up behind us. Finally he said, "Get on."

Mutely I obeyed.

He didn't comment, but simply restarted the bike. Once

the light changed again, we were back in traffic as if nothing had happened.

By the time we arrived in Memphis, I think we'd exchanged maybe five short sentences, and those were simply for the purposes of navigation. I wasn't angry so much as hurt, but being hurt was making me angry. I hadn't been the one to start shit in traffic. I hadn't done anything to encourage the fools in the sedan, and I hadn't done anything wrong by thanking Alamo for thinking I deserved respect.

But I was the one being given the cold shoulder.

"If you want to go somewhere else, that's fine." I met his gaze and held it. I'd put up with a lot, and honestly, being ogled by strangers hadn't felt that disrespectful. Having my *friend* act like this, on the other hand, felt a lot like disrespect.

"I'm here with you," he said. He didn't sound particularly pleased about it, though, and I wanted to hit him for it.

Instead, I walked into the bar with a silent biker at my side. Alamo wasn't being rude per se, but it was pretty obvious that he didn't want to be with me. He looked about as happy as a man who just had his bike trashed. He hadn't. Traffic had been decent. The weather was perfect. Aside from that one incident, everything was good, but he was acting as if he was miserable.

Abruptly I spun around so we were face-to-face and asked, "If you didn't want to be here, why'd you agree?"

"What?"

"You heard me." I folded my arms over my chest and leveled a glare at him. "If you want to be a jackass about being with me, you can turn around and go. I'll call the bar and have someone come out and fetch me home."

"I came with you. I'll carry you home." He matched my glare, as if he had a right to be angry. He didn't. I hadn't done a thing that was wrong, and I wasn't going to be treated poorly for no reason. I'd had enough of that in my life.

"Don't do me any favors." I started to walk away, and he caught my wrist in his hand.

The moment I glanced down at his fingers where they were curled around my wrist, he released me. "I like doing you favors, Ellen. We're friends, darlin'. Friends do favors."

"We're friends?"

"I thought so," he said carefully.

There were a lot of other things I wanted to say. When he thought I didn't notice, he looked at me like we were something a lot different than friends—unless he meant the sort of friends Noah and I had been. When we had been on the road just now, he'd been ready to rip into people for looking too long at me. When I touched his arm or kissed his cheek, he tensed like he was under siege. I couldn't decide if it was interest or distaste. He was far more confusing than I knew how to handle.

"Go sing, darlin'," he said softly. "I didn't mean to frighten you back there on the street, but you're safe with me."

I startled at that. I didn't want to laugh at how wrong he was about my reasons for being upset, but I did need to clarify one thing. I shook my head and told him, "I'm not afraid of you. I grew up with the club. My closest playmates were . . . bikers' kids like Killer and Noah."

Alamo said nothing.

Deciding that blunt might be best, I added, "You're acting like you don't want to be here. *That's* the problem."

For a heartbeat or three, he didn't reply. Then he shook his head and told me, "There's nowhere I'd rather be, Ellen . . . Now go sing. Your voice is like to calm even the most savage beast."

Chapter 9

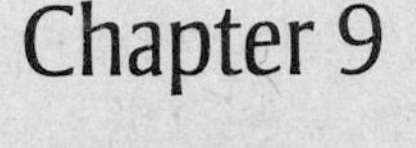

BEING ONSTAGE WAS LIKE BEING DRUNK, BUT WITHOUT any unpleasant side effects. When I sang, the world clicked into order. If I was sad, I let my grief into the song. When I was angry, my rage fueled the lyrics. When I had an audience, I felt like all of the people watching me were lending me a bit of strength and energy. I'd heard people call it a high, but that wasn't quite the right term for me. When I was singing, I became stronger. If I didn't need the music to channel an excess of emotion, I simply become *more.* I became sexier, confident, and *alive* when I was in the right mood.

When I finished singing and walked over to Alamo, he was looking at me exactly like I wanted. I could see the desire in his expression. Once you've seen that look, that almost lean-in, that simmer in someone's eyes, you recognize it when it happens. In that instant, I knew he wanted to kiss me. It was right there, a possibility that I desperately wanted, but he took a step back from me.

"You're incredible," he said.

I took a step toward him, and he flinched like he wanted to back away. I tilted my head up and looked at him, holding his gaze and refusing to pretend that I didn't see the hunger there. I couldn't force the words, though, couldn't ask why he was retreating from me.

"Thank you" was all I managed to say.

He nodded. "So . . . I don't know what the plan is now. Are you done or—"

"I am." I didn't intend to back up, but then he folded his arms over his chest, and I felt it like it was a slap. All the confidence from singing felt smothered by that gesture. It was foolish, but for a heartbeat, I felt crushed.

Never again, I reminded myself. I wouldn't waste my energy where I wasn't wanted. I wouldn't settle for half. I wanted to be drunk on desire. I wanted to be unrestrained. I wanted to be adored and feel as powerful and complete as when I sang.

"Can you take me home?" I asked.

Alamo nodded again. He remained physically distant, although his words were kind. He complimented my voice, telling me that he was "honored" that he'd gotten to hear me twice—and then he took me home. I was glad he liked my voice, but I wanted him to like all of me. When he let his guard down, he obviously *did*, but I wanted it completely. Instead, he was all but running from me. It made me feel like I was sending out a creepy stalker vibe or something. The truth of the matter was that friends don't avoid one another the way he was dodging me.

Since Alamo was running more hot and cold than I could handle, the next few times I decided to sing in public, I drove myself. My poor car wasn't really up to the extra miles, but it was what I had, and I didn't feel like begging for attention. Honestly, I was starting to think there was something wrong with me. For years I'd been resigned to clandestine meetings and no proper dates—except when I went out with people in my attempts to get over Noah. Now that I was over him, I was interested in another man who seemed to want nothing to do with me. It was hell on my self-esteem.

But I couldn't say that I was shocked over the next few weeks when Alamo continued to keep his distance. I couldn't even say I was shocked at how close Aubrey and I became either. I was focused on being a good friend, singing, working on my designs—any and everything but how lonely I was and how ridiculous I was for being interested in Alamo.

Of course Aubrey and Killer's drama was doing a great job of distracting me here and there too. Earlier in the day, she'd called and said she needed a friend.

I'd taken her to a movie, a distraction we obviously both

needed, and afterward we started to talk as I drove us to the diner.

A part of me was dumbfounded when she stared out the front window and said, "Zion is leaving the Wolves for . . . us, me, however you say it."

I whistled. "Damn. You tamed—"

"No. I didn't. We hung out and—"

"Hey," I interrupted, glancing her way briefly. "Not a criticism. Like I said, he was bound to fall hard when he fell. I just underestimated how hard."

"I'm scared," Aubrey whispered. "What if he's making a mistake? What if I'm not worth it?"

There were few things she could've said that would establish this was not a mistake. That happened to be one of them, though. I might fail at my own love life—or even just *having* a love or sex life—but I knew enough to be sure that *she* wasn't failing. She might not see it, but she was head over heels in love. Killer, of course, hadn't bothered denying that he was in love. They were the real thing, even if Aubrey was still afraid.

Gently I told her, "Sweetie, the fact that you're even worried about that instead of what if *he* hurts *you* is proof that he's not making a mistake."

She gave me a tremulous smile.

I hoped that this meant good things for both of them—and that it meant that Aubrey would be staying here in Williamsville. It seemed crazy that Killer would leave the club. He had *never* had commitment issues. It was Noah who had struggled with that . . . and me. I didn't think much of it until recently, but I wasn't much better than Noah had been. I didn't commit to singing. I didn't date anyone I might've ended up with for real. Instead, I fussed over design, which I enjoyed but wasn't a passion for me the way singing was. I stayed with a man I *knew* wasn't going to date me openly.

I could blame Noah for our years of half togetherness, but the fact of it was that I was responsible too. Killer was the only one of the three of us who knew what he wanted. He wanted Echo's approval, so he spent years training and became the club enforcer. He wanted Aubrey, and he'd been dogged at pursuing her. The other women before her? He barely learned their names. He wasn't rude, but he was clear. Noah and I had both played at being half in, half out. Noah was a Wolf, but not. I was devoted to the club, but never involved with a Wolf who wanted a relationship. We both played around at school, pursuing careers that weren't *the one*—and we'd dated people who were never going to be the one.

I shoved those unpleasant revelations in a box and returned my focus to Aubrey, who was silent at my side now.

"Aubrey?"

"Mmm?" She stared out the car window.

"Talk to me," I ordered. I was trying not to press her for details, but my patience was wearing thin. Her ups and downs with Killer mattered to me. They were both people I cared about. I was rooting for them, hoping that they'd actually found a solution to what could've been an insurmountable problem.

Aubrey and I had made it to Mama's Grub and Grill, and she was still quiet. Obviously, there was more going on than she had said so far. She was already a dear friend, and as I'd never really had close female friends, I was still trying to figure out what was normal. I wasn't entirely sure what was "normal" for girlfriends—and considering that what I wanted to talk to her about was an area I was lousy at *and* it involved my childhood friend, the whole situation was a little weird.

But I was a Southern woman, and that meant that I knew that tea and food were step one of sorting out most troubles. That was why we were at Mama's Grub and Grill. It was a little family diner. The front of the building was actually a shiny trailer that had been attached as a room expansion to the diner a few years back. It was a quick and dirty way to add a room, but it worked and I liked the look of it. Aubrey stopped and stared at it briefly, but then she smiled. That was one of the things I liked about her: She was surprised now and again by things that were not unusual here, but she adjusted and saw the upside rather than turn up her nose. I appreciated that my newly transplanted friend saw the beauty in the South rather than dismissing it.

"Let's get a table," I suggested as we crossed the lot toward the diner.

Aubrey nodded, her gaze taking in pickup trucks and battered cars. It was far from a classy joint, but there wasn't any place that had better food—except my mother's table.

We weren't even in the door before we were stopped by the roar of a Harley. I hoped for a heartbeat that it was Alamo or even Killer. It wasn't. The biker most awkward to run into was the one blocking our way.

"Are you okay?" Noah asked in lieu of a greeting. I was fairly sure he was talking to Aubrey, but his gaze was on me.

"Yeah," she said.

"She and Killer sorted things out." I crossed my arms. It wasn't that he was a bad guy. He was still my friend, and I wanted to sort out my lingering anger with him, but I also wanted him not to screw up the good thing that Aubrey had found with Killer. I leveled my best glare on Noah and warned him, "And *you* best not be stirring up trouble."

Then I linked my arm with Aubrey's, led her around him, and headed toward the front door. I opened it with a jerk, and I led her past the hostess stand and to a booth. I'd been coming here too long to bother waiting to be seated. None of the regulars did.

When I looked up to see Noah headed toward us a few moments later, it took far too much effort not to get ugly. I didn't *want* to fight with him, but he was so willfully obtuse sometimes that I couldn't help myself either. Aubrey was none of his business, and she wasn't going to speak freely with him there. He had to know that.

Noah slid in beside me just as the waitress came and handed us two menus.

"Sorry, I can bring another one," she said.

"Nah, I'll share." Noah scooted closer to me, using the menu as an excuse to move in far too near me.

Once the waitress turned away, I glared at Noah again and slid the menu toward him. "Here. I don't need it."

He leaned back and draped his arm over my shoulder. "Me either."

He grinned and didn't move away. It stung, the way he was being casual and easy when I was realizing how unhealthy we'd been for years. Then he added, "Burger, fries, strawberry shake . . . and onion rings unless you're free for a ride."

I flipped him off, but I said nothing. My temper was burning to burst out. I wasn't going to repeat this same pattern that we'd been locked in. I knew it wasn't fair of me to expect him to have an epiphany just because I did, but my temper wasn't sparked just by that. Even if I hadn't realized what a fucked-up mess we'd made of things, I would be angry at his casual attitude right now.

"How did you know where we were?" Aubrey asked Noah, drawing me out of my thoughts.

"Miss Bitty."

"My mama," I interjected.

"Right." Aubrey frowned in confusion. "But we just decided to come here."

Noah laughed. "You were upset. That means Ellen would bring you here. Comfort food. It's how the South works."

Despite myself, I smiled. When he was sweet like that,

I remembered the boy who had been my friend. He was the one who took me to buy tampons the first time because I didn't want to have a "you're a woman now" conversation with my mother. Back then, every milestone led to tears and wishes that my father was there. The idea that my father would want to hear about my first period was ludicrous, but my mother had put him up on a pedestal at that point, so she didn't hear a lot of logic. Noah Dash was my best friend—and now we were acting like strangers.

And I didn't know how to get us back to being friends.

By the time we ordered, I felt less tense. Aside from that brief moment, Noah was acting like himself, seeming like my friend again. I looked at Aubrey and pointed at her. In a faux serious voice, I warned her, "There will be spilling of secrets. Don't think this reprieve means I'm letting it go."

"Yes, ma'am," she said.

Noah laughed. "Someone else unwilling to face your wrath. Smart move, Aubrey. Smart move."

I flipped him off in reply. Rather than take the hint, Noah hauled me closer and tried to kiss my cheek. It was a step too far.

I shoved him away so hard that I almost slid out of the booth.

Noah scowled. "What the fuck was *that*?"

"You're pretty, but . . ." I shrugged, trying to make it a joke.

I really didn't want to have this conversation, not here, and not in front of Aubrey. She had no idea that we had a history, and I wanted to keep it that way. For the first time in all the years of secrecy, I was the one who didn't want to tell anyone about what we used to be. It was a sad sort of funny that I now wanted the exact opposite of what I had wanted, but I saw no need to talk about what we no longer were. Doing that would only cause pain. It was precisely what I didn't want.

"I'm pretty but *what*?" Noah sounded genuinely hurt as he echoed my words, and I hated that my heart ached. I didn't want this. What I wanted was to shove it all into the past and try to be friends. What I wanted was to make it crystal clear to *both* Noah and Alamo that I was single, and that I was not going to go backward. I was working on the future, and dwelling in the past was useful only in that it made clear what I *didn't* want.

Instead of looking at Noah, I shrugged again, took a sip of soda, and said lightly, "Let it go, Noah."

"Ellie—"

"Drop it." I elbowed him. I looked at Aubrey. "He's just jealous because I'm not interested."

Noah's snort was his only reply, but his body grew tense.

"Poor babe's been pining for me since we were . . . what?"—I glanced at Noah and tried again to sound lighter—"ten years old?"

"Only because everyone else was afraid of your temper," he teased back with a little smile. "Seriously, Aubrey, she was the scariest kid ever. Even *Killer* was afraid of her."

"Respect, not fear," I corrected. I took another drink and

looked back at him. I met his gaze and said, "Unless you want to start a fight, Noah Eli Dash, you best be minding that tongue of yours. I'm still in possession of that temper."

He stared at me for a long moment before saying, "I haven't forgot anything, Ellie Belly."

"Ellen," I corrected tersely.

Something in my tone must've been revealing because Aubrey kicked me under the table and said, "So Ellen and I went to the movies . . ."

He looked at Aubrey, and the conversation shifted to an intentionally innocuous topic. I almost wanted to interrupt him on more than one occasion and ask him to notice how much better we were as friends, but there was no way to do that until Aubrey wasn't at the table.

I got my chance about twenty minutes later when she went to the ladies' room.

Pitching my voice low enough that no one would overhear me, I asked, "What are you *thinking*?"

"What?"

"We *split*, Noah."

"We were never together," he corrected, almost automatically.

My temper spiked, and I kept myself from shoving him by sheer willpower. "Well, whatever we were, it won't be happening again, so mind the space a bit."

He frowned at me. "What did I do that you're so mad?"

I sighed at the sheer immensity of his cluelessness. "I'm not mad, Noah. I just don't want you to get in my space or make cracks about being with you. Everyone else might think you're just being flirty, but I *know* you."

"So saying I want to see you is *wrong* now? I thought you weren't mad. That sounds a lot like mad." His voice was going as rough-edged as I felt. "I'm trying to figure this out, Ellie, but you're not making it easy."

"There's nothing to figure out." I met and held his gaze. "Let it go. I'm done. I've been done. We're *done*."

This time he sighed. "Well, when you feel like telling me what I did, let me know. I want things to be right with us again."

My anger fled like he'd just dowsed it with ice water. "I do too, but the right *I* want is us being friends."

"Me too," he started.

"No," I corrected. "*Friends*, Noah. Not what we were. Just friends."

Then Aubrey started toward us, and I said, "Drop it."

He frowned again, but by the time Aubrey slid into the booth, he looked like he had when she left. I was grateful for that, at least. The rest would get sorted out in time. Either he'd believe me eventually or he'd have no choice but to believe me once I was seeing someone else. I'd prefer that he accepted the truth before I started dating anyone, but if I got a shot at getting past Alamo's walls, I was going to take it and damn the consequences.

Chapter 10

A FEW DAYS LATER, MY OWN DRAMA WAS THE LAST THING on my mind. I was standing in my laundry room, a pair of jeans in my hand, and singing loud enough that Mama had opened her bedroom door. She was still tiptoeing around me about it, but she and I both knew that I was becoming increasingly comfortable with it.

I got a call from Killer's number. We weren't much on phone calls. In fact I couldn't remember the last time he'd just up and called me. "Killer?"

"No, it's me," Noah said.

I felt the jeans fall to the floor, vaguely hearing the thump as they landed on the ground. I didn't even need to ask to know something was wrong. I could hear it in Noah's voice, and there weren't a lot of reasons Killer would surrender his phone.

"Is he . . ."

"He's okay, Ellie." Noah sounded as rough as I suddenly felt. "He's going to be okay, at least. Unconscious still, but the surgery went—"

"Surgery?"

"He was shot," Noah said.

The simple words made me shake. There were things that were a reality in our world. Getting shot or arrested was always a risk, especially for Killer. It was why I was grateful that Noah hadn't been patched into the club when Killer had been.

"What happened? I thought he was getting out and—"

"Not work. There was a break-in at Aubrey's place." Noah explained the whole mess, and all I could think was that everyone was lucky that Killer was going to be okay, especially when Noah added, "And Echo's openly admitting he's Killer's dad. He's here, and so are Aubrey and Mrs. Evans."

"Yeah? That's something, right?"

Mama walked in and looked at me. I guessed that my lack of singing was a big whopping clue that something was wrong, but my voice carried enough that she knew to come check on me.

Her arms wrapped around me as Noah said, "Apparently, he and Echo sorted that out earlier, and then . . . this."

I closed my eyes and leaned against my mother. "Killer's okay, though. You promise?"

"Yeah. Pinkie swear."

I nodded, even though Noah obviously couldn't see me. Then I added, "You be careful, too."

"They arrested the guys who—"

"Just say yes, Noah. You two have been my best friends forever. No matter what we are now, you're my friends. Tell Killer I love him . . . and you."

"Ellie—"

"Not that sort of love, Noah. Not for either of you. Friend love. 'I'd be crushed if you died' love. That's all." I felt tears on my cheeks, and all I could think about was the last time the phone rang with bad news. Then it was my father. It was me holding Mama as she crumbled. It was the end of normal.

"I'll tell him," Noah promised. "We care about *you* too, Ellie Belly. I know Killer does, and I . . . I miss us being friends."

I nodded again, but all I could say was, "Be safe."

Then I disconnected and told Mama, "Killer was shot, but he's okay."

My mother straightened up and looked me in the eye. "I'll call Dar and see what Echo needs. We'll look in on that schoolteacher of Echo's too."

"They're all at the hospital." I rested my forehead on her shoulder for a minute. "He's okay. Killer's okay. He could've . . ."

Mama stroked my hair. "Hush, now."

Tears were streaming down my face. I didn't want to

mention my father, didn't want to think about that horrible night—or any of the ones that followed. If not for Echo, I don't know that my mother would've known how to get back on her feet. He wasn't all handkerchiefs and soft words. He'd given her a couple of days, but then he was . . . tough. I remember him telling her to get it together. I remember him telling me to call and check in with him or Uncle Karl every other day, and then eventually it was every week.

Right now, the man who had pulled us to our feet was hurting. His son—*my friend*—was hurting. My ex and my only female friend were both hurting too. I didn't know what to do, but I wanted to do something.

"How do I . . . what do I do?" I asked Mama.

She kissed my forehead. "You come into the kitchen with me, and we make a few dishes to put in Killer's fridge. We call the other wives and daughters, and we make sure that they know, so everyone's Wolf is taken care of. Then we look after those that don't have old ladies or daughters."

I straightened and stepped back. I knew how to do this. Wolf families don't falter. We were tougher than that. *I* was tougher than this. "Right."

We walked to the kitchen, and Mama went to the table with her phone. Mine rang again. It felt surreal, but having a focus was all that I had to keep me from crying.

She looked at me and motioned me to go. "Take it in the parlor."

I wasn't even through the doorway when I heard her say, "Dar? It's Bitty."

"Hello?" I answered.

"Did someone tell you?" Alamo asked by way of greeting. "He's okay. The surgeon said he'd be a hundred percent fine."

"Yeah." I smiled at the fact that he'd opened with reassurances. "Noah called."

There was a pause, and then Alamo added, "I know you three grew up together. Do you want to come over? I can fetch you or send someone or . . . I don't think Dash ought to be driving. He's shaky, and Echo's keeping him near."

I laughed despite myself. Echo wasn't going to let Dash too far out of sight, as rattled as he must be, but that wasn't something that was my place to point out. The family background was complicated. Dash wasn't Echo's kid. Neither was I. That didn't stop Echo from paying a fair bit of attention to us, as well as to his actual son.

"Ellen?"

"I'm guessing there's a pack of Wolves there," I said mildly.

"No reason you can't be here if you want to. I'll tell Echo myself if you want," Alamo offered.

I could hear the sounds of the hospital PA system in the background. I didn't want to be there, not right now. "It wouldn't do Killer any good for me to be there," I said. "I'd only be coming to make myself feel better . . . You'll call me though if anything changes, right? I mean, maybe I should—"

"He's fine," Alamo stressed. "But I can call or text updates. Hell, I can take his picture and text it."

My tears made my eyes blur. "I'm sorry. I just . . . he's not supposed to get shot. The last time someone did . . . he died."

Just then I couldn't make myself say *who* that was. I couldn't think about my father dying. All I could do was remind myself that I'd had two separate people verify that Killer was going to be okay.

"How about I come get you tomorrow as soon as you're up to it? I'll tell Killer's old lady that you're coming. Maybe she'll go home for a nap if you're here." Alamo sounded like he knew exactly the right things to do, and I had to wonder what sort of crisis sent him out of North Carolina that he was so damn calm.

"Is eight too early?"

"I'll be there or send someone else if you want. Just tell me what you need, darlin'."

"A ride to see Zion," I said. "Eight a.m."

"I'll be there," Alamo promised.

The next few hours were a blur. Mama and I cooked and talked. She talked mostly about the early days of marriage, about Daddy singing in the house, but neither of us mentioned the long-ago night when the phone call about a shooting was about him.

I sang. It didn't fix anything, not truly, but it made me feel better. Maybe part of that was because it made Mama feel better too.

"So Dash *and* Alejandro both called?" she asked mildly about an hour into our marathon cooking session. We were done with a pair of casseroles and had started to prep lasagna.

"I'm not dating either one of them." I stared down at the noodles I was rinsing.

"Riding with them?"

There was something awkward, even at my age, at having my mother bluntly ask if I was having sex with two different men. "Noah and I used to, but . . . we're better as friends."

"Your decision or his?"

I looked up and met her gaze so there was no doubt as to my truthfulness. "Mine."

She nodded. "And Alejandro?"

"He's a friend." I squirmed under her attention, turning my back to her and trying to avoid the topic.

"Mmm."

There was no way to pretend that noise was anything other than doubt, but I wasn't taking the bait. I started singing, knowing full well that she'd let the subject go if I kept on. Even when she wanted an answer, Mama rarely interrupted me midsong. It was a trick my father had taught me years ago. She knew it too, but still went along with it. The only thing she did was give me one of her "you ain't hiding a thing, missy" looks. I swore they ought to give her a patent for that look, but I wasn't pretending that I'd given a full disclosure. I shrugged and started singing "Down to the River to Pray."

Mama let me dodge the conversation, and we cooked with little conversation after that. The most she said was a song title here or there or a small note on Daddy or me and Killer and Noah when we were kids. I knew that she was trying to make me relax enough to sleep, and maybe she was doing it for her own nerves too. It worked, though. By the time I crawled into bed, dawn wasn't far off, but I was past my tears and I slept without nightmares.

Chapter 11

ALAMO WASN'T A STRANGER TO TROUBLE. HE'D COURTED it like it was an art form for a few years before he realized that Zoe required a parent. Admittedly she was self-sufficient to the point that he was somehow enough for her, but he wasn't sure he'd have figured out how to be an adult if not for her. Between being there for her and coping with his own stupidity, he'd thought he was ready to handle whatever drama came his way, but he was at a loss right now. Ellen wasn't *his* to look after, but he felt compelled to do so all the same.

And the biker he'd ask permission of was the one who was laid up in the hospital bed.

He did his part while the club members were in and out

of the waiting room. Dash, for all of his idiocy in regard to Ellen and the club, had stepped up and was standing where Killer should be, where he would be if he was able. Alamo didn't know Killer as well as the rest of the club, but in the months he'd been here, he'd come to value him as a friend. There was always something awful about one of the club brothers getting injured. This was worse, though.

The result was that come dawn Alamo was still in the waiting room. He'd caught a nap in one of the uncomfortable chairs, which was more than Dash had managed. He had stood at Echo's side as if he'd stepped into Killer's boots between one breath and the next. Both Aubrey and her grandmother seemed grateful for his presence there, and Echo obviously was. By morning, though, he was the only one still there who hadn't slept.

It earned Dash a little of Alamo's respect, enough that he walked over to Dash and offered in a low voice, "I can look after them if you want to take a breather."

Dash tensed. "I've got it."

They weren't ever going to get along, and the offer wasn't going to change that reality. It was, however, the right thing to do. Alamo held up his hands. "No disrespect. I know you can, but you'll do them all more good if you catch a couple hours."

Dash looked over at Echo, who was obviously watching them. Even now he was keeping his eyes on everyone and everything.

"Killer's going to be fine." Dash wasn't relaying anything

they didn't all know, but as the night went on, it had been a sentence said more and more often as if they all needed to repeat it to reassure themselves.

"Everyone will be." Alamo looked over at Aubrey and her grandmother. They were both leaning on Echo in some degree of sleep. They'd been in with Killer, but the nurse suggested he'd rest better if they left.

Alamo suspected she'd meant "leave the hospital," but Echo wasn't willing to tell Aubrey's grandmother she had to leave, and *she* wasn't willing to force Aubrey. So they all three stayed—and Dash stayed on guard. Everyone else had left by now.

"Look, man, I don't like you any more than you like me, but we care about some of the same people." Alamo kept his voice pitched low. He was fairly sure there was nothing that went on in the club that escaped Echo's attention, especially if it concerned Killer, Dash, or Ellen, but that didn't mean that they needed to discuss it in front of him.

Dash didn't reply.

So Alamo opted to be even more direct. "Killer's good people, but even if it were you in that room, I'd be offering. We're in the same club."

"Fair enough," Dash said after a long moment. "I'll take two hours, but I'm not leaving. Killer says you can handle whatever comes, and Echo trusts you, but if something happened to any of those three, I'd be needing a hospital bed because Killer wouldn't forgive me."

"Understood." Alamo gestured to the back of the room

where he'd been. The light overhead was out, which was probably not intentional, but it made that little nook darker. One of the Wolves' old ladies had turned off all the televisions earlier. So, between the silence and dark, it was about as comfortable as it could be in a hospital waiting room. "The corner over there is quiet enough."

"If they need me or Killer asks for me or—"

"I'll wake you," Alamo assured him.

It was probably about as friendly a conversation as they were capable of having. The situation with Ellen made it impossible for them to be friends or even comfortable acquaintances. Alamo wanted to punch him more often than was reasonable, strictly speaking. He *knew* it was a little unfair, but it was what it was. Ellen stood between them, not because Alamo was trying to take what wasn't free to take, but because he thought Dash was an ass for the way he treated her. The fact that Alamo wanted to treat her right didn't factor in as much as the fact that he was regularly incensed that she was unhappy—and that Dash was at fault. If a man was lucky enough to have someone as talented and assertive as her, he ought to be proud to carry her wherever she wanted to go. Instead, she was left calling him for rides because Dash couldn't be bothered.

Thinking about that wasn't going to improve his odds of being civil to Dash, though, so he shoved those thoughts aside and walked over to Echo. One of the nurses looked up as he approached. She hadn't looked at Dash with that same sort of apprehension, but some people have an easy charisma that makes them seem safe even when they're wearing the same sort of leather jackets and riding boots. Dash had this, the charm that leaders needed. Alamo was a lot more like Killer: *Brute* and *brawn* were the kind of terms people used to describe them. It wasn't the patches proclaiming them as Southern Wolves or even the 1% patch. If it had been, the nurses would look at Echo that way too. He was obviously the man in charge, obviously the one who kept the rest of them on leashes—or released them from leashes when necessary—but even though he wore the same patches, the nurses smiled at him. Some people simply had that indefinable trait. They'd make great leaders, politicians, heads of state, or even cult leaders. Alamo didn't envy them. There was a weight to that kind of thing.

Alamo, on the other hand, was perfectly content to be the sort of man who did the dirty work. He had the skill and the lack of guilt. Like Killer, he was a good soldier. Unlike Killer, Alamo had zero urge to be anywhere other than among Wolves. He couldn't imagine life without the club, and he'd be damned if he looked long at a woman who wouldn't share that sentiment. He could respect Killer's decision to leave the Wolves for Aubrey, but the cold truth was that he wouldn't be able to find a woman attractive if she wasn't as devoted to the club as he was. Family was essential, and this was the only family he'd ever known—other than Zoe, of course.

Echo looked up at him when Alamo came to stand near him. He was unobtrusive about it, far enough away to give him privacy if he needed it, but close enough that there wasn't anyone going to get close to him without Alamo's allowing it. Being Echo's guard meant taking any bullet or blade before it was even in spitting range of Echo—or in this case, Aubrey and her grandmother too.

"Good work getting the boy to relax," Echo said. "Killer would appreciate it."

"He's not leaving, but he agreed to grab a couple hours."

"It's better than nothing." Echo nodded, and then he leaned his head back against the wall and closed his eyes. He didn't point out that he knew that Alamo had stayed of his own accord, and he didn't acknowledge the fact that he could've *ordered* Dash to take a break. He didn't have to, though. Echo didn't answer to anyone—with the possible exception of the woman currently resting her head on his shoulder. He let both Killer and Dash make their own choices as much as possible. No one called out that it was training for the future, but everyone knew it.

Now that Killer was stepping away from the Southern Wolves, that left only one likely candidate for Echo's heir. Whether or not Dash saw it, Alamo was well aware that Dash was the most obvious choice for following in Echo's steps. Truth be told, he was a far better choice to be the next president anyhow. Killer was . . . a triggerman, a problem solver of the sort that Alamo was. Dash was the kind of man who could handle politics and finances and all the business parts.

Unfortunately, that reality would mean that sooner or

later Alamo was going to have to decide if he needed to pull up stakes and move to another chapter. If he and Dash couldn't sort out their antipathy, Alamo would need to leave.

The thought of it was frustrating. He was tired of moving, tired of being unsettled. He'd been in Tennessee only a short time as it was. Needing to think about moving again was depressing, but it was just another reminder not to get too attached, not to get involved, not to think about roots. He'd learned that lesson as a kid, and even though he *wanted* roots, life didn't make that easy. It was just one more reason that he shouldn't look too long at Ellen. He just needed to find a way to remind himself of those reasons when he saw her because a few minutes in her company made it hard to remember to use logic.

Chapter 12

By the time Alamo arrived at my house the next morning, I wasn't a mess of tears anymore, but it was a close thing when I saw that Mama was already up and in the kitchen preparing a basket to take to the hospital.

"Echo's old lady called and said you were going in to see Killer." Mama had a thermos of coffee in her hand. "This is for you, though. Don't let that pup have anything them doctors don't say he can have, you hear?"

"Yes, ma'am." I accepted the thermos and went to open it, but she held out a cup.

"This is for now. That's for when you get sleepier and don't want to leave Killer's side." She pointed at a backpack. "There's other things in there. He's going to want a few odds and ends to be comfortable, and Echo doesn't need to be carrying them."

I glanced at the bag. I didn't need to ask to know there was a weapon of some sort in it, unregistered and probably lacking a serial number. I wasn't going to open the bag to look either. If someone stopped me, my surprise would be real no matter what they pulled out of the bag. Of course, the ideal was that no one stopped me. If they did, I had to trust that Echo would provide the best defense possible. That was the part of being in this family that was hard to explain: some of us were more able to take certain risks. Echo was protected at all costs. He was essential, the man who kept all the balls in the air, who handled the hard calls, who made the choices that kept the chapter—Wolves and their families—safe, but also made the choices that resulted in business income. Wives and children could be called on to make contributions, just as Wolves did. Mama had volunteered herself, and now me, over the years because we didn't have a man in the house to share the obligation.

All told, I could see why Aubrey had issues with the club. I didn't, but I understood how a person could. I suspected that if she knew the whole of it, she'd have a lot more reasons to complain. Some wives were kept a bit more in the dark, but Mama hadn't been and she was raising me to be independent but still loyal to the family. I took no issue with it. I did my part when the opportunity was presented to me.

I met Mama's gaze and nodded. "Got it."

She rewarded me with a proud smile and opened the door. "Alejandro? Did you want something to eat before you go back to the hospital?"

"No, ma'am. Thank you, but I don't want to put you out."

She waved him off. "Nonsense. I was making eggs for Ellen anyhow."

Every last one of us knew she was lying, but it was one of the polite sort of lies that was allowed. He was visibly exhausted, and whatever Echo had said to Mama had predisposed her to be kind to Alamo. I didn't have the heart to tell him resistance was futile. He'd figure it out like the rest of the club had.

For a moment he stood like a small mountain in my doorway. I couldn't say whether Mama or I was happier to see him there. She loved any excuse to look after one of the Wolves, and I . . . well, I just liked seeing him. Going to see Killer wasn't for any sort of reason I liked, but it was less awful because of Alamo.

Mama poured a cup of coffee, pointed at the table, and turned her back to fetch the eggs from the fridge. She knew as well as I did that he was too much of a gentleman to disobey her. He was a Wolf *and* a Southerner.

"How is he?" I asked, pulling out my own chair. I wanted to go see Killer, but I wasn't going to ignore my mother's courtesy toward Alamo. I wasn't a fool.

"About as well as you can be after getting shot." Alamo walked into the kitchen and lifted the cup of coffee Mama set on the table. She'd offered to feed him, and he refused. She had the prerogative to ignore that refusal—which she obviously was since she was cracking eggs into a bowl.

"He sent Echo and the women home," Alamo added.

I kicked out his chair. "Sit."

He gave me a look that might've quelled someone not used to bikers. He was a lot of muscle and leather, and I had no doubt that it intimidated most folks. I wasn't most folks, though. My only reaction to his scowl was a fluttering of my pulse, but not from fear. I was too used to bikers and their old ladies to find a scowl daunting.

Back when we were kids, Killer had suggested that I'd never be able to date anyone other than a biker because buttoned-up sorts were too easily cowed by my forthright ways. At the time, I think he was putting in a good word for Noah, but the observation still held true. I kept trying, but sometimes I thought that the more mainstream a man was, the less able he'd be to hold my attention. The ones who stood a chance, who were assertive even though they didn't ride, seemed to think that because I was surrounded by bikers, I was easy. I got that it was just a stereotype, and I had no issue with a woman owning her sexuality. If I'd *wanted* them, I'd have no guilt in *having* them. What I'd learned early on as a girl surrounded by tough women was that there was a difference between choosing to have sex and feeling *obligated*. I didn't do obligated, not even when I was with Noah. The fact was that I didn't feel any guilt over wanting my pleasure, but I sure as hell wasn't going to do it just because some uptown man—or a biker—paid me a few compliments.

That didn't mean that Killer was wrong about what it took to hold my attention, though. He saw it well before I did: I was more than a little swayed by a man with attitude and the skill to back it up.

"Do you want peppers? Onions? Cilantro? I don't have any jalapeños or—"

Alamo laughed. "Just plain ol' eggs, ma'am. I don't need anything particular just because of my genes."

Mama put one hand on her hip and gestured with the spatula she had just pulled out. "No lip, Alejandro! Echo tells me you don't have a mother, so consider this your warning: I adopt strays when I can. Killer and Noah both spent more than enough time at my table." She shook her head. "Not that Uncle Karl's a bad cook, mind you. Surly old bastard might be better than me, but we don't talk about that."

Alamo looked like he'd just stumbled into a mess of confusion. He glanced my way, and I debated not taking pity on him, but . . . the rest of us had spent years dealing with Mama, so it wasn't entirely fair to expect him to know what to say.

Then again, I wasn't sure my words were any more benign than hers. I grinned and told her, "I don't feel particularly brotherly toward Alamo, Mama. No need to go adopting him."

She snorted in laughter and pointed the spatula at me. "Scrambled or something else?"

I couldn't quite bring myself to look at Alamo. I hadn't outright said what my feelings *were*, but it wasn't a big leap to understand what they were. I hadn't ever lived like caution was the answer to any question—except when refusing to sing—but thinking about Killer's getting shot made me want to take a few more risks.

Alamo held his silence. Not that I expected him to remark when we were in the kitchen with my mother, but a half hour later when we were climbing on the bike, he was still without comment. That clarified it, I guessed: he simply wasn't interested.

I needed to stop putting myself out there and move on, then.

When we pulled in at the hospital, I slipped off the bike and said, "Thanks. "

"Do you want me to—"

"I got it," I cut him off. "Thanks for the ride, though." I tried to smile, but I suspected it looked strained. "You should probably sleep anyhow. I could've driven myself actually. I should've. Sorry I bothered you and—"

"It wasn't a bother, darlin'. " He frowned at me and stood. "You need to stop putting words in my mouth."

I nodded.

"Do you mind telling me what happened here?"

"Nothing." I straightened the bag on my shoulder. I didn't feel anything in it through the fabric that seemed like it could be a gun, but knowing Mama, I was sure she'd wrapped it up in a shirt or a pair of jeans or something. She wasn't stealthy with her words, but that was a choice. The woman was cagier than a fox even on her worst days. If a woman could run the club, she'd be more than able.

Alamo was still staring at me, and although I knew that whatever answers he wanted weren't written on my skin, I still squirmed and turned away.

I didn't make it four steps before he fell in at my side.

"You're like to give a man whiplash, Ellen," he said quietly. "I don't know what I did wrong, but if you feel like telling me, I'd be obliged."

I glanced up at him and shook my head. "You didn't do anything, I just need not to trouble you for favors."

He sighed, but that was all the answer he offered.

We were almost at the front door of the hospital when he glanced at the bag I was carrying. "For Killer?"

I nodded.

"I can carry it." He didn't speak any more overtly than that, but there was a question in his gaze.

"You can't." I repositioned it again, not because it was truly awkward but because it was heavy on my mind and felt more weighty on my shoulder than it really was. Knowing my obligations to the Wolves and being fine with them didn't mean I was unaware of risks.

"Are you sure?" Alamo offered.

I stopped midstep and locked gazes with him. "If you were to get picked up, it would inconvenience the club, especially with Killer in the hospital." Then I resumed walking. "Anyhow, I'm sure everything is worked out."

My theory was proven right as I saw the guard at the door of the hospital. He wasn't a Wolf, but his cousin was. He stepped in front of the metal detector to hug me, exclaiming, "Ellie!"

The alarm went off. His gun was visible, as was his badge. The faux sheepishness he had for setting the alarm off was remarkably convincing.

"Sorry!" He wasn't overly loud, but the folks in the lobby would've heard him all the same. He looked at Alamo. "It was probably my gun that set it off, but protocol . . ."

It sounded like he was apologizing, but there was a question in there too.

"Not that carrying's illegal, just not in the hospital," he continued.

Alamo didn't look at me. He simply held his arms out to the side. I reached over and held open his vest, so it was clear that there was nothing hidden there.

"I got this, Ellie," the guard, whose name I couldn't recall, said with a laugh. "Go on and step aside, li'l bit."

So I stepped out of the way while the guard patted Alamo down. A moment later, he waved Alamo forward. "I was sorry to hear about your cousin, Ellie. He saved old Beau's life, the way I hear it. Bullet's not much of a reward for being a hero."

I made polite replies for a moment, looking away, letting tears well up. It wasn't hard to do. My grief and worry over Killer weren't far from the surface as it was.

A few moments later, Alamo and I were walking through

the hospital corridor to Killer's room. It was far from easy being there, thinking about the way this could've gone, thinking about someone I called family being hurt, but it could've been a hell of a lot worse.

Big Eddie was standing against the wall outside Killer's room. He looked up when he saw us, and the glance he sent my way was anything but subtle. His opinion of my relationship with Noah had been made clear repeatedly.

I shook my head slightly. I wished there was another answer I could give, but nothing was going to happen with Alamo. He'd made that clear, and I needed to just accept that his flirting was without intent to deliver. It was harmless, and I needed to let go of any hopes I still had.

I put a hand on the door, but I didn't open it. Instead I said, "I appreciate everything, but I want to see Killer alone."

Alamo nodded.

"That goes for *you* too," I told Big Eddie.

He shrugged. "I'm just holding up the wall and keeping that boy from deciding he'd rather check himself out before the doctors—and Echo—decide he's clear to leave. If Killer had his way, he'd have left when Aubrey did. Echo had to swear to personally stay on Mrs. Evans' sofa just to get that one to agree to take a nap last night."

I couldn't even pretend I was surprised. Killer had dedicated himself to every martial art he could, as well as marksmanship lessons, in order to keep Echo safe over the years. Since he'd fallen for Aubrey, he'd been more than a little focused on her safety, and I suspected he'd be worse after a home invasion.

"I won't keep him awake long," I told them both. "I just need to see him."

"Echo said you'd be by." Big Eddie gave me a sympathetic look. "He's going to be just fine. I promise you. If he wasn't, Echo and Aubrey would both still be in there. They went home for sleep, though."

He didn't come right out and mention my dad, but I knew that he was aware of why I needed to see Killer. I suspected Echo was too. I nodded and pushed open the door.

Killer was in the hospital bed. Wires and tubes were connected to him, and he was paler than he should be. I wouldn't say he looked harmless, even now. He did look more vulnerable than I liked.

His eyes opened, and he smiled at me. "No' said you'd be here."

"Noah gets a few things right," I said as I walked over to the chair beside the bed.

"He was scared," Killer said slowly enough that I knew he was on narcotics. I'd seen other Wolves in the hospital and recognized that determined speech; it was as if even now they had to be too damn stubborn to admit weakness. I could *see* the IV tubing, and I *knew* he had been shot. I could see the bandages, but . . . he still had to try to sound invulnerable.

"I'm okay, Ellie Belly," he said when I met his gaze. He'd obviously been watching me study him.

Tears filled my eyes again. "You're the closest thing I have to a brother or cousin or—"

"I'm *fine*, Ellie. Look at me." He reached out, and I tried not to notice that his hand was shaking.

"I know that," I snapped as I took his hand. "If you weren't, I'd be yelling at you." I took a couple deep breaths. "All I could think about was . . ."

"Your dad," Killer finished. "You and No' both."

It was odd hearing him use the silly name we'd both called Noah as kids. Noah claimed to hate it, but we all knew that was a lie. "How come you didn't have a nickname?"

He squeezed my hand and said lightly, "You *do* remember that I was christened something other than Killer, right?"

I rolled my eyes. "It's not the same. We were the only ones who ever called him 'No' and you two were the only ones who called me 'Ellie Belly' . . . which is not a very flattering name, by the way."

He shrugged and winced. In true Killer fashion, he glared at his bandage, as if the wound were something sentient he could intimidate.

I giggled. Seeing Killer being himself was enough to get rid of the illogical worries that had brought me to see with my own eyes that he was okay. It wasn't that I doubted any of them when they swore he was fine. I'd just needed to see that.

"I feel like I just got you back in my life, and you go and do *this*," I chastised. Despite my best efforts, my voice cracked a little as I added, "You need to stay safe. I need you to be safe."

He stared at me, and I knew there was a secret to share that would involve his not being safe. I knew it the way I'd known he was holding secrets when we were kids.

"Whatever it is, don't tell me yet," I said quickly.

"I'll be careful . . . doing whatever it is," he promised.

"I don't want to know today." I stood and released his hand. "I just needed to see you. Now that I have . . ."

Slowly I lowered the backpack from my shoulder.

"Mama said Echo wanted some things brought in. These aren't *yours*, but I know how you are with your blankie."

He quirked his brow again. "Blankie, huh?"

I shrugged and said, "Do you want it on the chair here or closet?"

"Right here." He held out a hand. "Tell Big Eddie to come in on your way out. He'll get me situated so I'm able to sleep."

Carefully I leaned down and kissed his forehead. "Listen to the doctors, Killer."

Then I left, only to find Alamo still in the hallway waiting to carry me home. Big Eddie gave me a bone-crushing hug, and I went out far more relaxed than I had arrived. Seeing that Killer was alive and himself was all I really needed in order to go home and rest.

And even though I'd said I didn't need Alamo to wait, I couldn't deny that I was grateful that he'd done so. Both he and Noah had done what I needed them to do as I tried to keep my heart and nerves together. Killer might not be blood family, but I wasn't sure if I'd be able to keep from falling apart if he had been more seriously wounded.

My family wasn't exactly traditional, but it was *mine*. Killer, Noah, Alamo . . . they all mattered enough that in that moment, I was simply grateful that they were all safe and well.

Chapter 13

WHATEVER PEACE I'D FELT TOWARD BOTH NOAH AND Alamo ended within days, unfortunately. Noah was as underfoot as a body could be. After all the times when I'd wanted his attention, I had it now that I didn't. Alamo, on the other hand, was back to his disappearing act. Sometimes I swore they conspired to make me want to strangle them both—Noah for being a lousy friend and Alamo for acting like I was trying to stalk him but claiming we were friends. Men sucked. It was that simple. Mama was right that they were about as worthless as old Confederate money . . . except I couldn't help wanting them to get their heads out of their asses.

My patience wore thinner and thinner over the next few

weeks as Killer healed. I snapped at any and everyone who crossed my path. Even Aubrey wasn't safe from my moods of late. It was just like when we were kids again in some ways. Killer was the peacekeeper, the one person who seemed to be able to tell me to rein in my increasingly volatile temper.

Tonight I was stuck sitting at the bar with Noah, and this time neither Killer nor Aubrey was there to help me avoid losing my temper. Worse still, Alamo had walked out not twenty minutes after we'd arrived. Sometimes I wanted to round everyone up who was making my head ache and then one after the next line them up and have a "come to Jesus" talk with each and every one of them.

Tonight I'd start with Noah.

He shot me sideways looks, pulling his attention from the bartender for a moment here or there. She wasn't as good as Mike or even as good as Aubrey had become, but she was sweet and available. That meant Noah was going to take a run at her.

It used to be that he didn't do that in front of me. Maybe this meant he was finally accepting the truth of our new situation. I wondered if there was any good way to ask him that without him misunderstanding. This was the trouble with sleeping with friends: it made returning to friendship-only status awkward.

"You okay, Ellie?" he asked in a low voice, one far too familiar for my liking.

"Always." I sipped my drink and smiled. I didn't want to fight, not really, not again. I *wanted* him to ask me how we got so messed up, maybe apologize for being so damn stupid. As it was, I had the sneaking suspicion that he'd scared off several guys on campus who had seemed interested in me at first, but then suddenly vanished. They obviously weren't keepers if one biker—no matter how much he scowled—could send them running, but still, I wished we could get past this.

"Something happen?" Noah pressed when I kept my silence.

I shook my head.

He stared at me for several moments. We both knew I was lying. I'd done a lot of that lately. It wasn't a solution, but I wasn't left with a lot of choices. If I wanted to be around Aubrey and Killer, that meant dealing with Noah. If I wanted to not argue, that meant accepting Noah's refusal to talk about what we *weren't* anymore. It meant pretending we'd only ever been friends. That was the only way I knew to carry on without fighting.

"You're quieter than normal lately, Ellie," Noah said, pressing again. "Did something happen?"

"I was just surveying the options."

Noah narrowed his eyes, but said nothing.

"Don't be like that," I said with a nudge. "It's not like either of us are having any fun sitting here watching them dance."

I nodded to the dance floor where Killer and Aubrey were all entwined like lovesick puppies. I was happy for them, but sitting here with Noah was harder than usual. Idly I asked Noah, "Did Alamo say if he was coming back?"

"Does it matter?" Noah asked, a familiar edge to his voice.

"Maybe." I wasn't scared of Noah. Sure, he *could* be a bit intimidating, but even now that we were barely speaking, I knew that deep down he was still my friend. Maybe dating a biker would help clarify things—not that I really needed another excuse to want to see Alamo.

He was another mystery, though. Any attempt I made to talk to him was thwarted. I repressed a grin at a stray thought of putting both Noah and Alamo in a room and explaining that I was well over Noah and was intrigued by Alamo. Wouldn't *that* just be fun for everyone?

"I thought we had a no-friends rule," Noah said.

Quietly, because there were always people listening at the bar, I said, "You offered 'friends with benefits' to Aubrey months ago. She asked for my advice about it." I shrugged. "I figured our old rules expired when we stopped . . . whatever we were doing."

"Whatever we were doing?" Noah echoed. "That's what we're calling it now?"

I hadn't been trying to start this conversation, but I was tiring of ignoring it. So I kept going, "They were stupid rules anyhow. We were kids. It's not like what we had mattered . . . and Alamo's not exactly your *friend*. From what I can see, he barely tolerates conversation with you."

Noah ignored the point, as he always did lately, and said, "That thing with Aubrey wasn't a big deal, anyhow. I wasn't going to ever stand a chance with someone like her."

My mouth opened in shock, but I didn't know the words to explain how rude he was. Sure, Aubrey was beautiful, but I wasn't exactly fugly and he'd stood a chance with *me*. Any urge to be gentle with his feelings vanished.

"Fuck you. Seriously, just . . . fuck you, Noah," I said.

"Whoa! I didn't know you were getting to be good friends with her when that happened. You know I don't mess with your friends, and you don't mess with mine. The rule stands. We had a spat, and then she was there while you were mad at me. I didn't mean to make you *angrier* by chatting her up . . . and nothing happened anyhow, not really. I don't know how long I'm to be doing penance for whatever pissed you off before her, or if that was added to my sentence or what's happened in between, but that doesn't mean anything changed about *us*."

I stared at him in blatant shock. "You don't think anything has changed?"

He shrugged.

"We're *done*, Noah. We were done months ago. I didn't walk out like we were fighting. There was no penance. I left you. What we were doing was toxic. I deserve better than that. We both do. Maybe you don't want it right now, but someday you will. Maybe that's why you noticed Aubrey. You started realizing that you could have an actual relationship and that meant looking at someone new and—"

"That wasn't what happened with her," he started.

"She told me everything." I shook my head. "You and me? We were a mistake, Noah. We're never going back to that."

"Why? We had fun, Ellie," he said. He offered me the sort of smile I used to find endearing. Tonight it just made me wonder if he'd been manipulating me all along.

I slid off the barstool. "I need air."

I took a deep breath, stepped around him, and walked away. I kept walking out the door and into the parking lot. He didn't follow, and I was grateful for that small victory.

There were only a few motorcycles in the lot tonight. It was strange to see it so empty, but there was obviously something going on out of town because they'd all left in a thunderous roar earlier. Now it was just a few stragglers in the bar and our little group. Until recently Killer would've gone with them, and that was perhaps the oddest thing—seeing them all roll out without him.

I leaned against the wall, wondering if Alamo had gone with the club on tonight's event. I didn't know where they went or why. In a lot of cases, it was best not to know.

The door opened with a screech. The hinges were intentionally left unoiled to make a loud noise on opening. Bikers weren't keen on being startled. Neither were those of us who grew up around them.

Killer came outside, obviously looking for me and just as obviously not making a big thing about it. He hadn't been the easiest person to talk to the past few years, but that had changed a lot since he'd gotten with Aubrey. Of course, getting shot had probably been a factor, as had Echo finally owning up to being Killer's dad. A lot had changed, and with it, Killer had too. He'd become more approachable, closer to the person I'd known when I was a kid.

"Are you okay?"

I had wiped my tears away already, so aside from my red eyes and the fact that I was standing outside alone, there was little proof that I was not okay. I smiled with effort before saying, "You know Noah and me. We argue."

Killer shook his head and staunchly declared, "It's his fault. Always has been."

I laughed. "That's not what you used to say. 'Ellie Belly, you're too much of a hard-ass.' Or 'Ellie Belly, you're going to make Dash have a mental breakdown.' "

"I have no idea what you're talking about," Killer said lightly.

"Liar."

He lit a cigarette, glanced at me sideways, and muttered, "I'm going to quit. I promised, but . . . not yet." He took a long drag, savoring the smoke, and then exhaled before adding, "You know he cares about you, right?"

"I do. We're friends." I reached out and took Killer's cigarette without bothering to ask. We'd all three started smoking as kids. I was the only one who'd mostly quit. Tonight, though, I wanted a couple moments of nicotine peace.

"He thought you'd forgive him forever," Killer said. "He figured you and I would both forgive him for the things he said to Red. I forgave him already."

“He’s not *my* cousin,” I said drolly.

Killer grinned. “He didn’t stand a chance with Red. We all knew it.” Killer paused and waited until I looked at him before adding, “Just like we all knew you two weren’t going to end up working out.”

“Yeah, well, he somehow doesn’t get that.” I ignored Killer’s outstretched hand, and after a frown he lit a second cigarette. I didn’t feel like sharing, even though it was his cigarette.

Killer scanned the parking lot in the way he always had. Even though he wasn’t part of the club after this week, he still acted like he was on guard duty most of the time. I wondered briefly if the Marine Corps knew that their new recruit was already trained and in better shape than most seasoned Marines.

“You two have been hopping back into bed since he figured out that you weren’t just one of the guys. No one knows what changed, but whatever it was, Dash thought you’d get over it.” Killer didn’t ask outright, but it was obvious that the question was there.

“He forgot my dad’s death anniversary,” I admitted in a voice almost too low to hear. “The week I walked out on him . . . he’d forgotten.”

Killer winced.

“Of all the people in the world, Noah was the one who shouldn’t have forgotten.” I shook my head, staring out into the street rather than looking at Killer. “I think I could’ve kept forgiving him for tossing me aside. I think I could’ve even pretended not to notice the proof that there were other women even when we were together the same week. I forgave a lot."

"You did," Killer agreed. "I never got why."

"We both lost our dads." I shrugged, trying to find the right words that explained without hurting Killer's feelings. "You had yours. No one said it, but Echo was always your dad. I had Mama, and Noah had . . ."

"No one," Killer finished. "I get what you're trying to say, but we both had Uncle Karl. He was a good dad to both of us."

"Having someone leave or not say they're your dad isn't the same as your dad *dying*." I thought back to sitting outside wrapped up in blankets watching the stars with Noah, talking about our dads being dead. We kissed the first time that night. It wasn't like we were trying to exclude Killer, but his dad was still there. His mom wasn't dead either. Me? I had my mother, but my dad was dead. Noah was alone. I thought about that night over the years when I got mad at him. I made a lot of excuses for him that I wouldn't for anyone else.

"You know Echo's going to try to draw him in now," Killer said. "He told me that if I'm not going to stick around, that leaves Dash to fill that role and see how things are done. He doesn't like not having someone around that he can groom to be his heir. Crazy old man thinks he's a king or something."

There was a new sort of ease when Killer talked about

his father. As a rule, people didn't call Eddie Echo crazy—unless it was a tale of what a badass he was. *That* sort of crazy was okay.

"Noah isn't like you," I said carefully. "He could be like Echo . . . but he's not . . ." My words drifted off. There was no nice way to say that Noah wouldn't be as comfortable with shooting or beating a man. "He *could* do it, but it's never going to sit right with him."

"Echo knows that." Killer sighed. "Noah's better with money and planning. I wasn't ever going to be able to run the club. Thought about that when I was in the hospital. I don't have any grief with it. I'd already decided to leave by then, but Echo . . . he needs to let Dash be himself, and that's not a triggerman."

As casually as I could, I asked, "What about Alamo? He seems like he's staying, and he's . . . more like you."

Killer stared at me for a minute, shook his head, and told me, "You need to get things straight with Dash before you go asking about Alamo."

There I was trying to be gentle, and Killer had to be an ass. Seriously, I got that he and Noah were family in a way I wasn't, but this was a step too far. I dropped the cigarette to the parking lot and ground it out with a bit more energy than maybe I needed to use. "I *left* Noah. It's been six damn months. How much straighter do I need to be?"

"I'm saying this as your friend, Ellie. Talk to Dash when you're both calm and sober. Let him know that you're not coming back. Echo doesn't need trouble in the house over a woman, even though that woman is one we *all* know and love. You got me?"

I nodded, and he went back inside and left me there alone. Maybe he was right. From the sounds of it, he knew more than I did about Noah's idiocy. How the man could think that I'd be back was beyond me, but obviously he was delusional.

Tonight, though, I wasn't up to any more confrontations. I had an interview with Southern Belle Industries on Monday. It wasn't a lot of money if I got it, but it was a potential door-opener. So I was going home and sorting through my portfolio of designs and the closet of clothes I'd made from those designs.

I walked over to my car and opened the door, thinking of one of Mama's few favorite phrases that wasn't from the South: "A woman needs a man like a fish needs a bicycle." It was an old feminist phrase coined by a lady called Irina Dunn, which was a tidbit I'd learned myself. Mama just knew she'd read it on a T-shirt, and she liked it so much that it had become a standby phrase in my home.

I had no need for a man *or* a bicycle. I might want a man, but I didn't *need* one. What I could use, though, was a job. That meant succeeding in this interview.

Chapter 14

MY PREPARATION FOR MY INTERVIEW WAS AS THOROUGH as I could make it. I'd dressed carefully, prepared, and even scored a relatively decent parking spot so I wasn't walking too far in the humidity. Walking inside the office building made me think of those day spas that were trying awfully hard to be fancier than they really were. Lipstick on a pig could go only so far, and a nondescript office building in the South was still what it was no matter how much lipstick was applied. It wasn't New York or Paris or Milan—and truth be told, I wasn't expecting it to be. Those places, I suspected, were all perfectly fine, but my take on the world was more loving what you are than trying to be something you weren't. That went for clothes and buildings as much as it did for people.

After a brief wait in a remarkably uncomfortable chair in a room with the sort of soulless music that made me want to sing out loud just to drown out the noise, I was called back to a stark office.

The walls were covered with framed magazine covers and assorted other pages. It was more of a "look at us" wall than decoration. The office itself was mostly windows and minimal furniture.

"Ellen Gillham," the woman who was apparently interviewing me read off the papers in front of her. She glanced at me and gestured at another stiff, modern chair.

"Yes, ma'am," I said as I took my seat.

She looked at me again in silent assessment. Her expression, like her tone, couldn't have been less enthusiastic if she were paid to be so. Her glass and metal desk was almost completely barren, and the only eye-catcher was the vibrant red of her shoes. Staring at her feet seemed a little too submissive for my taste, but I silently awarded her points for the tactic.

After a few moments, she looked back at the file, skimming my résumé and letter.

"Pitch me," she said.

"Okay . . . well . . . I'm interested in joining the Southern Belle team. I've been working on my associate's degree and—"

"Do you have any skills that set you apart?" She was now

examining her nails—which were apparently *terribly* engrossing.

"My portfolio highlights—"

"I don't need a designer," she said blandly, not even looking up from her manicure as she continued to study her fingertips as if there were lottery numbers written on her perfectly tipped claws. When she finally looked up, she added, "Everyone thinks they're special. They're wrong."

For a moment, I considered letting my ugly words fly free. My designs were *good*, and I was a fabulous singer and a great daughter. Maybe I wasn't what *she* thought of as special, but I was a far way from common. I opened my mouth to tell her that, but she spoke before I uttered a word.

"I'll go through your designs, and if they're actually worth anything, I'll pass them on," she said. "Chelsea at the desk will validate your parking."

And at that, I was apparently dismissed. The whole interview, if it could even be called that, was over in minutes. It wasn't the biggest slap my ego had ever taken, but it sure as hell wasn't fun.

I wandered around until I found a little country and bluegrass bar I remembered from years ago and went inside.

"Do you have any use for a singer for a couple songs?" I asked the bartender. "My father, Roger Gillham, used to sing here sometimes and . . ."

The bartender looked at me and said, "That don't mean you can sing, sweetheart."

"True, but . . ." I closed my eyes and started to sing Alison Krauss' "Down to the River to Pray."

When I was only a couple of lines in, he cut me off and said, "Point made. I'm not paying anything, but you want to sing, go on ahead."

By evening, my mood was tolerable enough that I could drive home without feeling like my temper and disappointment were going to rise up and choke me. I should've left a bit earlier, but I hadn't expected the sort of storm that was thundering around me now.

The rain was making it damn near impossible to see the road as I drove back home. Singing had been good, but the reason I'd driven into town was an interview that had *sucked*. The only cure—yet again—was more music or someone sweet to improve my mood. Since I was (a) single and (b) in my Civic in the middle of a downpour on a back-country road, I was singing along with the radio, flipping between country and classic rock stations, and venting my ugly mood by belting out songs.

My car was my sanctuary when I needed to sing loudly, but even after my afternoon of music and my current loud and unrestrained singing, it wasn't curing what ailed me tonight. When even singing wasn't curing my foul temper, I knew it was the sort of day best forgotten.

Then I heard the *ka-thunk*.

"No, no, no!" I jabbed the button to turn off the radio, but I didn't actually need to hear more to know what it was. My car tugged to the left, and the feel of the road under my wheels was wrong. I had a flat, and it wasn't just a slow leak either. That was a sudden jolt, which meant the tire blew . . . which meant that I had to pull over.

I killed the engine after I pulled as far off the road as I could get without ending up in a ditch. At least the shoulder wasn't terribly narrow. On the other hand, there was exactly no light out here. I kept my driving lights on so if anyone did come down the road they wouldn't rear-end me.

The *swish screech* of my wipers was louder now that the music had stopped. My tire was blown. My blades were bad. My bad day just kept getting worse. I took a breath and hoped things were as bad as they were going to get. I snatched up my phone and looked at it. No bars.

"Really? *Really?*" I pounded the steering wheel a couple of times. There were a dozen things I'd rather be doing at midnight on a Monday. Even sorting laundry sounded a whole lot better. I leaned into the backseat and waved my phone around again on the slim chance that there might be a magic spot where I had reception. There wasn't.

No signal. No lights. No one in the passenger seat to lend a hand.

I debated walking; I was only a few miles from town. I debated trying to wait out the rain; it had to stop sooner or later. I had no idea when, though; I wasn't exactly a weather watcher. Neither walking nor waiting seemed wise. Traipsing along an unlit back road in the rain put me in danger of getting hit or picked up by someone dangerous, and staying in my car would mean sleeping here with only a locked door for protection. I had my gun with me, but that wasn't something I was eager to use if there was a better option.

Both of my potential plans so far meant I was risking ending up in a bad situation. I didn't think people were inherently dodgy, but that didn't mean I was going to go looking for trouble either. Sleeping in a car alongside the road was only marginally better than walking along the road . . . which meant I needed to woman up and change the flat tire so I had another option. That was the smartest and fastest solution. It just meant that I was going to be cold and filthy too.

"This just keeps getting better," I whined. Maybe it was stupid, but I didn't want to ruin my best outfit. I'd worn it to the interview to highlight my skills as a designer. Destroying it while changing a flat *after* the disastrous interview was too much to bear.

Lightning illuminated the sky, providing a flash of brightness that made quite clear that the road was getting nearly impassable. I needed to change the flat and do it soon.

"Lousy day just gets lousier by the damn minute," I muttered as I glanced in the backseat hoping to find something a little less nice to wear for wrestling the spare out of the trunk and sloshing around in the mud and rain. At least I had a pair of old boots there. If I had to sacrifice my new shoes . . . well, let's just say that I'd be more likely to go barefoot and hope there weren't any broken bottles.

"From awful to fucking ridiculous." I pulled off my shoes

and shoved my feet in the worn-out combat boots. If I hadn't cleaned my car, this wouldn't have happened. I usually had several outfits in the car. Clothes were a passion. I designed them, sewed them, and I'd hoped to be getting an internship writing about them.

Now I was looking at having to sacrifice my new favorite blouse to mud. I'd hand-stitched it and I'd be damned if I was going to let it get destroyed today on top of the rest of the day's disaster. I looked outside again. Not a single car had passed in the fifteen minutes I'd been sitting here. Mud, rain, and darkness were all I could see. I should've stayed in Memphis tonight and taken another turn on the stage. I'd only gone onstage to sing again a couple of times so far, but it was like that first cookie after a long diet: I wanted more.

Maybe tonight's fiasco was God's way of reminding me that I wasn't doing what I was supposed to be doing. Now that Echo had pointed it out, now that I realized that I might be able to look after Mama if I let go of my reasons for refusing to take the stage, I felt like there was a compulsion to just do so. I felt guilty, though, for not realizing it till now, so I'd opted to drive back home rather than tell Mama I wanted to stay in Memphis and sing. The result appeared to be that I was stranded in a downpour with a flat tire.

With another sigh no one was around to hear, I unbuttoned my blouse, set it aside, and debated. I was already down to a skirt, gray stockings, black calf-high boots, and a bright blue pantie and bra set. I shucked the skirt.

Aside from the boots and stockings, it was a lot like stepping into the rain in my swimsuit. The combat boots over stockings looked a bit crazy, but it wasn't like anyone was going to see me. "What the hell . . ."

I picked up my little handgun and opened the door. I was willing to change a flat in my underthings rather than ruin my clothes, but I wasn't stupid. Deserted roads were dangerous if the wrong sort of people came along. Fortunately, I'd spent most of my life around the Wolves. Bikers might get a bad rep in a lot of places, but they were my family—and they'd taught me to handle a gun and fight dirty if I had to fight at all.

I popped the trunk, put my gun to the side, and heaved the spare out so I could get to the jack and lug wrench.

By the time I'd loosened the nuts, my hair was drenched. I shoved it back, hating the way the tendrils felt as the rain washed all the product out. I didn't even want to guess what my makeup looked like.

I had the car up on the jack and the nuts off without much trouble. Lack of light made it slower, but it was going just fine—until I started shivering. My clothes wouldn't have made a difference, but I was cold enough that I wished I'd had that tiny extra layer of fabric just then. I dropped one of the lug nuts and had to get my phone to use it for light.

"Seriously?" I let out a frustrated yell as I scanned the mud and gravel to find the missing nut.

I spied it, only to realize that I'd done so because of a flash of headlights.

"No. No. No." I scrambled to the back of the car, snatched up my gun, and tried to calm myself as the driver of the truck rolled to a stop behind my car. I stood there with a wrench in one hand and a gun in the other. If I were a different sort of girl, I might've tried to cover myself, but modesty wasn't as much of a defense as a wrench or a bullet.

The headlights were all but blinding me, and some part of me was cringing at the way I had to have looked. Wet underthings clinging to me didn't leave a whole lot to the imagination. My hand shook for a moment.

"Ellen?"

I lowered my gun. My hand still shook; whether from the cold or burst of fear, I wasn't sure.

"Alamo," I said, my voice shakier than my hand. "Come to rescue me yet again?"

He laughed. "Anytime you need me."

My heart clenched at his words.

"I can usually take care of myself," I said, despite my best efforts at being nice. I hated that he was seeing me a mess again.

He, of course, looked both gorgeous and collected, and while I wasn't exactly in need of rescue, I couldn't help drinking in the sight of more than six feet of firm muscle and menace. If that wasn't enough to make me smother a sigh, a glance at his face would do. He was the best sight I'd had all day.

"What are you doing out here?" he asked.

"Taking a shower. Care to join me?"

He grinned. "I save my cold showers for *after* I see you, darlin'."

I rolled my eyes. Alamo might tease now and again when the mood struck him, but I was fairly sure he found me about as attractive as an angry rattler. A guilty voice whispered that maybe seeing me like this might change his mind, but I didn't want his attention if he wanted me only for the exterior. I was an all-or-nothing girl these days.

I folded my arms over my chest and said, "I dropped one of the lug nuts."

"Was that before or after you thought changing your flat while *naked* was a good idea?" He pointedly didn't look anywhere but at my face.

"I'm not naked." Any lingering fear I had gave way to a touch of embarrassment and anger. He was in his usual jeans, T-shirt, and jacket. I had a handgun, a pair of boots, and not much else.

He shucked off his leather jacket and draped it over my shoulders. "You're going to freeze out here."

"I'm fine," I lied.

Alamo's jacket hung down far enough that my hips were covered. Add to that the fact that riding leathers were thicker than the stuff that people wore for fashion only, and I was weighed down by heavy, warm leather. The sheer pleasure of it left me momentarily speechless.

I hadn't realized how cold I was until I felt warmer. A small sigh of pleasure escaped me. "Thank you."

His voice was gruff as he ordered, "Just . . . get in the truck, woman. I'll get this."

Maybe it was sheer stupidity, but I hated looking like I needed help. Alamo was a good guy. I knew he wouldn't razz me over it, but that didn't erase the urge to prove myself.

"I can change it myself. Like I said, I dropped a lug nut. Just let me find it," I said as I started to squat down.

He caught my arm. "No."

"Your headlights are a lot better than my phone. Once I get—"

"I'd rather not have my coat in that mess." He nodded toward the mud that was oozing up over my boots. "I know you could change the tire, Ellen. We *both* know it."

I looked at him, trying not to shiver again. He released his hold on my arm.

"I also know that you're already cold, and I'm not interested in arguing. This road's not too long from washing out. That's why I was out here. Echo sent me and a bunch of the guys to check roads." He softened his voice a little and added, "How about we both agree that you're a badass and you get in the truck?"

I wanted to argue. That was my first instinct most of the time. Being an outspoken girl in the South meant flaying the chivalrous hide off boys, and then later, men. It meant needing to prove myself. My mama had taught me that. She was a single mom determined not to raise an idiot.

"Ellen?" Alamo prompted.

I looked at him. The headlights behind him cast enough

light that I could see the rivulets of rain outlining muscles that were the fantasy of many a woman at Wolves & Whiskey. He'd been my fantasy since he'd picked me up the day I left Noah—not that it mattered. He'd do this, flirt for a heartbeat or two, but then he avoided me like the plague. I was beyond sick of it, and I simply wasn't having it anymore.

"I'm more than able to do this. I don't need you. I haven't called you for a favor since—"

"Since I took you to see Killer at the hospital," he finished. "Trust me, darlin', I noticed."

"Really?" I glared at him and decided that being blunt was past due with him too. "I'm surprised you noticed anything, the way you dodge me."

He said nothing at first, just stared at me.

"I'll change my own damn tire," I snapped. "Just let me find the lug nut."

"Stop." Alamo wiped rain off his face and said, "Please . . . get in out of the wet and let me do this."

"Why?"

"Because it'll be faster, and because you're a sensible woman, and because . . . I *want* to." He sighed. "I don't mean to piss you off by staying clear of you."

"You admit to doing it, though?" I pushed.

He let out a growl. "If I admit it, will you get in the truck?"

"Yeah."

"Yes, I avoid you. Happy now?"

"No, but I'll get in the truck," I said.

He held out his hand for the lug wrench.

I handed it to him. Then I walked over to his truck and climbed into the warm cab, drawing in the scent of fuel, cigarettes, and whatever shampoo Alamo used. It was a kind of minty smell that was uniquely him. The underlying scent of cigarettes was a little out of place. He didn't smoke. A lot of the Wolves did, though, so it wasn't surprising to smell the undercurrent of it in his truck.

I closed my eyes and let the warmth soak into my wet body. It wasn't a minute later that I closed my eyes. I meant for it to be just for a moment. It had been a wretched day, and the night hadn't been any better. Honestly, the only good thing had been Alamo.

At least that was what I thought until I opened my eyes again to realize that the truck was moving. I blinked and turned to him. "What the hell?"

"You were asleep."

"And you couldn't wake me up?" I pulled the jacket closer around me. "Now I need to get my car and—"

"I already called Dash and told him to send someone to bring it round the house before seven. I didn't know what time you had school." He glanced at me briefly, and then averted his eyes as soon as they fell on my stocking-and-boot-covered legs. He cleared his throat. "Sorry I don't have a blanket or towel or something. I wasn't expecting to find a naked woman with a gun alongside the road."

I steadfastly ignored the mention of Noah.

Alamo pointed at the heating controls. "You can adjust

the temperature if you need. I wasn't sure if you would be too warm with the jacket, and the windows were already fogging up from the wet on us both."

I glanced his way, despite my best efforts, studying the man beside me again. He was as wet as I was, and without his jacket, his T-shirt and jeans did nothing to hide his build. He downplayed his size most of the time, wearing loose shirts and being careful not to come up on people unawares. He was subtle, but I'd noticed.

Alamo was the sort of man who would look intimidating even if he wasn't cut. His sheer size was impressive. Once you realized that he worked out too, it was damn near impossible not to drool . . . at least that was *my* reaction to him. Maybe not everyone felt that way, though.

I looked out the window. It was a lot easier than looking at him. I didn't date Wolves often. Sure, I'd gone on a few dates here and there, but Alamo was confusing. Mixed signals did nothing good for any woman's ego. They also led to heartbreak in the end more often than not. Noah had already taught me that lesson. I didn't need a refresher course.

I'd never committed to even a semi-serious relationship. I think I was twelve years old the first time Mama had explained that nothing good could come of it—and I was pretty certain that the last such lecture had been this month. She loved the Wolves the way a mother loves the worst-behaved of her children, but she reminded me often that loving a Wolf was a life-changer . . . as if I somehow didn't get that. My father died when I was twelve, shot on a job for the club. It was the beginning of a lot of years of hearing Mama tell me that love was a mistake.

Unfortunately, a lifetime of hearing her say that relationships were unwise didn't make Alamo any less sexy.

We drove in near silence. The whoosh of the wipers and the tapping of rain on the truck were the only sounds other than the wheels on the road. It was peaceful, and I was tired enough that it was lulling me to sleep again. When I noticed that I'd started slumping down in the seat, I forced myself to straighten up. "Where are we going?"

"Miss Bitty might still be awake if you want me to carry you home," he offered. "I brought your keys, your gun, and your clothes that were on the front seat."

"Thank you," I said quietly.

"I locked your car up too."

"Thank you," I repeated, realizing that he was being as courteous as possible, and I'd been a lot less than gracious. "Sorry if I was bitchy."

"You were wet, frightened, and tired." He reached out like he was going to pat me or something, but then his hand returned to the wheel.

"Still . . ."

"It's all good, Ellen. You haven't ever owed me an explanation for anything. That hasn't changed tonight, darlin'."

We lapsed into silence again until he asked, "Do you want me to take you to your house or . . . ?"

"No. Mama's got ears like a soldier," I said, thinking

about trying to explain why I was coming home wet and muddy and mostly naked. If she saw me like this, I wouldn't ever hear the end of it.

"Maybe Aubrey's awake . . . or Dash. If you called him, he's up." I looked around for my purse and saw it on the floor. I hated the idea of dealing with Noah on top of everything else, but it wasn't like my day was going to get a whole lot worse. "Maybe I could crash on his sofa."

Alamo cleared his throat. "Dash wasn't very pleased about me calling. He's . . . busy."

I snorted. "You mean he's got some girl there."

"He was worried about you, though," Alamo added quickly.

There was something off in his tone, enough so that I asked, "Why would I care what Dash is doing?"

Alamo didn't answer. Instead, he was silent long enough that I was about to repeat my question when he said, "If you're not going home, you can stay at my place tonight. I know Killer said he and Aubrey were out tonight, so she's probably still with him."

I looked out into the night, not sure what to do. Maybe it was better to go home and deal with Mama's nagging. Being alone with Alamo wasn't exactly *un*appealing, but I didn't want him to feel beholden. He had just admitted that he was avoiding me, and while it didn't make me feel particularly warm and fuzzy, it did clarify that I had no business trapping him.

"Ellen?"

I glanced over at Alamo.

"I have a huge tub," he said. "You can take a hot bath and get the mud off you."

I smiled at the image of Alamo in an oversize bathtub . . . and then I flashed to the thought of him standing up out of that bath. The truck seemed a lot warmer all of the sudden. I wasn't trying to replace anyone, including Noah, and I certainly wasn't looking for what Killer had found. That didn't mean that I was blind to the deliciousness that was currently dripping wet and only inches away from me.

"That sounds perfect. Thank you for being there for me . . . *again*."

Chapter 15

WHEN WE REACHED ALAMO'S HOUSE, HE PULLED under a carport and cut off the engine. "Hold tight for a second, darlin', and I'll grab your door."

The carport was only a few steps from the house, but I was glad I wouldn't be stepping directly back out into the wet. I was still damp, but I wasn't cold. Getting a cold shower once tonight had been more than enough.

A moment later Alamo came around to open my door. I wasn't opposed to chivalry. I didn't *expect* it as if it was my due, the way some women did, but I could appreciate a man treating me like I was precious. I turned to climb out of the truck and had to decide between keeping the jacket on my body or having my hands free.

Before I could decide what to do, Alamo put his hands on my waist and lifted me out of the truck. "Come on inside."

"Let me get my things," I started, but when I stepped forward, I realized I had the same problem. There really was no way to keep covered and do much else.

From the brief heated gaze as Alamo saw the expanse of skin that I inadvertently flashed as I stepped away from the truck, he wasn't complaining yet.

Seeing the tightening of his jaw, his deep inhalation of breath, and his lingering glance made me happier than it should have. I wasn't vain, but the way he always seemed to run from me made me a little crazy sometimes. I smiled and gathered up my purse and clothes, letting the jacket gap just a bit wider.

"I dropped your gun and keys in there." Alamo nodded at my bag, eyeing it warily as if a woman's purse was inherently dangerous—or maybe he was just looking for somewhere to stare after the way he'd just responded to seeing my bare skin. I was certainly *hoping* that was the case. I didn't want to manipulate him, but what woman doesn't like being appreciated?

Alamo motioned me toward his house. It was only a half dozen steps between the carport and the small covered porch on the front of the house, but those steps were enough that I realized again how cold the rain was. I was grateful for the continued shelter the moment we were on the porch.

He unlocked the door and opened it for me to go in first.

Being treated so politely was *almost* enough to make me forget that I was wearing next to nothing. He was unusual. I'd seen him laughing and carrying on with the rest of the younger Wolves, but he was always exceedingly polite to women. Even when he was walking away from me over and over, he wasn't hurtful or rude. Tonight, though, he appeared to be letting me into his home.

He locked the door behind us, and I heard the telltale beeps of an alarm being set. "I'll write down the code for you. Most of the club has it, so it's nothing."

"You don't need t—"

"I don't want you to feel trapped," he said firmly.

I looked away again and took in what I could of his home. The house wasn't huge, maybe a three-bedroom at most, but it was surprisingly orderly—not that I expected him to be a slob, but I'd never been inside a man's house that was so neat and clean. It was simply furnished too. No clutter had accumulated anywhere. I could see a giant television, a dark brown leather sofa, and a coffee table that looked as if it had been made out of an old engine. The table had a clear sheet of glass seeming to float above the engine. There was one book on the table, and that was it. No bottles or dishes or ashtrays were scattered on the surface of the table.

In the entryway where we stood, I noticed a small stand with a bowl, presumably for keys, and a few pieces of mail addressed to Alejandro Díaz.

"I don't want to track mud everywhere," I said. "If you want to move past me, go ahead . . ."

"I'm not any cleaner than you are," he pointed out. He paused, glancing at my mostly bare legs, and added, "I'm just wearing more clothes."

At that simple reminder, everything felt slow and heavy, as if we were wading through thick summer air. It was a feeling that came over me far too often when I was with Alamo. Sometimes I thought it was my imagination, but other times I thought it was the heft of words we both weighed and rejected without speaking them.

I stepped a little farther to the side when I realized that he was bending down to unfasten his boots. It seemed strangely intimate to be standing in his house like this. I wanted to pause and wonder over the fact that I was in *Alamo's* house. He was a very private man. All I knew was that he'd moved to Williamsville from somewhere in the Carolinas, had a sister, and was maybe twenty-seven or twenty-eight. I hadn't even been sure of his full name until tonight. Using names other than their Christian names wasn't uncommon for bikers, but I'd grown up in the midst of the Wolves, so I knew most of the club by their given names too, especially the younger bikers. In their cases, we'd gone to school together. It was only the men who came to the Tennessee chapter from elsewhere that I didn't know.

It was only Alamo I wanted to know better.

Being allowed inside Alamo's house after he'd so constantly put distance between us felt like an invitation to know him better, and I wanted that. Unfortunately, I also wanted to do it when I wasn't doing a striking impression of a wet cat. I tried to toe off my boots. It was a slow process, but the alternative was bending over. Alamo's jacket was long, but not so long that it would cover my ass if I bent down to take off a boot. Putting my nearly bare ass in his face was . . . either rude or a blunt invitation that seemed wrong after he'd rescued me.

So I stood there trying to think of another solution. My poor brain wasn't having much luck with this dilemma either. I swore I wasn't as daft as I'd felt tonight. Clearly my lousy day wasn't doing wonders for my mind.

After Alamo pulled off his second boot, he looked at me. "Do you want help?"

My hand tightened on the jacket, holding it together at the middle. "That would be nice," I said in a voice I didn't entirely recognize.

Alamo squatted in front of me, paused, and looked up at me. "Balance yourself on me so you can lift your foot."

I put one hand on his shoulder. Touching him made me far too aware of his position—and of how little I wore under his jacket. I shivered.

"Lift."

Silently I obeyed. He tugged my boot off. He was being a complete gentleman, but I was thinking about him in ways that were far from ladylike. It wasn't new. We'd ended up in these tense moments since the day we met. Right about now was when he usually ran or retreated or whatever he called it.

Tonight, though, his fingers grazed my calf as I lowered my foot. I drew a sharp breath. Part of me was embarrassed. The rest of me wanted to ask if he could turn my lousy day into something good.

"Lift," he said, quieter this time.

He removed the second boot, still acting as chivalrous as if I were a nun. Instead of pressing the moment, he retreated again. He set my boot to the side and stood. "Let me show you where the bathroom is."

I followed him, leaving wet footprints on his floor. He was leaving a trail too, and I noticed how very small my feet were next to his. I liked that he made me feel like a waif of a girl, despite not being one of those model-thin types. I might love fashion, but I couldn't ever have been a model. My body wasn't made for being that thin.

The house felt silent, and the sense of everything being strangely intimate continued to build again as Alamo started the bath and picked up a jar of pale purple bath crystals.

"Salt?"

I nodded and looked around the room. It was a surprisingly large bathroom, even though there was a massive slipper tub in the center of it. I'd expected a garden tub or even one of those regular tub-and-shower combos, but extra-long or something. This was neither. It was a tall, wide, old-fashioned-looking slipper tub.

Alamo didn't look at me as he poured the salt in, but he obviously saw my curious look because he said, "I like to soak, not with all that smelly girlie stuff, but in hot water. I got permission from the landlord to add the tub after I moved in. Regular tubs are too small."

"I didn't say anything." I smiled at his vaguely defensive attitude. "The only thing I *might* ask is how much it would cost to use this sometimes."

"My door's always open to you, Ellen." He had that soft tone that I remembered from the night he'd picked me up half a year ago—and that he'd used earlier as we stood in the rain. I wanted to believe he reserved it for me. I'd never heard it when he talked to anyone else, but then again, I rarely heard him talk to any women.

"As long as I call first, right?" I teased, trying to end the renewal of my foolishly hopeful thoughts.

"No need." He met my eyes and added, "I don't have a woman right now. Haven't since I moved here."

"I've seen you with girls. There was that blonde—"

"Dating doesn't mean they're in my house . . . or my tub. I don't make a habit of bringing women to my home." He shrugged. "I like my space. Killer's been here. Echo. Mike. That's really about it. This is my home, darlin', and that's not where I'd let just anyone wander about. Women I went out with once or twice aren't the same as you, and to be clear, Ellen, dating doesn't mean they're in my bed."

"I wasn't saying you—"

"Actually you *were*," he said, cutting me off. His voice grew harsh as if he was angry, even though I didn't know why. He shook his head and added, "You think just because Dash and Killer can't keep it zipped that we're all like that."

"Killer's all but married to Aubrey already," I corrected. I was still feeling protective of Killer. Ever since he'd gotten shot, I was prone to forgive most any offense and defend him ferociously. I crossed my arms and pointed out, "He's a one-woman Wolf now."

Alamo nodded. "True. Aubrey's good people, even though I can't see how a sweet girl like her fell for a prickly bastard like him. He's a lucky man." He met my eyes. "But Dash is a fool."

"Because?" My voice grew all wobbly when I asked. I hated that he thought ill of me for my past with Noah.

Alamo shook his head, but he didn't clarify. He never brought it up, never mentioned the day we'd met. I wished he would. I wished he'd just tell me that he thought I was an idiot or a slut or whatever it was that he thought. All I knew was that when Dash's name came up or Alamo saw me talking to Dash, he turned away. Maybe *he* had never made a mistake, but that shouldn't mean that he judged me for one I made a long time ago.

"Right, then." I took a breath and stepped closer to the tub and, consequently, closer to Alamo. There was no way to check the water and hold the jacket closed—or avoid bending over. Truthfully, though, I wasn't sure I wanted to either. I wasn't careless with my body, but I wasn't a prude either. If he was going to think I was a pass-around girl, maybe he'd end this ridiculous distance between us. There was no reason for him to know that I could count my bedmates on one hand and have fingers to spare. I hadn't been with anyone since Noah and I split.

I let go of the edges of the jacket, letting it gap open. Almost involuntarily, Alamo dropped his gaze to the middle of the bright blue bra and then down to the matching panties that I'd exposed. Earlier, it was dark enough and I was cold enough that I wasn't sure what he'd thought. I knew this set was a good choice for me though. The blue was a nice contrast against my pale skin, but it wasn't something predictable like black or red.

He took a moment simply staring at me, and I felt like my skin burned where his gaze touched. I rolled my left shoulder so the jacket fell off that side, and then pulled it forward over my right side. It looked as practiced as it was. I might not have a long list of ex-lovers, but I'd spent more than a few hours learning how to make myself look natural and relaxed at things that were terrifying. My body wasn't perfect, but whose is? Confidence was sexier than physical perfection.

Seeing Alamo's eyes darken was renewed proof of that truth.

"Here." I held his jacket out to him. "Thank you for keeping me warm. Sorry it got a little wet. I guess I was pretty soaked." I ran a finger along the inside of one of my bra straps. "I appreciate not having to ride home in just this, though."

His gaze tracked my hand as he accepted his leather without looking at it. He watched as I propped a foot on the tub and rolled one of my stockings down. When I repeated the action on the other one, his hand fisted on his leather jacket.

I bit back a smile.

Once he looked back at my hand, I slowly slid it down my hip until I reached the top edge of my panties. I paused, enjoying hearing the quiet exhalation as he waited, and then I started to slide my panties down.

"What are you doing, Ellen?" His voice wasn't as soft and comforting now. He sounded like he was struggling. I loved that I was finally getting a reaction.

"What does it look like?" I paused in my disrobing.

He looked at my mostly naked body. "Either trying to seduce me or getting naked so you can get in the tub."

"Does it have to be one or the other?" I asked softly.

He tossed his jacket toward the door, and the next moment he grabbed me and yanked me closer. After months of barely being within a foot of me before stepping backward, he had me so close that his wet jeans were harsh against my now-bare legs.

I looked up, and he caught my mouth in the sort of kiss that made me think every other man had been doing this *very* wrong. My arms twined around his neck, and he lifted me up so I didn't have to stretch.

I wrapped my legs around him, cherishing the strength

in his arms as he moved to support me with one hand under my ass. His T-shirt was sopping wet, and worse yet, it was between me and his skin. I started trying to tug it up.

Bare stomach. Bare chest. I could feel each wet, hard inch of Alamo as I tugged the shirt up. I wanted to look, to touch, but seeing that exposed skin meant stopping kissing him.

I pulled back only long enough so I could get the shirt over his head, but as soon as I started to do so, he lowered me and my feet touched the floor again.

"No. I don't do halfway, Ellen." He stared down at me. "I can't do this. I can't mess around with someone under club protection."

My kiss-addled brain clearly wasn't working right. Seeing the bit of a tattoo that was visible above his belt wasn't helping. I wanted to see the rest, to see him. He, however, was stepping backward.

"What do you mean?" I managed to force my gaze higher so I was looking at his face. The wet T-shirt clung partway up his chest, baring skin I'd finally been able to touch. He was right there. He'd been kissing me. Now? Nothing but a glimpse of bare skin that was distracting me from my attempts at conversation.

"Protection?" I repeated stupidly.

"I'm not going to start shit in the club for a one-nighter," he clarified—or seemed to think he'd clarified.

My temper washed back over me. I'd been doing so well, telling myself I didn't mind that he thought I got around or that he thought I wasn't attractive or whatever his drama was, but his words hurt enough that I was suddenly furious instead of aroused.

"Okay," I said as carefully and calmly as I could. "You're not from here, so maybe you're confused or something. I'm not under protection. My father was a Wolf, but he's gone. I'm not anyone's old lady, *and* I'm an adult. I can choose my own bedmates without anyone's approval or permission."

Alamo shook his head. "Then maybe you need to tell Dash that."

"Excuse me?" I stepped back and crossed my arms over my chest again. "That was a *long* time ago."

"Was it?"

"I'm not the one in his bed tonight, in case you forgot that," I snapped.

"And I'm not interested in being a revenge fuck because he stepped out on you again," Alamo said just as sharply.

"Now you listen here, Mister Judgmental." I pointed my finger at him like he was a misbehaving child. "Not that it's any of *your* business, but I haven't been in his bed since the day I climbed on the back of your bike."

Alamo looked . . . surprised. There was no other word for it. He hadn't expected that answer. It was obvious in his expression.

There were only a few possibilities: Dash had lied to Alamo, he'd presumed rights that weren't his and told Alamo I was off-limits, or Alamo was simply confused. I wasn't particularly pleased with any of those possibilities.

"Then . . . that doesn't make sense," Alamo said, frowning now. "You're not with Dash?"

"I'm not with Noah," I stressed. "I have *not* been since the day you picked me up in the alley."

Alamo shook his head. "That's not what I heard. He made it very clear that you were under his protection, and I was to keep my hands off."

"That was *months* ago!" I pointed out. "Before—"

"Not before," Alamo interrupted. "After."

This time I was the one shaking my head in confusion. I opened my mouth, but there wasn't anything I could say other than calling Noah or Alamo a liar. Finally I managed to say, "Oh."

My temper was dowsed, as was my libido.

"I don't poach, Ellen. He said you were his, and . . . he hasn't rescinded that. He's *repeated* it in case I forgot." Alamo took a step back, as if being close but not touching was as difficult for him as it was for me. Gently he asked, "Why do you think I've stayed clear of you?"

"Because you aren't interested," I said, but my voice lifted at the end, making it seem like a question instead of a statement.

"Christ, woman! I stayed away because I forget myself when you're near." He laughed, not like it was funny but like he was uncomfortable. "Killer's been on my ass about it too. I don't want trouble. I tell myself that over and over, but then I see you, and all my logic starts evaporating."

Again all I could muster was a quiet "oh."

I wanted to say more. I wanted to call Noah or Killer. Hell, I wanted to call Echo, but it was the middle of the night, and my wanting a man wasn't the sort of emergency that justified calling Killer *or* Echo. And Noah needed to look me in the eye when we sorted this shit out.

Unfortunately, that all meant that I was standing in Alamo's bathroom, nearly naked and having been kissed like kisses were art, and I was *still* going to bed alone. I'd wanted Alamo more and more over the past few months. He was kind and funny and sweet and sexy. Here I was in his house, and I was no closer to progress.

"I'll get you a shirt you can sleep in," Alamo said after several moments of staring at me in silence. "I'll leave it outside the door so you have privacy."

And then he left me there, and I felt like screaming again. My day wasn't ending any better than it had been going since I'd left for the interview. The difference was that this time I could blame it on one very specific person: Noah Dash.

Chapter 16

ALAMO WALKED INTO HIS FRONT ROOM AND HUNG UP HIS jacket. Knowing that Ellen was naked in his tub wasn't doing wonders for his resolve. She'd seemed genuinely confused when he'd mentioned Dash, although Dash had all but hung a "do not touch" sign on Ellen six months ago.

Alamo had followed the rules. He'd kept it light and easy, and he hadn't smacked Dash despite seeing him flirting with everything with a pulse. He'd kept clear of Ellen as much as he could—and to find that she and Dash weren't even together was infuriating. Maybe they did this regularly. That had been what Alamo had assumed, that they were one of those insane together-apart-together couples.

Tonight, though, Dash was in bed with some girl while Ellen was cold and stranded. There was no reason he couldn't have come to pick her up tonight, or have taken her to sing or to see Killer in the hospital. Honestly, Alamo couldn't understand why Dash wasted his time with the girls he did when Ellen was around—or why she put up with it if they *were* actually just on the outs—but relationships weren't exactly his thing.

He'd had exactly two that were anything semi-serious, but in both cases they'd fallen apart over Alamo's prioritizing Zoe or the Wolves over his then-girlfriends. If he met a woman who didn't think his devotion to his family was a problem, maybe he could consider settling down. He wanted to. Unlike a lot of the bikers he'd known in his life, Alamo wasn't interested in the women who waited around like groupies hoping to be upgraded into something more. He'd moved to Tennessee for a clean start, and he wasn't going to mess up because he broke club rules. The Wolves were family. Aside from his sister, they were his *only* family.

That didn't change the fact that Ellen was in his thoughts far too often. After her comments tonight, he was starting to think that Dash had simply marked Ellen as off-limits in case he wanted her back later. It didn't matter, though. Being interested in Ellen didn't change the fact that she was off-limits until Dash rescinded his claim.

Alamo grabbed a beer out of the fridge. It wasn't what he wanted, but what he *wanted* would land him in trouble—

and he had plenty of that dogging him already. After he'd put a beating on that asshole in North Carolina, he'd worked to put that rage away. He'd slipped here and there, especially when the car full of jerk-offs in traffic had been eyeing Ellen.

He'd hoped that the fact they had Carolina plates was a coincidence, but he'd been a bit wary afterward. Nothing else had surfaced since that day, though, so he was hoping that mess was in the past. If not, he'd deal.

The one thing that set his temper on edge faster than lightning was someone disrespecting a woman he cared about. Zoe and her roommate Ana were both careful to remind him that they could hold their own in many cases, and he was grateful for that. Honestly, he couldn't fathom even dating someone who wasn't ballsy because his temper simply wouldn't bear it. It wasn't like he'd ever so much as raised his voice at a woman, so he wasn't worried that he'd hurt one. It was more that he worried that he'd get so protective over one that he'd hurt someone *else*. His little sister's friend was crying on their sofa that night, and he'd just snapped. Afterward, the guy he'd put in the hospital had claimed he hadn't seen his attacker, and the girl offered Alamo an alibi.

Thinking of his sister made him realize that he'd gotten so caught up in Ellen that he hadn't checked his phone. That was the first time in months that he'd failed to check in with his baby sister. He went to his jacket and grabbed his phone from the inside pocket. He couldn't get it to check for messages earlier because the jacket was wrapped around a nearly naked woman, and he wasn't about to go pawing at her to find his phone.

He turned it on to see eight texts from Zoe. He was relieved, even more so as he scrolled through them all. That was the trade-off they'd agreed on when he moved. He was willing to go and let her stay there, but she had to keep him updated on where she was. Some people might think it was a little excessive, but her regular—and often smartass—texts were a salve for his constant worry at being away from her.

As he read the long scroll of messages, he smiled. Apparently Zoe and Ana had been out to a movie, bought coffee, stopped to buy tampons, and then headed home. She also pointed out that they were back home and the door was locked. Oh, and that they *both* needed tampons, so "Hey, no worries that anyone's knocked up!" He snorted and texted back that the immaculate conception might be her greatest life achievement if she could pull it off one of these months. Her reply—"I could've gotten laid! One day it'll happen"—was instant and accompanied by a picture of her sticking her tongue out at him as if she was two, not twenty.

Knowing she was home and safe always made him sleep better. The past year or two, he'd felt the same about Ana. They were his responsibility. He'd failed by missing Ana's text the night she was attacked. He hated worrying that he'd fail them again by being a state away, but they weren't willing to move or to agree to his moving back home. These nightly texts were what made it possible for him to sleep.

He tapped out: "Check in with Nick this weekend too."

"Yes, dear."

"Either you let the Wolves know your schedule or I move back."

"Already called N," Zoe replied. "Stop worrying. We're both fine."

He smiled and typed, "Love you, lobita. Sleep well."

Her reply was as routine as his last one had been: "Love you too. Kisses."

His guilt over not checking in earlier lingered, but his sister and Ana were both fine. Ellen was too. That was the important thing. The thought of all of the things that could've happened earlier made him want to grab Ellen and elicit promises that she'd never end up alone along the road again. He couldn't, but he wanted to.

Instead, he went into his room to get changed out of his wet clothes.

Walking out a few minutes later to find Ellen standing in the living room wearing nothing but his T-shirt made him reconsider his earlier decision about not calling Dash to ask why he claimed she was off-limits when she knew nothing about it. Alamo wasn't looking for trouble—*still*—but it seemed absurd that the woman he wanted was here, single, interested, and still forbidden.

"I didn't realize you were out here," he said stupidly. "Let me get you a sweatshirt or something."

"This shirt works," Ellen said. She stood there with her hair in a towel, her body barely covered in black cotton, and her nipples visible through the shirt like an invitation he wanted to accept.

Instead he said, even more stupidly, "It's cold."

He went right back into his room and pulled out the heaviest, longest shirt he could find. He grabbed a pair of sweatpants too. They'd be too big, but maybe she could use a belt or tie them in a knot at the hip or something. He needed not to see her, needed some sort of reminder that she was out of his reach, and she wasn't doing anything to remind him of that. He had to.

Ellen's expression when he returned to the main room made him stop in the doorway. She looked like she wasn't sure if she was angry or hurt or both, and he didn't know what to do with that. Women usually fit into three categories in his life: his sister and her friends he wanted to protect, brief hookups, or strangers he didn't notice or chose not to notice. Ellen didn't fit in any of those. She wasn't someone he wanted to be with for a brief encounter—and he sure as hell didn't feel brotherly toward her.

"You thought I was with Noah," she said finally. "That was why you called him when you found me earlier along the road. You think I'm his . . . what? A woman who takes scraps?" Ellen's hands went to her hips, the movement easing the hem of her shirt higher. "I put an end to that the day I met you. Noah hasn't been in my bed in *half a year.* When he told you that, it was right after you picked me up, right?"

"Yes, but . . ." Alamo held his hands up in surrender.

"Well, that was then, and this is now. Tomorrow, if he brings my car here before I'm awake, you drag his sorry ass in here and wake me. You're about to owe me an apology."

"An apology?"

"For not just asking me," she explained.

"Yes, ma'am." He tried to keep his emotion out of his voice, but there was something fabulous about a woman in a temper. He wouldn't want to be on the receiving end of it, but seeing her like this made him certain that she'd be everything he could want in life. There was nothing inherently *wrong* with women who were sweet-tempered. They just didn't appeal to him. Ellen did. He'd done his level best to ignore it, but it was far from easy to do so.

"Alamo?"

"Yes, ma'am," he repeated.

Ellen crossed her arms over her chest, and he thought she was going to turn her temper on him for woolgathering, but instead her voice grew soft and she asked, "Can I get a pillow and blanket for the sofa?"

Alamo blinked at her and realized he hadn't told her he had a guest room. It wasn't typical of single guys, but he had a sister who visited often enough that there was no way he could have a house with only one bed. Doing so would mean *he* had to try to sleep on the sofa, which was far too uncomfortable for him and had been since he was too young to drive, or that he'd be asking a woman to sleep on the sofa. That was completely impossible for him. He might not have been raised by the classiest people, but he was still a Southern man and that meant that he was duty-bound to treat women like the precious creatures they were. No exceptions.

"Come on." He led Ellen to the room Zoe used and felt like an idiot for not already thinking to see what clothes his sister had left behind. Admittedly, seeing Ellen wet and nearly naked hadn't done great things for his higher-level processing, but he felt foolish. "There are probably pants of some sort in the dresser. They're small enough that they wouldn't fall off you like these." He held up the pants and shirt he held in his hand.

"Can I still borrow the sweatshirt?" Ellen asked.

She stepped forward, and Alamo felt like retreating—almost as much as he felt like grabbing her. He wasn't going to piss off the club. He needed them, not just because they were family, but because they'd help him keep Zoe safe if her father ever got out of the joint. Wanting a woman, even one as amazing as Ellen, wasn't enough to risk his sister's safety.

He tossed the shirt at the foot of the bed and took several steps backward.

"Thanks," she said.

He nodded. It was ridiculous trying to find the line between being rude and keeping his distance. He was always careful with her, trying to avoid even one-on-one conversations. Having her in his house made that a lot less than possible.

They stood there awkwardly for several moments. There

were a lot of things he wanted to say, questions he wanted to ask, explanations he wanted to offer, but words weren't his thing. He thought about what he wanted to say, but still ended up picking the wrong words and saying something even stupider than the ones he had spurned.

After another few silent moments, he mumbled, "If you need anything, I'm here."

He felt a little like a coward, but he didn't know what to do with Ellen. He didn't want to make her uncomfortable, and if he stayed there, he'd either say something he shouldn't or reconsider his decision to call Dash and ask why Ellen was off-limits if they weren't still together after all. The smartest thing he could do was exactly what he had been doing all along: stay clear of her as much as possible and avoid being alone with her.

Right now Ellen was still out of bounds.

Chapter 17

A FEW HOURS LATER, I WAS ALREADY AWAKE. IT WAS TOO damn early, but no matter what time I went to sleep, I *always* woke early. I hated it. It was as if my brain kicked on whether or not my body was ready to engage.

That didn't mean I was getting out of bed yet.

I'd been stretching and trying to decide if I wanted to get dressed in proper clothes or get coffee first. Coffee was essential, especially at this hour. Unfortunately, getting to the coffee required movement—which *might* require clothes. I had Alamo's shirt and a pair of leggings I'd found in the dresser, but it was pretty casual to be walking around in front of a man I wasn't sleeping with.

I didn't even want to ponder why he had a bunch of women's clothes. They were all the same size and style, so I was fairly sure they were all the possessions of one woman. I had a couple of T-shirts from exes, but that was because they were comfortable. Since nothing in the dresser would fit Alamo and I was pretty certain that he didn't wear women's clothes, *that* clearly wasn't why he kept some woman's clothing.

None of which helped my "dressed first or coffee first" question, which—as with many other mornings in my life—seemed very pressing and large. Usually it was answered by whether or not my mother had an overnight guest. It almost always made me feel skeezy to have a stranger see me in my jammies, especially a stranger who had slept with my mother. Today, though, there were no strangers—only Alamo, who had seen me in my pseudo-pajamas, as well as seeing me in a lot less. Soaking-wet underwear didn't hide anything, so I was leaning toward getting coffee before getting properly dressed. If not, with the way my luck had been going, I'd spill coffee all over myself and the only clothes I had with me. Deciding to get up hadn't made me energetic, though.

Then I heard Dash's voice.

I was up and out the door so fast that I was surprised I hadn't tripped. I tore into the room and pointed at him. "*You!* You ought to be grateful I'm not kicking your ass right now."

Dash took a step back. His eyes widened, and his mouth opened. "I brought your car," he said, holding up my spare key like a peace offering. "I got someone to pick me up here too in case you were sleeping."

I snatched my key out of his hand. I had no patience to wait to hear what else he had to say—or desire to let him keep my key either. That was a right for friends, and currently Noah Dash was dangerously close to losing that title.

"Why does Alamo think I'm your fuck bunny?"

"My . . ." His attention shot to Alamo, and I knew that there were words he would be saying—or possibly saying with fists—if I wasn't standing in the room.

"Fuck bunny," I repeated, crossed my arms over my chest and tapping my foot exaggeratedly like a thumping rabbit. "You better get explaining."

"I never said . . . Ellie, come on. You know I wouldn't talk trash on you." Dash stepped forward.

My hand shot out, palm flattened on his chest. He was obviously strong enough to keep moving, but he stilled at my touch.

"Explain yourself," I ordered.

"All I did was say you were under my protection . . . but that was when we . . ." Dash started. "We had a fight, but I thought we were still . . ."

I smacked him up alongside the head.

"Hey!" He ducked back, clearly expecting another smack to follow.

So I didn't disappoint him. This time I slammed my palm into his shoulder. "And what do you think people will *think* when you say some shit like that? Huh? Do you think they'll say, 'Oh, that Dash, he's a meddling ass'? or will they say, 'Ellen's giving it up to Dash again'. You tell me, Noah Dash. What will they *say*?"

He glared at me. "I'm just trying to look out for you."

"Liar."

"Ellie, when I first did it, I was just trying to make sure that no one treated you poorly." Noah gave me the same sort of pitiful expression that had worked wonders when we were kids *and* had still worked when we were adults. It was as good as an admission of guilt.

I stared at him, letting the facts sift through my sleep-deprived mind. If he was guilty, that meant he'd fucked up. I rolled what I knew over in my mind, and in a sickening flash of clarity, I realized that he had lied to me—and not just a little. If he had said I was under his protection, that meant he'd all but announced that we were sharing sheets.

In a remarkably steady voice for a person five seconds from tears, I said, "People knew about us. When you acted like we were a secret, people *knew*. You treated me like I was only worthy of slipping into your apartment after dark, but they knew. The whole goddamn club knew!"

"You're taking this all wrong," Noah said.

He looked at me, and I knew what he still wasn't saying. He thought I'd come back to him. I had already decided I wasn't going to, but I'd hoped we could be friends. Right now I wasn't even sure I was going to be able to continue to call him a friend.

"All that time when I wasn't allowed on your bike, when

you didn't want people to get the wrong idea, they *knew anyhow*. You can't have it both ways, *Dash*. You can't treat me like I'm your property when you won't own up to it." I took a deep shuddering breath. "You did, though . . . You treated me like I was yours, but you never meant for it to be true. I was a fool."

"Ellie, come on. I just wanted to keep you safe. You know you're special to me, and I just couldn't stand the idea of the rest of those asses taking advantage of you. You know how guys are." He reached out like he'd hug me.

I stepped back. Tears would fall if I let him touch me, and that wasn't okay. Maybe it never would be again. He was breaking me.

I shook my head. "We're done here."

"Ellie—"

"We're *done*, Noah, and I expect that you'll tell Mike to let the Wolves know that you rescind your protection." I blinked so my tears of anger wouldn't spill. "Just . . . stay out of my business, Dash. I don't want to even speak to you."

"Ellie . . ."

I shook my head again. "Before you go, tell Alamo that I'm *not yours*, since I never was. You tried to have it both ways, and you have *nothing* as a result. Fix it."

At first Dash didn't reply. Then he stared unwaveringly at me as he told Alamo, "Ellie's not under my protection, but if you think that this means she's—"

"It's none of your concern what I am," I interrupted. "I don't even want to lay eyes on you. If I were a man, you'd be on your ass right now. The *only* reason I'm not punching you is that I don't want to embarrass myself in front of Alamo."

"You need to understand—"

"I understand everything I need to," I interrupted. My temper was so close to boiling that I was starting to shake. "I was an idiot for putting up with this as long as I did. You didn't want me enough to treat me right, but you didn't want anyone else to give me what you refused. *Fuck. You.* Noah."

He stared at me for another few moments, and then he turned and left without a word to me or to Alamo. Once I heard a car door slam, I pulled out a kitchen chair and sat. If I didn't, I was likely to fall down.

A few moments later, Alamo put a cup of coffee in front of me. "You take your coffee black, right?"

I looked up at him and nodded. I felt like I should be embarrassed. He always seemed to see me when I was a wreck. First the day I had left Noah, and then when Killer was shot *and* when I was dripping wet, tired, and nearly naked. Now, as icing on that awfulness, he got to see me angry and hurt. I hoped he remembered the other times, either when I was singing or we had ice cream or there were people around.

As I thought about his actions, I realized that all the times when I thought he was uninterested, it was all about the fact that he was influenced by Noah's lies. It shifted my understanding of almost every single encounter Alamo and I had ever had.

I met his eyes and said, “I swear my life isn’t as messed up as it looks.”

“It looks fine, Ellen.”

I snorted.

“You had a bad relationship situation, some amazing secret trips to sing, a perfectly understandable worry over Killer, and then a car breakdown,” he said with a shrug. “It’s not so awful.”

“And I can’t sing around the people who love me, and I keep flirting with you like some desperate—”

“Any man with half a brain would be interested in you, but I can’t ignore direct orders.”

“*Echo*?”

Alamo shook his head. “Killer. Dash warned me off. Killer said that Dash’s claim was no different from the rest of the club.” He shrugged. “I figured you two must’ve still been together. One of those couples who are back and forth all the time.”

“According to Noah we weren’t ever a couple,” I said. “I don’t love him. I don’t want him. I haven’t in a while . . . but I was already disgusted with myself for being *that* girl, you know? To think that everyone knew just makes it worse.”

“I’m sorry,” he said. “I had no idea it was a surprise to you.”

I wrapped my hands around the cup, which had a footprint, the UNC logo, and the words *Tar Heels* on it. It was an odd reminder of where he'd come from, of the fact that he had people and a life he'd left behind.

"I'm glad you didn't know it was a surprise, then. I'd rather be mad at just him than both of you," I told him bluntly. "You're probably the only one I'm not on the verge of getting ugly with . . . well, and Echo. I'd never disrespect him. But Killer? He should've said something. Hell, Big Eddie could've told me."

Alamo was silent as he finally poured his own coffee. Once he sat across from me, he said, "Point taken. Well, then, I'm sorry you found out the way you did."

"Thanks." I thought about how many bikers knew, and I wondered if my mother did too. Did everyone just assume that I was in Dash's bed all this time? I wasn't even sure I wanted to know. I didn't have the energy to start yelling at the whole lot of them, and to be honest, I just wanted to move on.

For a few moments, I debated the wisdom of my impulses. It wasn't that Alamo was a real rebound, though. I wasn't intending to use him. The fucked-up mess I'd had with Noah was in my past as far as I was concerned; it was only Noah and everyone else who had missed the memo.

"Just so we're putting it all on the table, I want you to know that Noah and I were together as kids, and then . . . I don't know . . . now and again we fell into old habits. But that all ended the day I met you." I looked away from my mug and met Alamo's eyes. "Not because of you or anything weird, but I wouldn't be with one Wolf and be thinking about another the way I've been thinking about you."

"You don't owe me explanations about anything," Alamo said carefully. He was eyeing me the way I suspected he'd watch someone he thought capable of pulling a knife—or, for example, stripping down and kissing him in his bathroom.

"I know, but . . ." I tried to think of the right way to say it. Sometimes I wanted to be less blunt than I was, but I'd never quite mastered that skill. Maybe it was being raised around Wolves and their women, or maybe it was just who I was. Either way, I was deficient in the Southern lady area. I met Alamo's eyes and said, "I just didn't want you to think I was the sort to flirt like I did if I had something going with another man. I'm not like that."

"Darlin', you don't owe me or *anyone* an explanation," Alamo said, just before he smiled that sweet flirtatious smile he passed out easily to women at the bar, including the female bartenders, but only rarely offered me. I liked it, liked being the one in his focus.

"There's been no one in my bed since the day we met," I added. "No one has a claim or right to be there either."

"Good to know." He took a sip of his coffee before asking, "Are you saying the job's open?"

I laughed. "For the right man. You applying?"

"I think I am," he said.

Then we sat and enjoyed our coffee in silence. It was wonderful to finally be speaking openly and to get the sense that he was receptive to my interest after all. I guess I hadn't imagined the way he'd watched me.

Being quiet with him was a weirdly comfortable thing, despite the fact that he'd just seen me five seconds from flaying the flesh off Dash. I shook my head. He'd *also* seen me nearly naked. All told, we should be a whole lot less relaxed than this, but we sat in peaceful silence. I liked it, the way he could be there without needing to fill up the space with words and questions. My own brain was noisy enough that sometimes people who were too filled with talk made me tense.

My mother was the opposite. Silence bothered her. She said my father had been like me; "still waters" was what she called my quiet spells. I wasn't so sure that was right. I wasn't exactly thinking anything deep or earth-shaking. It was more like my mind needed space to sort through thoughts and ideas. Silence was sometimes what I needed for . . . I guess what you'd call mental updates. I kind of visualized it as my mind plugging into some far-off server and downloading software updates. I wasn't going to *say* that, but it was the visual I thought closest to the way my body slowed.

Then it would pass, and I'd be me again—loud and bold, fearless and silly. The Ellen people saw was never as quiet as I was in my private hours each day. I needed that time, though. I was a wreck without it. I built quiet time into my routine. If my mom and her latest date weren't awake yet, I'd take my quiet when I had coffee. If not, I'd go outside or into my room. If all else failed, I'd take a bath or a long walk.

"Usually my silence bothers people," I said finally.

Alamo shrugged. "I like it." He met my gaze. "And I like that you're relaxed enough around me to be silent."

I stared at him. I'd thought that he had no idea how rare it was for me to be so at ease, and part of me wanted to run far and fast because I felt like he'd figured out one of my secrets. The rest of me, however, wanted to curl up next to him and go back to sleep. I had the sneaking suspicion that I could do that with him, that I could sleep soundly, that I could maybe even *sleep in* if he was at my side.

"Since we cleared that bullshit about Dash up and I'm not one for subtlety, what do you say to taking me for a ride?"

Alamo looked at me again, and then he returned to drinking his coffee. He didn't reply until he needed a refill. I liked that too, the way he wasn't rushing to answer. It made the silence shift into something charged with possibilities—and like most things with him in the past day, it made me think about what he'd be like naked. He was deliberate at almost everything, and I closed my eyes briefly against the images *that* thought evoked. I had the feeling that deliberate attention from him would be . . . everything a woman could want in bed.

"A ride?"

"Today," I clarified. "Not because I need to go somewhere. Not a favor. Just you and me and your bike."

He stood, walked over, and refilled his cup. He lifted the

pot and looked at me inquiringly. I held my cup out, and he topped me off.

"It depends on what you're looking for, Ellen."

"Nothing. A little stress relief." I paused, thinking of the number of times when I felt like we were on the edge of a conversation and he'd retreated. Now I understood why. I was furious with Dash, but I was also feeling cheated that I could've been here in this moment before now.

In a level, firm voice, I said, "This right here? It's good. I've wanted to talk to you alone so many times, but you always walked away. Coffee at your table is nice."

"But?" he prompted.

I grinned. I liked this straight-up negotiation and honesty. A lot of men were intimidated by women who spoke their minds. Sometimes I thought that Killer had been right when we were kids and he'd suggested that I was so blunt as a way to scare people off. It made it easy to see who was a runner. It worked, though. If they couldn't handle me in conversation, they sure as hell couldn't handle me any other way. Alamo seemed like he might be able to handle me, so I didn't try to mince words.

"But I want a ride," I said. "Not to carry me to work or as a favor, but a ride. No destination. No plans. Just a tank of gas and go. I hope you're going to stop walking away when I try to talk now that you know I'm available, but either way, I'm glad that whatever happens next is just between us."

I looked him over and let myself enjoy the very details I'd been training myself to ignore. He was fit and intimidating, and it looked like he'd be able to handle any trouble we came across. It did good things for the libido I'd been trying my damnedest to quash.

Alamo didn't reply, but he was grinning at my assessment. He leaned back and let me take a good long look. It was about as subtle as I felt, and I drew in an appreciative breath. Sometimes women thought that men didn't like being ogled, but that was sheer foolishness. A man wouldn't work to look that good if he wasn't wanting someone to notice. I was noticing, and for the first time since we'd met, there was no reason to pretend otherwise.

"Today I'm in a foul mood, and I want to be on the back of your bike," I said. "Riding with you without having to keep my distance will put my mood to rights."

"Is that all you want today? A ride?"

I paused, debating the wisdom of my next words, but I figured I was either all in or not at all at this point. I'd lost months because I had no idea he thought I was forbidden. I took a sip of the coffee I was cradling, hoping to sound less nervous than I really was, and said, "Sex at the end would be perfect, but I'm not demanding it."

"*Damn*, darlin'." He didn't look away. "An offer like that's enough to make a man offer all sorts of promises."

"No promises. No strings," I clarified quickly. "If we work well together, we can make a habit of it. Just to be clear, though: I'm not looking to be your old lady, and if there is one back home, I need to know. I'm not a home wreck—"

"There isn't," he interrupted. "There's no one."

I debated pressing the matter. There were an awful lot of women's clothes in his guest room for a man without someone in his life, but I trusted him. If he said there wasn't a woman, there wasn't. I knew him well enough to know that. Maybe there had been one, and she was gone now. Maybe he was holding on to the past. I didn't know, and if we were going with no strings, it wasn't my business. He was a good man with a sexy body and a custom bike. That was all I wanted in that moment. If I'd been looking for a relationship, I'd have a lot of other questions, but that wasn't what this was.

"Ride. Sex if it happens. Repeat if it's worth it. No strings either way," I clarified so we were both sure of where we stood and what was on the table. I tilted my head to stare into his eyes and asked, "So . . . are you in?"

"I'm in," he confirmed in a slightly rougher voice.

I finished my coffee and stood. "Meet me at my house in two hours then," I said, and then I went to get dressed and go home.

Chapter 18

If I was lucky, I could slip in, get changed into something to ride in, and then get out without an interrogation from my mother.

I wasn't lucky. Mama was waiting in the front room, the one she always called the "parlor" like we were some sort of gentrified people. We weren't. We were just regular people. We weren't on assistance, but we hadn't ever been money either. She earned enough at her job to pay the bills and buy groceries. The house was paid off because it was my father's. That was it. We weren't struggling, but we weren't headed off on luxury cruises either. I was hoping to change that now that Echo had pointed out that I could do so with my singing, but I wasn't sure that I could. These last few months were the first time I'd truly considered it, and it was both exciting and intimidating. I was starting to get back to being comfortable enough with the idea of singing in public, and I'd made some money doing it. Now that my internship was a wash, I was going to throw myself into it.

"Ellie?" Mama called when she heard the door close. There was a slim chance it would be anyone else. No one else walked in without knocking or calling out. Seeing my mother and one of her boyfriends wasn't comfortable for anyone.

I usually called out too—unless I was trying to slip up the stairs without stopping to chat. I bit back a sigh and answered, "Yeah, it's me."

Instead of darting upstairs as I had planned, I went into the living room. Mama was sitting on the sofa with a cigarette in hand, smudged eyeliner that told me she'd been crying, and a brittle smile that warned me that she was in what I often called "determined happiness." She was dressed in a pair of jeans so tight that if she stood, everyone and their cousin could tell she didn't wear underwear. The shirt she had on was some frilly number that was utterly unsuitable for sitting around the house at this unholy hour. There were only two reasons for her to be dolled up so early—either she was just getting home or she was newly single again. The shirt wasn't the worst of it, though. She had on her black leather vest, the one proudly proclaiming that she was the property of the Southern Wolves. She didn't wear it outside the house. Daddy had been gone since I was still in elementary school, and she hadn't belonged to anyone since him. Wearing that vest meant she was single. She always wore it around the house when she and her latest split up. Usually, there was a lot of chain smoking, and once in a while she'd throw a huge meal and fill the house with bikers. Echo always slipped me money for groceries afterward, not that we always needed it, but just because widows were under his care. I hadn't thought much about that until he'd pointed out that we didn't need to be under club care. I had another option.

"Tell me you had a better night than I did. Tell me you were out *there*"—Mama waved her hand in a wild gesture in the general direction of the world beyond our house—"celebrating getting that dressmaking job or something."

"Nope. I had a flat tire coming back, and I didn't get the job," I told her as I slumped into the chair across from her.

"That sucks." She sighed.

"Yeah."

"Harry went back to his wife," she announced in the same heavy tone I'd used. "He thought I could still scratch his itch after he moved home. Idiot."

"He snored like a rabid beaver anyhow. I could hear him clear downstairs." I bit my cheek as soon as the words were out. It was a silly game we always played when her lovers became exes.

"Smelled worse than that," she added sagely.

"Probably the foot fungus."

Mama sighed again and took a drag off the cigarette in

her hand before saying, "Poor Harry. He just couldn't bear living on his own, and when I said I wasn't looking to let anyone move in here, he said he was going back home."

There was no actual sympathy in her voice, and I knew that "poor Harry" wasn't how she really felt. She was livid, but Mama was a Southern lady. She might look like she wasn't particularly ladylike, but poverty and manners weren't mutually exclusive. It took effort to get her to break manners and say what she really meant—and that was my job.

"Bless his heart." I uttered the Southern truism with a fake sigh.

Mama didn't miss a beat before saying, "Well, the Good Lord sure hasn't blessed anything *else* of that man's. Harry was so small in his drawers that I think his exes might all still be considered virgins."

"Dodged another bullet," I told her, wondering if these post-breakup conversations had ever been any different. We'd shared some version of these same lines for as long as I could remember. I didn't know if there was a time when she cried or raged about a man. Honestly, I'd come to think that if she ever cared enough to feel that much for a man, she'd chosen to never spend another night with him. It was the ones who mattered *least* who seemed to get to stay the longest.

My mother was, in her way, still faithful to my father after all this time. It wasn't the sort of faithfulness most people would understand, but I had figured it out years ago.

Her heart was safe from anyone else's getting into it the way he had. The rest? They were distractions. The only one who stood a chance was Big Eddie, and he was too much of a gentleman to push his luck. I suspected he'd been waiting for Mama to be ready to be with another Wolf, but the closest he'd seemed to be able to get was a few conversations with her. I didn't understand them.

And I wasn't sure I wanted to know. The idea of a stepfather halfway between our ages was weird to me—and I knew that my mother wouldn't take up with a Wolf unless she meant it as more than a passing fancy. Everyone knew that.

After a few moments, she sighed. "I'm not sure I'm up to cooking a big meal this time, Ellie."

"So don't."

"Traditions are what keep things in order." Mama lit another cigarette, holding the new one to the still-glowing cherry of the one in her hand. "I like to have the family over when I'm blue. It helps."

I didn't know what to say to that. I got it; after all these years, I had to. I just didn't like it. I went over to her and kissed her cheek. "Let me talk to Echo or to Uncle Karl. Maybe we can have a party or a potluck. Aunt Dar might have ideas too."

My mother reached out and squeezed my hand. "You're a good kid. I don't understand half of what you say most of the time, but you're a good kid."

"Hush, you." I had to deny it, that was part of the rules

too. She didn't get me, though—never had, never would. Most of what I liked wasn't what made sense to her, and the one thing I thought we should have in common—bikers—was a source of stress between us.

We still had a no-lies rule, so I paused before heading up the stairs and said, "I'm going riding."

"With Noah?"

"No."

"Noah's a good boy," she started.

I held up my hand before she could start singing his praises again. The son of Eli Dash could do no wrong in my mother's eyes. "Alamo."

"Does Noah know?"

I sighed. "It's none of his business, Mama."

"I have no issue with Alejandro. He seems like a good man, but Eli's kid—"

"No." I tried to keep my temper down, but after finding out that Noah had been meddling in my life, I wasn't feeling as charitable as usual. "Dash might be worse than *you* when it comes to committing. When he falls, I'm going to sit back and hope the woman's got a boatload of patience."

Mama nodded. "Men are nothing but trouble. If it wasn't for sex or carrying things, I couldn't see a single reason to keep any of them past the first night. Your father was the only one worth keeping."

She lit another cigarette and glanced at the picture of my father that hung on the wall.

"Go on then," she said, shooing me off with the hand

holding a cigarette. "I'm sure you've got better things to do than sit here while I get all maudlin on you."

I gave her a kiss on her well-rouged cheek and headed upstairs.

Once out of her hearing, I had to decide if there was anyone to update. She expected it, even if she didn't mention it. Harry hadn't done anything wrong, not in a "needs an ass kicking" way, so updating the club wasn't necessary. I called my aunt Darlene quickly, filled her in, and decided that was enough. Mama wasn't keen on Echo or the others knowing her business most of the time, so I respected her wishes as much as I could. Plus, of course, Aunt Dar was the longtime wife of one of the Wolves, so if she decided to share my mother's single-again status, that was on her.

Family situation resolved, I started to go through my clothes to find the right thing to wear for my date with Alamo. As much as I wanted to wear something super-sexy, I also needed something that wouldn't result in road rash if we ended up laying the bike down. Alamo wasn't an unsafe rider by any stretch, and Williamsville was a very rider-aware town, but accidents still happened, and I was fairly sure that Alamo was the sort of man who wouldn't even let me on the bike if I wore a cute skirt to ride. Jeans were unavoidable; so was either a vest or a jacket.

Growing up around bikes and bikers meant that I also had a variety of boots for the occasion. I grabbed one of my favorite pairs: knee-high distressed black leather, sturdy but high-heeled, straps and buckles that looked more piratical than anything else. Tight jeans, tall boots, riding jacket . . . which left me with the girlie touches. I was all about independence, but I always preferred the girliest underthings I could find. Alamo had already got a glimpse of the blue set, so I looked through the options. Pale pink? Too soft. Red? Too predictable. Purple was a good compromise.

The top was the biggest challenge, so I went to get my shower while I let that thought stew. I'd missed this, primping for a night—or afternoon, in this case—out with someone. Maybe Alamo would be the perfect solution: a strings-free relationship with a beautiful man on a Harley. As long as he wasn't looking for strings, we could have something good now that I'd solved idiot Noah's attempt to keep the Wolves away from me.

Unlike Aubrey, I had no issue with being someone's old lady. In truth, if I ever decided to take dating seriously, I was more likely opposed to being with a man who *wasn't* a Wolf, but serious wasn't on my to-do list. Right now, that list was pretty short: relax and ride.

Chapter 19

ALAMO WASN'T TERRIBLY SHOCKED TO FIND KILLER ON his porch an hour later.

"I crawled out of a warm bed with Red to come check on your dumb ass," he said. Most of the Wolves wouldn't show up unannounced, but Killer had been the club enforcer since he was old enough to pull a trigger for Echo. The normal rules weren't ever something he considered.

"Don't recall calling you," Alamo pointed out even as he found an ashtray.

"Big Eddie called after he dropped Dash off here after getting Ellie's car." Killer tapped the tip of his cigarette on the counter. "I'm leaving town soon. Dad's going to ask you to step up."

Alamo stared at him. He'd been here only a short while. Gaining any position of importance with Echo himself was unexpected. On the other hand, Dash would be shit at being an enforcer. It didn't take a genius to see that he was more brains than violence. Carefully Alamo said, "I'm not looking to start trouble, but I don't want to be taking orders from Dash, especially right now."

"I get that, and so does Echo." Killer shrugged. "You did right by us with that mess over with the pricks who tried to screw with the girlie bars."

That had been more of a showing that they had the muscle and manpower than anything. Another club had tried to start some shit at a strip club that the Wolves owned. The manager called. The Wolves rode over to the little roadside dive and made their presence felt. It was just business.

He shrugged. "It wasn't a thing. I'm good with a fist or two."

"And that's what Echo needs," Killer said. He cupped his hand around his cigarette as he lit it. After a long drag, he muttered, "I'm going to miss these."

Alamo shook his head and grinned. "Little slip of a woman's got you whipped, boy."

"Damn straight she does," Killer said. "Red's worth it." He inhaled again and crushed his mostly unsmoked cigarette in the ashtray. "Didn't say I was *opposed* to quitting for her, just that I'll miss it."

After a moment, he continued, "You're going to need to sort your shit out with Dash. I'm not going to be here to keep you two in check, and Echo's not as nice as I am."

Alamo snorted.

"Dad needs someone to do my job," Killer said, clarifying exactly what position was open. "Dash . . . would be a fine president if that's the way things go, but he has no stomach for violence."

"Are you saying I do?" Alamo asked lightly, even though Killer was affirming his own theories of the situation.

"I know you," Killer said bluntly. "You'd keep him . . . *them* safe. Dash is an idiot sometimes, but he's my family. Echo . . . it would be bad for the club if he got hurt, and I need someone I trust to make sure that doesn't happen. I suggested he look to you."

Alamo nodded. "Aside from the part where I need to take orders from Dash, it's doable."

Killer laughed. "Boy's not going to end up president any time soon. My father's not stepping aside, and Dash isn't even ready to step up. For now, what you'd need to do is keep my father safe, do what he thinks needs doing. I'll talk to my cousin before I go." He paused, and then when Alamo said nothing, he prompted, "Is that a yes?"

It was an honor. They both knew it. Being recommended by Killer was a testament of his trust. Being offered a position by Echo was even more remarkable. Not all clubs handled things the way this one did, but Echo was like a king. Alamo had heard stories of his devotion and ferocity before arriving. Since joining this chapter, he'd seen proof with his own eyes. Echo was well worth taking a bullet for.

"I'll keep your father safe," Alamo swore.

A visible tension dropped from Killer's shoulders. He looked less strained, and Alamo wondered how hard this decision to leave the club was. Maybe it was easier because Killer was blood family to Echo, so there was still a tie to the club, but maybe that actually made it harder. Leaving Zoe in Carolina to move to Tennessee was difficult in a way that Alamo hadn't expected. She was a student, an adult, and thoroughly capable. He'd still felt like he'd left one of his lungs behind, stretched out on the sidewalk where anyone could trample or ruin it. If something happened to Zoe, Alamo would be more devastated than if he lost an actual lung. He realized that Killer was feeling a bit like that when it came to leaving the club, especially his cousin and his father.

"I don't like Dash, but I'll do my job there too."

Killer nodded. "That's why I recommended you."

They stood in a heavy silence filled with the kind of topics that neither man really discussed comfortably until Alamo wondered what was left on Killer's mind. After several moments, he had his answer. Killer added, "I count you as a friend, but that doesn't change things. Ellie's good people. She's got no father or brother to do this, and I didn't do it with Dash when he started sniffing around her . . . but I'm doing it now." He met Alamo's gaze and said, "Don't hurt her. If you do, I'll be paying you a less friendly visit."

"Not a whole lot of Wolves stupid enough to issue me threats."

Killer nodded again. "Not a lot who would be able to take you down. Don't forget that I'm one of those that can. I should've put Dash into a wall years ago for how he treated her, but . . . I let myself think they could sort it out. That was a mistake, but I'm not making another one where she's concerned. Think of her as my sister. You hurt my sister, and I'll be paying you a visit."

There were a lot of things that could be said, and maybe if they were different people, some of those things would need saying. Neither of them was big on explaining the details—nor did they need to. Killer had stood up for Ellen, but not in the territorial way Dash had done. He'd simply pointed out that there was someone who would take up for her if needs be. Alamo respected him for it.

"We going to paint each other's nails next or you want to see if there's any races on the television? I have an hour or so."

Killer flipped him off and grabbed the television remote.

Chapter 20

I WAS ALL BUT READY TO START PACING LIKE A CAGED BEAST as I waited for Alamo to pull up outside. I was ready, and I'd never succeeded at patience. I examined my outfit again, fussing and reconsidering for what felt like the eighteenth time. I'd found a shirt that was layers. Underneath was a soft black camisole. On top of that was a deep crisscross V-neck in a sheer fabric that felt like I'd imagine clouds must, soft and almost intangible. I'd gone with mauve for that layer, and then I'd embroidered button tabs that gathered and pinched the fabric up slightly at mid-biceps. I'd made it myself, like most of my favorites. The unexpected benefit of being poor was that I'd had to find a way to create clothes with less. I repurposed things, shopped the bargain bins at the fabric store, and haunted thrift stores. It resulted in an eclectic style that was often both practical and varied.

Tonight, admittedly, my style was a little swayed by my audience. I wanted Alamo to want me badly enough that he couldn't see straight, so I was straddling a line between biker babe and girlie girl. Hopefully it would work.

It had been years since I'd gone riding for the sake of riding. Sure, Noah had given me a lift, and sometimes we'd gone riding, but with him there were strings. I hadn't realized how many until today. Even with him, it had been a good eighteen months since we'd gone for a relaxed ride. It had become an issue. We'd meet up and go where there was no chance of being seen, no risk of our status as friends with benefits being found out . . . at least that was what I thought. He'd obviously been a little less concerned since he'd put me under his protection.

The older bikers acted a lot like I was a little sister or a favored niece. It was always a joy to even get a ten-minute lift to class or home, but it wasn't quite the same as a long ride with no goal other than enjoying the machine and the biker. With the older bikers, I kept my distance as much as I could on the back of the machine. You'd never guess it by the way a lot of women were on bikes, but it wasn't technically necessary to wrap around a biker like a barnacle clinging to a cliff. Riding was an excuse to be close, but it wasn't actually *necessary* . . . just fun.

So I kept my distance from the older bikers, especially the one memorable time Echo himself gave me a ride to school.

I felt like the queen of badasses that day. The club president let *me* on his Harley.

The younger bikers were mostly hands-off with me, and I now understood why. The renewed thought of Noah's meddling made me want to scream, but I had a much better plan for all that emotion. Now that there was no obstacle, I could simply be with Alamo, and that was exactly what I was looking for today. It wasn't a casual decision—or one I made often. I could count my bed partners without needing all my fingers, but I wanted to add one more to the list.

A small voice whispered that what I really wanted was for it to be the *last* one I added to the list.

I heard Alamo before I saw him. I watched as he roared down the street and felt a bit like a child about to open a present. In the street outside my house was a beautiful Wide Glide, chromed-out hot-red detailing on the tank. Astride that beautiful Harley was Alamo. He looked up at my window as if he knew I was there.

I waved. I wasn't about to start playing coy. He already knew I wanted him.

After I checked my lipstick and hair one last time, I grabbed my jacket and helmet, and then I headed downstairs.

"Going now," I called out to Mama as I walked past her and opened the door. I stepped out and pulled the door shut behind me before she could reply.

Alamo was still astride his bike, and it occurred to me briefly that he was preening just a little too. I thought back over seeing him at the bar, and I had to wonder if this was something bigger for him too.

"How long?" I blurted out.

"How long what?" he asked.

"How long have you wanted me?"

Alamo took a breath before making an approving sound and saying, "You're something else, Ellen."

"Yeah?"

He reached out and pulled me closer. I went willingly. There was always something intoxicating in being grabbed by a man I wanted. I liked it, the possessiveness and impatience of it. Being wanted was a powerful feeling. The only way to get closer was if I straddled his leg or tried to slide onto the bike in front of him. I ended up with his knee between my thighs, and one of my arms around his neck. The other hung at my side so I didn't drop my helmet.

I tilted my chin up and kissed him.

It was everything I could want, as good as our kiss in front of his tub. He might be quiet, but he applied that same sort of attention to listening to my body, responding to every cue I didn't even realize I'd offered. He kissed like I was an exam he wanted to pass—and I was pretty sure that there wasn't much that would curl my toes quite like his kisses.

I wanted to find out, though, enough that I wasn't sure I wanted to take the time to ride. I loved riding as much as any woman who has experienced the freedom and bliss of being on a Harley with a beautiful man. After a couple of kisses, however, I was willing to bet my voice that I'd enjoy sex with Alamo even more than a ride.

When he pulled back, he answered my almost-forgotten question. "Since I met you, Ellen. I wanted you the day I met you. You were fierce even though I knew you were hurting, and you were bold, and God help, you have a body that would make a saint want to sin." His hand was splayed across my low back. He slid it down over the curve of my ass. "And I got to tell you that I've never been mistaken for a saint."

I lowered my hand from his neck, trailing it down his chest and to his very defined abs. I stopped at his belt buckle. "Good."

He smiled. "Climb on the back, woman, or we're going to end up missing the ride part of this date."

"Date?" I didn't squeak the word, but it was a close thing.

"Date." He cupped the side of my face with one hand. "I heard you on the no strings, but I want to get to know you better, so this *is* a date. I want you, but not just in my bed."

"So . . . what does that mean?" I was feeling vaguely panicked at the idea of losing Alamo before I even had him, but I didn't want any confusion on what this was.

"It means that I want to *talk* to you too. It means that if you're riding with me, you're going to have to tolerate being with me in public. Is that a problem?"

"No . . . but I'm not looking for anything heavy. I mean—"

"How about we start with a ride like you said earlier?"

I stepped back a little further and put my helmet on. "We could talk in bed . . . just ride to your place."

Alamo shook his head. "Let me take you out. We can ride down toward Memphis, grab a bite, and talk."

It struck me as funny that the last man in my life wanted me only in private, and I had hated it. But right now I wanted to be alone with Alamo more than I wanted a date. "Oh . . . right."

Obviously, he could tell that I was a little confused because he said, "Ellen?"

I looked at him, thinking back to the day we met.

He obviously misunderstood my silence, though, because he said, "I want you, darlin'. Told you that already." He gave me a wry smile. "Wanted you these past months, and learned to cope with it. I can cope for a few more hours so I can take you out first. You deserve that: being treated like a lady. Let me do it."

I melted a little at his words and thought back to his words this morning. He'd accused me of holding out everything he could want, but I was fairly sure that he could be accused of the exact same thing. I kept that truth to myself and climbed onto the back of his bike.

He glanced over his shoulder at me. "Comfortable?"

"More than," I admitted. "I've a helluva bike *and* you between my thighs. It's a good day."

"Yeah? Well, then how about you pretend you're a Harley virgin and move a little closer? You're way back there like this isn't your first ride."

I laughed, but I eased forward. This time, for the very first time, I slid so close that I looked like one of those nervous girls who were half sure they'd go flying off the back. I twined my arms around him and pressed my chest to his back. It felt good not only to be allowed to be this close to him but to know he wanted me there. "Like that?"

"*Just* like that."

"Remember that later when we're stopped and do this face-to-face," I suggested.

He laughed. "I'm sure I can think of more than a few ways we can do this, and with a sight fewer clothes."

"I'll hold you to that," I said lightly.

The bike roared to life under us, and I sighed happily. I knew Harleys were machines, but there was something primal in the roar of a bike's engine. The rumble felt like I imagined a lion's roar echoing across the miles would, like there was something here to be in awe of and feared, and the sort of man who could handle that sort of raw power was the sort of man I wanted by my side and in my bed. I'd dated men who didn't ride, but I felt they were all missing something. It was, to me, a lot like the difference between a tiny little dog who wore outfits and a wolf. Little dogs were cute, but if I needed to be protected, I'd pick the wolf every damn time.

Alamo was *all* wolf. I leaned my cheek against his shoulder, extra grateful that he wanted me close. This was how it was meant to be, intimate and natural, not hidden, not all tense and awkward, not rolling in self-doubt. I felt vaguely sad for the people who'd never experience the thrill of riding and angry that Dash had stolen this joy from me by falsely marking me as his.

Alamo had given me back a pleasure that words couldn't begin to explain, and he'd done it without realizing it. I squeezed him and said, "Thank you!"

He didn't reply in any way other than speeding up a little, but that was answer enough for me. Much like sex, the best rides weren't about a lot of words. A few instructions here and there weren't amiss, but it was the action that mattered. I laughed aloud, both in joy and at my inability to be around him for more than a few minutes without my brain ending up focusing on sex.

Once we hit one of the smaller roads that would take us to I-40 eventually, I leaned forward as much as I could and said, "Open it up."

A few moments later, we were cruising at speeds that made me want to whoop in joy. The throttle wasn't wide open, but there was a limit to how fast we could ride safely, even on a nearly empty road like this. This much speed made the engine switch from a low rumble to full-out growling. There was no other motorcycle that could compare with a Harley for sheer attitude, and that roar was the sound of bliss. Any woman worth her salt answered only one way to the not entirely joking question of "ass, gas, or grass" to pay for a ride. Much like a man who could fight, dance, or drum, a man who rode a Harley well was usually a man worth bedding. Alamo was a confident and masterful rider, and it made my entire body hum with pleasure. I wanted to have that same confidence focused on *me*.

The next hour was spent enjoying this little bit of heaven, but we eventually slowed as we started to come up on people. This far from Williamsville was still Wolves territory, but it was a little less remote, so there were state police to contend with instead of just our town sheriff. With stateys, there was a bit more probability of being hassled just for being on a bike. Add in the colors visible on Alamo's jacket, and the odds of getting pulled over in some random town increased further. There was nothing illegal on either of us. I knew that without asking, so it would be most likely only a speeding ticket. I was still glad that Alamo wasn't one of those bikers who had more attitude than sense.

Now that he'd slowed, we could speak a little, but I was still content with the silence.

A few minutes later, Alamo rolled up to a red light.

I used the pegs to stand and lean forward. It wasn't a move I'd try with just anyone, but despite the massive weight of the bike, I knew Alamo held us steady. So I twisted around his side and bent down to kiss him. It was an awkward position, and it drew a few honks from other cars. One person hollered, "You go, girl."

When I pulled back from kissing him and sat down, I was grinning like an idiot. It was just a quick kiss, but it was exciting to be able to do it, to kiss him and not care who could see us.

"What was that?" he asked.

"Just checking," I said.

"On?"

"Whether it really was that good to kiss you or my memory was faulty," I said cheekily.

He shook his head. "You're something else, Ellen."

"I am." It was liberating to be treated like my audaciousness wasn't off-putting.

The light turned green, and we took off again with the delicious roar made only by a Harley. I let out a whoop of joy, and in short order we were on the freeway, sliding in and out of traffic, faster even that we'd been on the side roads.

Riding like this, with speed and curves, was a rush that I'd missed more than I'd realized. You can try to explain it, try to call up the memories, but that was akin to taking photos at an air show. Still images capture the blink of the dynamic aeronautic tricks, but they don't make you gasp the way the experience does. Riding was like that. No matter how much the memory was anchored, it was nothing compared to the experience itself.

We didn't speak another word until Alamo was parking the bike outside BB King's Blues Club. He cut off the engine and waited for me to slide off the Harley. I did so, pretending not to see the inevitable glances of passersby.

I took off my helmet and waited for him to stand.

He watched me curiously.

"What?"

"Gorgeous. Smart. Likes the blues. Attitude. Takes what she wants." He looked me up and down. "Gorgeous."

"You said that one already."

"It deserves repeating," he said.

I laughed.

"Tell me you're not one of those salad-and-water women now that this is a date, and I may just drop to my knees and praise Jesus," he said as he stood.

"You've *seen* me eat," I reminded him. "And I'm not exactly a waif either." I patted one of my hips with my free hand. "Real women have enough curves to be comfortable for long rides."

He grabbed me by both hips and jerked me toward him. "I like your curves."

"Good. You can explore them as much as you want after this," I offered.

"Count on it," he promised.

And I was. I was counting on a whole host of things that I hadn't even dared to admit to wanting to anyone but myself. Admitting them to him was invigorating. Knowing he wanted them too was even better.

Chapter 21

I WOULDN'T SAY THAT WE HAD A ROUTINE, BUT THIS WASN'T the first time we'd been to a club where I'd inevitably end up singing. This time, though, I was well aware that the attraction I felt wasn't one-sided. It made me bold enough to step up on the stage with a bounce that I hadn't felt in far too long. The man I wanted, the Wolf who had filled my daydreams, the person who made me feel like I deserved more out of life—he was watching me with a mix of approval and interest. It was a powerful feeling.

When the band beckoned me up, I stood like I normally would, but this time I bent down and brushed my lips over Alamo's. Then, satisfied that he was watching, I sashayed across the bar and held up my hand to the singer.

With a quirk of the lips, he took my hand and I stepped up. As soon as I was at his side, I told the band, "Etta James' 'I Just Want to Make Love to You.'"

It was a song I'd sung on this very stage, but never with such intent—or a public proclamation of it. The truth was that I wasn't going to even pretend to be meek or mild. It was as if all the ballsy impulses of the past few months were writhing under the surface, just begging to get free and announce themselves.

Once Alamo realized what song I was singing, he whistled like he was at a raucous concert.

I pointed at him and sang the chorus.

Most of the patrons laughed or cheered. That was the nature of a good blues bar: people were *real*, and they appreciated life. I felt increasingly alive every time I took the stage, and singing to the man I had every intent of enjoying only added to it. As much as I had wanted to stay in and get to know Alamo in the most fundamental way, I was glad he'd insisted on a date, not just because I was having fun but because the more we flirted, the more the anticipation built. It added a layer of new desire on the already powerful yearning.

Flirting so openly was exciting, and doing it from the stage was new.

When the set was over, I walked back over to the table, but I wasn't sure whether I was the predator or the prey. I felt like I was stalking toward him, but the heat in his eyes as he watched my approach made me feel like *he* was the one driving us forward.

As soon as I was near enough to the table, he caught my hand and yanked me into his lap. "Are you ready to get out of here?"

I looped my arms around his neck. "Depends on where you want to take me."

"Bed."

The sheer bluntness of it made me laugh in joy. I stood and snatched my helmet off the chair beside him. "Hell, yes."

He'd barely stood when his phone rang. I wanted to tell him to ignore it; I wanted to grab it and yell at whoever it was to go away, but I saw the look on his face when he glanced down. It was an expression I recognized without the next words he said.

"Club business."

I motioned toward it. "Go on. I'll keep."

He walked away and answered. I didn't point out that he didn't need to walk away to take work calls. I had been overhearing club secrets and business as long as my memories went back, far longer than he had, but the flat truth was that I wasn't his old lady—or an active Wolf's daughter—so he was right to walk away. I sat and listened to the music that was playing in the club while the band was on break. It wasn't what I'd prefer, but it was far from bad.

When Alamo returned to the table, he looked like he expected me to be angry, and I had to wonder if whatever woman he had in his life who'd left clothes behind wasn't good with the club. It wasn't unheard of. Both Aubrey and her grandmother had been willing to give up on the men they loved because they didn't like that aspect of the Southern Wolves. Admittedly, Mrs. Evans still loved Echo despite the fact they had been apart for years, and eventually she'd found a way to be with him but not be his old lady officially. In their case, it was simply time. They'd waited for years. With Killer, he'd left the club more or less so Aubrey would be with him. I wasn't like them.

"Hey," I said lightly.

Alamo looked at me.

"If you need, we can do a rain check on the rest of my plans," I said. "You're not getting out of giving the kisses I'm expecting, but if you have work tonight, that comes first."

The smile he rewarded me with proved that I hadn't misunderstood his worries. "You'd be fine with that?"

"My dad was a Wolf. My uncle is a Wolf." I kept my voice pitched low as I spoke. "If I had been a son, I expect I'd have been wearing club colors years ago. The club was *my* family way before you came strolling into Tennessee. They'll be my family if you leave. It's no big thing if you need to go to work."

"There you go again, holding everything out like it's easy," Alamo said in a deceptively calm tone.

I could hear history in those words, and even without the details, I understood what he was really asking was the same question I'd have to ask any man I thought about keeping: Do you accept that sometimes the Southern Wolves come before you? I was okay with that. I always had been.

This didn't mean that I wanted to be a woman he kept or that I was sure I wanted to keep *him*. So I didn't say anything for a moment. There wasn't anything I was sure I could say truthfully. We'd spent half a day together, and I was interested in more. I already knew I liked the look of him, and I'd had enough conversations with him in groups that it stung that he hadn't wanted more. Now I realized that he had but had been stymied by club rules, I wanted to get lost with him for a few days and see what this could be.

"We might not even suit." I softened the word with a smile, but I had to put it out there.

He picked me up, supporting me with his hands holding my ass, and kissed me—not a polite kiss meant for public, but an assault on my senses.

My legs wrapped around his waist, and my arms twined around his neck. I returned as good as I got, tongues dueling as we both tried to dominate the other. It wasn't until I heard applause that I pulled back.

"It looks like Miss Ellen's beau liked her singing too," the singer quipped as they took the stage again. "Maybe you ought to take him out of here before you set the house on fire, Ellen."

Alamo looked at me as he lowered me to the ground. "I need to go out, but if you wanted to wait in my bed, it would be more than enough reason to hurry home."

"Safely, though," I amended.

He smiled widely. "Darlin', I'm always safe. Just need to go deal with a thing, but it's nothing to fret over."

I'd seen that same glimmer in Killer's eyes when he had worked for Echo. The job in question was one that would involve violence. Back when we were kids, Killer had always said that a fight left him wired to the point that all he wanted was to follow it with a fuck. From the barely restrained excitement in Alamo's eyes, I suspected he felt much the same.

As a kid, I was more than a little disgusted by the idea of violence leading to sex—both because I didn't get the correlation and because I didn't much want to think about Killer doing *that*. Now, however, I got it, and I wasn't complaining about the adrenaline rush being redirected to something I'd benefit from, since it was Alamo who would be with me.

The ride home continued to be an exercise in flirtation. As with the rest of our day, it was obviously flirting with the intent to deliver. He gripped my legs or stroked my calves when we stopped at lights, and after the third light, I told him, "Two can play."

He didn't reply, but conversation was a challenge on the back of a bike.

More important, it was unnecessary. I slid my hands down his sides until I reached the bottom of his shirt. I felt him tense under my touch, so I waited, letting it drag out, extending the moment until my own patience expired.

Then slowly I eased my fingertips under the material. The skin under the pads of my fingers was newly free to explore, and there was something delicious about doing so while we were on his Harley. I'd never been an exhibitionist, but touching him as I had over the day so far was making me rethink that.

At the next light, he glanced back at said, "Payback's a bitch, Ellen."

"Are you telling me to stop?" I asked lightly. My hand dropped lower, not moving now, simply resting between his legs.

He arched forward slightly. "Not at all. Just warning you that if you're going to tease, I don't want any complaints later."

Far from complaining, I wanted to make him promise to deliver on that threat. I tightened my legs on either side of him and stroked my fingers down the seam of his jeans. "I'm not teasing. I have every intention to follow through."

He said nothing, so I continued the gentle motion of my hand until he slowed down the bike and ordered, "Stop, darlin'. There's a limit to what I can handle and still ride safely, and you've already passed it."

I felt as powerful in that moment as I had earlier onstage. It was good to be wanted, and even better to be wanted by him.

By the time we reached his house, my own desire had surpassed anything reasonable, but work didn't wait for such things. Alamo left me there inside his house with a kiss that promised everything else, and a quiet word of trust.

"I have no secrets I won't tell you if you ask, Ellen. Nothing like Bluebeard's wives hidden away in trunks. No rooms in my house are forbidden. Just be here when I get home."

"I will," I said.

A few hours later, though, I wasn't sure *where* to wait. It felt presumptuous to be in his bedroom, but I didn't want to sleep in the guest room and accidentally give the impression that I'd changed my mind. My hope was that he'd be back before sleep overcame me, but the few hours of rest the night before were starting to catch up to me. I changed into his sweatshirt, curled up on top of the covers in the guest room, and took a nap.

Chapter 22

I WOKE TO THE SOUND OF THE BEDROOM DOOR OPENING. For a moment I wasn't sure where I was or why, but the outline in the doorway brought it all back. I was at Alamo's house, in his guest room, and he was back.

He was also walking back out of the room.

"Stop," I said, sounding more asleep than awake.

"Ellen?"

"You shouldn't leave," I muttered, still blinking away the sleep. "I just napped, and . . ." My words drifted away as I tried to clear my mind. "I'm here. You're here."

"Is that a proposition?"

"Oh, hell, yes." I started to sit up so I could get out of bed and go toward him.

Before I could do so, he was at the edge of the bed. He scooped me up and walked out of the room, holding me aloft like I weighed nothing. I was fairly certain that carrying me like that was impossible. No one ever had before. Alamo held me effortlessly and walked to his bedroom.

I'd glimpsed it earlier, all simple lines and practical furniture. I hadn't lingered, though, feeling like it was an invasion of his privacy despite his parting words.

He lowered me to the mattress and looked down at me. "I've pictured you here."

It was no longer sleep that was tangling my ability to form words. It was him, the way he looked at me and the sheer unabashed *lust* in his expression. I swallowed, trying to think of something to say that didn't sound foolish.

"Do you know what I imagined, darlin'?"

I shook my head.

"Do you want to know?" His hands were on my bare legs, sliding up higher and higher.

This time I knew the right answer. "Yes," I said.

His fingers stopped at the edge of my panties, just as mine had done with his shirt earlier when we were on the bike. Unlike him, I wasn't trapped by circumstances. I held his gaze as I reached down and shimmied out of them, leaving only a shirt as a barrier between us.

He said nothing as he stared at me. It felt right to be silent then, only bodies and feelings between us. I wasn't so self-assured that baring my self was something I could do lightly, but any doubts I had faded as he drew a sharp breath.

In the next moment he had hands on my hips and was pulling me to him. There was something more intimate in this act, in the trust it took to let anyone near that most sensitive part of me, but I didn't feel the trepidation I'd felt when anyone else tried it. Alamo licked me and let out a guttural noise that made me feel like I was the sexiest woman in the world. He was everything a woman could want in a man, and he was worshipping *my* body.

Within moments, I knew that I'd been right about him: his careful, deliberate attention was heaven. If not for his grip on my hips, I would be arched halfway off the bed, but he held me steady as he drove me higher and higher. When I reached that blissful peak, he was still there, holding me to his mouth and driving me back up to nirvana.

My entire body shook with the force of my pleasure by the time he released me.

"Payback, darlin'," he murmured as he pulled me up to rest on his chest.

Then I drifted back to sleep in his arms.

THE NEXT MORNING, I woke up confused. It took me a moment to realize that I was in Alamo's house again, but not the guest room. I was in Alamo's bed, and he was holding me tightly.

I wouldn't have taken him for a cuddler, but I'd ended up with my head cushioned on his chest while I slept. He had an arm tight around my waist, holding me there. It was restful without being entrapping . . . at least it had been until I realized that I was nearly naked and in his bed. All the wanting that I'd been ignoring washed over me like the river escaping its banks after a heavy rain.

I splayed my hand out across his stomach and marveled at his taut muscles.

"If I play possum, will you keep going?" he asked in a low voice.

"Pants off."

"Yes, ma'am." He complied with a smile.

There was no need to waste more words when actions would serve us both far better. I wanted to explore, had wanted to do so since not long after we met, and now we were here. I slid my hand lower, dragging the edge of my thumbnail over his bare skin just hard enough to test his reaction.

Alamo's quiet murmur of appreciation made me smile. That was one of the things I appreciated about bikers: they usually appreciated both rough and gentle. As my hand wrapped around his cock, he parted his legs wider—granting me access and simultaneously pushing my leg back so he could touch me.

"Tell me what you like, darlin'." His fingers slid into already wet folds.

"Right now? Harder." My strokes sped. "Faster."

In barely more than a moment, he'd matched my pace.

The only sounds for several minutes were groans and breathing.

Soon I was grinding down on his fingers, but it wasn't enough. I didn't want just his hand. I wanted everything.

"Condom," I half asked, half ordered.

"Drawer" was his only reply.

It wasn't a battle of wills, not truly, but I saw the edge of it there. I opened the drawer, pulled out the packet, and looked at him.

"Am I still to be playing possum then?" he teased.

I grinned, tore the packet open, and in moves that were far more practiced than I'd usually admit to the first time with someone, I sheathed him.

He watched me with nothing but approval.

I threw my leg over him. For a moment I braced myself on my knees and looked down at him. There was a beautifully challenging expression on his face, and I knew that he wasn't going to let me keep control much longer. I wanted that, the fight for who was driving.

I waited, gaze locked, hovering over him. I lowered myself until we were touching, until it would take only a breath to be exactly where we both wanted to be, until it was a matter of which one of us moved.

And as soon as his hands came up to grip my hips, I slammed down just as he surged up. I let out a small animal noise at the perfection. We fit like he'd been custom made for my body.

He closed his eyes and groaned. In that moment, it was the most beautiful sound I could ever remember hearing.

When he opened his eyes, he ordered, "Take off the shirt."

"Gladly," I said. I wasn't as confident in my body as some women, but the way Alamo looked at me gave me all the self-confidence I needed. When I stripped off my shirt and he looked at me like I was a gift, I wanted to preen. To him, I was beautiful. To him, I was mesmerizing. I saw it in the way he stared. It was better than any rush I'd ever felt.

"Fucking perfect," he murmured.

And I felt like I was. Naked atop a gorgeous biker who was thrusting up into me like there was a prize for delivering the fastest, hardest orgasm of my life, I felt like I was a goddess.

When he followed that orgasm with several more, including the sort of leisurely sex that could be easily called making love, I was revising my stance and declaring *him* a god. Nothing had ever been this good, and despite my urge to keep my heart locked away, I was fairly sure he already had the key—and if he didn't, I'd tell him where to find it if he could make me feel *this* good regularly.

Chapter 23

I WAS STILL GRINNING WHEN ALAMO DROPPED ME OFF ON campus. My happiness didn't fade by the time class was over either. It wasn't simply that I'd ended my dry spell or even that I'd been with the man who'd been filling my mind when I let myself relax. It was that we *clicked.* There was something almost magical when two people fit so well.

"Did something happen?" Aubrey asked. She had waited for me after class.

I started at her question. I never quite bought into the idea that people could tell by looking if a person had recently been . . . satisfied. On the other hand, I still felt like I was doing an imitation of the Cheshire cat. I was *happy.* Casually I asked, "Like what?"

She shrugged and peered at me as if she could find clues. I didn't have the heart to tell her that she wasn't going to have any luck with intimidation. Between my mother and Echo, I'd had "the look" from the best. Aubrey was a sweetie, but she wasn't intimidating—at least not to me.

After a moment or two of trying to stare me down, she said, "You tell me. Noah took off when I said I was waiting for you. I know you two have had your issues, but I thought you were getting along."

I was so startled by her remarks that I simply blinked at her. My mind was so full of what had happened with Alamo that I'd set aside the other bits. The conflict with Noah wasn't *forgotten*, but it wasn't at the top of my mind. I considered not getting into it, but she'd been indoctrinated enough between her job at Wolves & Whiskey and dating Killer that I figured I could—and should—be blunt. "Noah told everyone I was under his protection. Idiot boy is the last president's kid and liable to be the next in line now that Killer's left. People think . . ." I looked at her to be sure she realized exactly what conclusion they would arrive at.

Aubrey's lips parted on a sound of surprise so low that I heard nothing. I saw it, however, and was glad that she wasn't offended. I'd hate to lose her friendship, but I knew that she counted Noah as a friend too. I felt horrible a heartbeat later when she thought about what she knew, what she'd seen when Noah had been with her at the same time as I was.

"You're not, though. Together with Noah, I mean . . . Right? When he and I were flirting, when he kissed me—"

"No." I cut her off before she could let that wave of guilt pull her under. She'd done nothing wrong. "What Noah Dash and I had ended before you moved here."

"How much before?" she asked softly as we walked through the hall toward the exit of the building.

"Enough that you can take your worry and guilt and shelve it," I assured her. I had become very fond of Aubrey over the months that I'd known her, but she was a little too sweet sometimes. It was probably for the best that Killer was walking away from the club. This life wasn't going to suit a woman like her, especially because Killer was far from fringe. He'd been in the thick of everything, and that would mean either lying to her or asking her to change. I was proud of him for choosing to be the one who made changes.

"Honest," I stressed, "Dash is my past. I thought we both knew that. He's always been out there wetting his wick worse than . . ."

"Worse than Killer was before he met me?" she finished in a joking tone. To my relief she bumped her shoulder into me. "I know Zion wasn't celibate before me. There was a reason he was called Ladykiller, right? I know." She shrugged, seeming so much calmer and confident than she'd been when I'd first met her. "That was before me. Now? He's *mine*."

I laughed at the edge of venom that had crept into her voice. She had grown at least a bit of an attitude being with

Killer. It looked good on her. Worrying about my drama with Noah wasn't what either of us needed. I'd rather think about Alamo, and Aubrey had plenty on her plate with Killer about to ship out to boot camp.

"So what's the plans for Killer's going-away party?"

"Echo and Zion are . . . negotiating. Echo wants a blowout. Zion wants them not to make a fuss." Aubrey shoved the door open with more force than strictly necessary. She wasn't in a proper snit, but she sounded like she wasn't too far from it. "The two of them! I swear they're absurd since Zion got shot and Echo agreed to him leaving the club. You'd think it was a wedding reception the way they try to draw me into it. I'm not the one going away *or* the father of him, but I'm stuck in the middle. Grandma Maureen won't tolerate it, though. She kicked them out halfway into dinner last night because they started bickering again, told them that they'd sort it out by tonight or *we* were deciding."

She paused awkwardly and glanced sideways at me. We were almost to the lot, and I figured she was headed over to the bar for work. She had continued on as a bartender even after getting with Killer. Most of the barmaids had a rule that they couldn't date a Wolf and still work there, but with Killer's leaving the club, that rule wasn't quite as applicable, I guessed.

I could hear in her voice that there was more she wanted to say. That tentative tone of hers had me debating between having mercy on her and forcing her to get there on her own, but she was also glancing at her phone semi-subtly.

Either she was running late or had another stop before work. So I prompted, "Spill."

She let out her breath in a big whoosh and, in a tumble of words, blurted, "There's a party at the bar tomorrow. Gran and I planned it, not huge, but not ignoring it either. Since Zion and Echo couldn't agree, we took over."

I couldn't help it. I laughed. "That's why you wanted me to keep tomorrow open? Sneaky thing. I thought you wanted a girls' night or a favor."

"You'll come, right? Even with you and Noah fighting, you'll come?"

I nodded. "I wouldn't miss it. Killer's family."

"He'll be glad you're there. At least he will when he realizes there's a party. Right now he's clueless. Echo is too. *Technically*, people aren't supposed to keep secrets from Echo . . . and I wasn't sure they would, so we've had to be a little stealthy. Mike knows, and Uncle Karl knows. Alamo too."

My ears perked up at that. "Alamo?"

"And Hershey and Big Eddie . . . and Noah. So far, Grandma Maureen just told the 'cubs' because they're all as scared of her as they are of Echo." Aubrey preened a little. The fact that her grandmother was the former—and renewed—love of the club president amused her. She'd gotten to see a side of Echo that very few people did. Noah and Killer had, of course. I had too.

None of that meant that Echo would hesitate to pull a trigger or order it done. Echo wasn't a house pet, no matter how much of his sweet side Aubrey had seen the past few months. He was ruthless, but he was ruthless for the good of the club. They were his family, and a Wolf would kill or bleed for family. I'd grown up knowing that, and I took comfort in it.

It was why I wasn't sure I could ever leave Williamsville. It was also why I knew I could do so if I decided to go. The club would look after Mama.

"So, party . . . ?"

"At the bar." She squirmed a little more.

"Spit it out, girl."

"Echo says you sing," she half said, half asked.

I tensed.

"Do you sing?" Aubrey pressed.

I used to sing at club parties. My father and I both did. Now that I was singing in Memphis again, I should've expected this request. I hadn't. I'd been so caught up in my personal dramas and my own slow return to singing that I hadn't thought about needing to sing for Wolves again. It wasn't that I didn't want to either. I just hadn't thought I was ready. Sometimes, however, being part of Echo's family meant that decisions were out of my hands.

As calmly as I could, I asked, "Echo brought it up?"

She nodded. "He was telling me that you had a beautiful voice, and that it was a shame that you didn't ever sing at the bar."

I nodded. There really wasn't another option before me. Echo spoke, and the rest of us obeyed.

"I know he's hoping that you'll sing, but he didn't want

me to ask until right before the party. He might not know *when* it is now that Gran and I did this, but he'd said before that we'd ask you the day before the party. I guess he wanted you not to have time to change your mind," she explained.

Sometimes I wanted to teach her to read between the lines, but I liked her for who she was, and I thought that between Killer and her grandmother *and* Echo, she'd be just fine. She wasn't stupid or even naïve. She simply didn't translate biker words and acts to regular ones. I smiled and said, "If Echo wants me there, I'll be there, *and* I'll be singing."

"Oh good! I was worried that you'd say no."

The relief in her expression was too much for me. I didn't want to take away her sweetness, but I had to point out the truth that was seemingly obvious to everyone but her. Gently I said, "No one tells Eddie Echo no, Aubrey. He wants me to sing. I sing. It wasn't a request. It never is with him."

"Oh." She frowned, and I felt a little bad as I watched her think over the situation. After a moment, she let out a groan. "How does he seem so nice when really he was giving you an order? He was, wasn't he? I was *delivering* his order."

I gave her a one-armed hug. "He *is* nice to the people under his wing. We're all there. You more than most. Between your grandmother and Zion, you're loved by the two people *he* loves."

Aubrey sighed again. "I know, but . . . I'm sorry. I can tell him I don't want you to sing or—"

"I'll be there, Aubrey. I'll sing for Killer. It's all good," I promised her.

Then I shooed her into the mammoth car she drove and waved her off. I didn't want her to linger longer, as I'd just noticed two guys staring at us. As Aubrey left, I glanced surreptitiously at them. They weren't looking at her quickly disappearing car, but at me.

Seeing unfamiliar faces wasn't entirely unheard of on the Williamsville Community College campus. There was always a mix of regulars like Noah and me who were taking their own sweet time to complete a degree and those who seemed to take only a class or two and then vanish. Seeing two strangers eyeing *me*, however, was atypical. Because I was the daughter of a Southern Wolf and had been a friend of other Wolves (or their kids) my whole life, people tended to give me a wide berth. If I had been a different kind of girl, I might think it was simple attraction, but I'd realized years ago that everyone attracts a *type*. There might be exceptions, but as a rule, women attracted men who had things in common with them. Maybe it was as simple as the way we responded to them, some signal we gave out unconsciously. Did I look back a little longer when bikers turned their gazes my way? Did I smile a little warmer for a man in worn jeans or a well-made leather vest? Did I take an extra breath at the sight of a good-looking tattoo? I went through a stage a few years ago when I tried to pay attention to it for a while—determined not to attract another man like the ones I'd dated so far, hoping to meet someone totally unexpected—but I'd never been able to figure out much of a pattern beyond the basic truth that we all have types whether we want to or not.

Khakis? Button-ups? They weren't the sort of men who looked my way very long—and I didn't do anything to suggest they should. Whatever reason these two had for watching me, it wasn't something good.

Chapter 24

ALAMO WASN'T GOING TO START DIGGING POSTHOLES for a white picket fence or anything, but he was feeling pretty good about the way things were turning out with Ellen. They'd still need to deal with the Dash factor. Larger than that, Alamo would need to decide if he could handle staying around, stepping up into Killer's role for the club, knowing that eventually it would be Dash he'd have as a president. Could he take orders from him? Would Dash be able to treat him fairly? Obviously he'd made progress in that direction because he'd been willing to trust Alamo to keep a watch over Echo, Aubrey, and her grandmother at the hospital, but that was a special situation. There was no way to determine if they could sort things out long-term.

For now he'd stay in Tennessee, but he wasn't about to start trying to figure out anything beyond the next year or two. What he could say for certain was that things were good for him here *right now.* That much he knew. Less than a year ago, he'd been forced to leave North Carolina because of trouble that he hadn't exactly *started,* but he'd certainly answered to the point of explosion. Despite the things he'd lost by leaving North Carolina, in moving to a new state he'd somehow ended up with a respected position and, potentially, a woman worth keeping.

All of which meant that he was expecting disaster to come knocking any minute now. If his mother had taught him anything in his childhood, it was that trouble likes a calm sea as much as the next person. The difference, inevitably, was that trouble turned a calm sea into the start of a hurricane as like as not.

So it wasn't terribly shocking when Zoe texted and said, "Coming up tomorrow."

He pulled out of traffic to reply. He hadn't been her brother and occasional father for all these years *not* to have learned a few things about his little sister. She was terse as a way to withhold information—often information he *should* have. It was her way of avoiding conflict, of aiming to keep those seas still and relaxed. By now it had the exact opposite effect on him. Her short, terse texts or messages raised alarms.

"What happened?" he replied.

"Talk tomorrow. Ana with me. Love."

Alamo scowled at the phone, even though his sister couldn't see his expression. They had been at an impasse often enough for him to know that pushing her wouldn't get him anywhere. That didn't mean he could skip asking questions. Trying to get a few details out of his stubbornly closemouthed baby sister wasn't easy, but it was necessary for him to have any peace of mind.

He texted, "Hurt?"

"No."

"Need escort?"

"Still no. Am OK. Coming up. LOVE." Zoe was far too fierce for her own good. If he'd had his way, he'd have sent her to one of those fancy private schools he'd seen on television programs, but that took a lot more cash than he had. Since he'd been fifteen, he'd taken work as a mechanic when he could find it. It was good honest work, and now that he was employed by the Wolves, he had that income as well. All told, he'd added to his savings over the years, dipping into it for Zoe's books and clothes and things. She had a fund given to her by her father, but it came with strings . . . and Alamo would rather work until he collapsed than have her tie herself even a little to her father.

He didn't remember the man well, but he knew that when Anthony Battista had been arrested, it was more than local news. He'd killed for hire—not that being paid or killing were inherently an issue under all circumstances. Alamo wouldn't be a Wolf if he thought that. However, Zoe's dad had reputedly enjoyed his work a bit too much. He'd made the news in that way that only the truly sensationalized crimes did. So accepting his money wasn't an option for Zoe, and forcing the matter hadn't ever been even a consideration for Alamo.

That meant focusing on earning so as to provide for Zoe. Luckily, they could get enough grants to cover Zoe's college tuition, partly because in-state tuition wasn't as high as tuition at a private college. It was still a bit more than he'd had saved, but with the grants, he'd made it work. Zoe didn't ask how, and he wasn't going to bring it up.

He was going to strangle her if she didn't get better about telling him secrets at a distance. Her refusal to put anything into type wasn't as much of a problem when they lived in the same apartment. Now that they were in different states, it was a huge pain in the ass.

Several more texts to Zoe went unanswered, but she finally sent a reply saying, "In class. Stop. Will see you tomorrow."

After another scowl at his phone, he shoved it back into his pocket and resumed his drive.

When he pulled into the lot of Williamsville Community College, he didn't have far to go to find Ellen. She was standing at the edge of the lot looking toward the main buildings of the tiny campus. She turned when she heard the sound of his bike, and the frown on her face was quickly replaced by a wide smile.

"Do you know any sexy singers in want of a ride?"

Ellen cocked her hip and looked him up and down in that

unapologetic way of hers. "Depends. Do you make a habit of lurking in school parking lots?"

"I might, but only if you're going to be in them," he said.

She laughed. "Good answer."

"Leave your car. I'll bring you back tonight if you want."

"What if I don't want?"

"Then I'll bring you back in the morning."

"Let me get my helmet out of the car." She sashayed to her car like she was on a stage and then looked back to make sure he was watching.

He was. "You trying to kill me with those hips, darlin'?"

Her laugh was lighter than he'd heard any time other than when they'd gone riding. "Honey, you ain't seen nothing yet," she said in an exaggerated drawl.

He grinned. "I like the sound of that."

Chapter 25

THE NEXT DAY I SPOTTED THE TWO KHAKI-CLAD STRANGers everywhere I turned on campus. The taller of the two seemed to be the alpha dog. Both were in their midtwenties, looked like they were lost en route to a country club, and had enough subtle signs of money that I knew they weren't community college students. I didn't recognize either of them, and I didn't see them talking to anyone in a familiar way. They spoke to people, but no one greeted them like they were friends.

I was very careful not to let them see me talking too long to my usual friends. I was already avoiding Noah, so that was easy. Aubrey was busy with tonight's party. I kept my conversations with everyone else to under five minutes. It was a little ridiculous, but until I knew who and what these two wanted, I was being cautious. I had no idea if they'd been following me long. I didn't think they had because based on today, they were far from stealthy.

By the end of the day, I'd run out of patience. I didn't *do* stalkee. Not now, not ever. I debated telling someone, calling one of the Wolves, but I also didn't do helpless maiden very well. I wanted something more concrete than "two guys keep watching me" before I talked to anyone.

So I waited for my chance. Once I was sure they were near enough to hear me, I silenced my phone and pretended to make a call. "I'm headed to the car. I'll see you soon."

Then I walked toward the lot as quickly as I could without seeming to be rushing. I stepped behind a truck with a massive lift kit and quickly crouched down. I stayed down and ducked behind several cars until I was on the far side of the lot, near my car in case I needed to reach it but well hidden.

I was parked in the outermost row near the restored El Camino that my friend Toby drove. He had it lowered so it would all but brush gravel if it hit a slight bump. I felt a little ridiculous hiding behind a car, but better that than being a victim because I ignored the pit in my gut.

I watched the two buttoned-up types look around the parking lot. The taller of the two made a remark to his companion. I couldn't hear the words, but I didn't need to hear it to know that he was angry or frustrated. The stiff body and wide hand motion conveyed that well enough—as did the other guy's tightening expression.

I hid and watched as they walked toward a Lexus that I'd thought was theirs. It wasn't sports car flashy, but it had that money feel to it.

"Well? Where did she go?" the taller khaki asked.

"How the fuck would I know?" the other answered.

"She should be here. That was her last class." Despite irritation, he seemed to at least be a little bit observant. That *had* been my last class of the day. On the other hand, my schedule wasn't terribly complex, and the campus was small enough that it wouldn't take long to suss out my schedule. That idea made me increasingly uneasy, though, because it meant that they might have watched me for a few days before I noticed. That made me feel both nervous and stupid.

The shorter guy was looking around the lot, and I tensed as his eyes raked over the area where I was hidden. His voice carried well as he said, "Well, we'd see her if she was here. That chick dresses like a blind vagrant."

Silently I flipped him off, even though he couldn't see my gesture. I was insulted, but I was also relieved that I wasn't imagining that they were following me. I didn't consider myself paranoid, but being stalked was unexpected. There was no way they meant anyone else, though, not with that reference to my clothes.

Once they got into their car and left, I stood and walked

to my beat-up Civic. It was about as well used as a car could get while still being functional. Right now, though, it felt like a fabulously protective castle. I wasn't scared per se, but no good comes of being stalked.

I had a few options. In my defense, I *did* know which one I probably should choose, but I didn't want to call in the Wolves unless I had too. I loved bikers, loved *these* bikers in particular, but they weren't renowned for being . . . cautious with their solutions. More important, Killer was on the way out to start his military career. He didn't need new trouble landing on his plate when he was trying to head to the door.

I suspected that Noah, Alamo, or Big Eddie would step into Killer's soon-to-be-vacant spot—at least temporarily. Even if they didn't, however, there were plenty of guys who could be called upon to handle any trouble. Adding to the things the club had to sort out right now was unnecessary if I could handle it myself.

So I was going to opt for the less wise path.

I couldn't decide if I was nervous or angry. Either way, my hands were shaking enough as I tried to put my key in the ignition that I dropped the whole ring on the floor of the car. I didn't want trouble, but I couldn't decide if there would be more complications if I took a minute to handle the stalkers or if I told Killer. Anyone other than Killer, Alamo, or Noah would go directly to Echo. Hell, Alamo or Noah would at least update Killer. The downside to being valued by the club president and the boys was that there was no way to turn that wasn't going to run the risk of angering them.

These assholes who were watching me had just put me in a bad situation. I wanted to hit them for it.

First, though, I had a going-away party to handle.

I was still shaking a little when I arrived at home, not visibly enough that Mama would ask harder questions than I could answer, but enough that she noticed.

"You'll do great, Ellie." She smiled reassuringly, meeting my gaze and giving me the same maternal smile she'd offered when I was a kid nervously about to go onstage with my father.

Tonight Mama was as dressed up as she had always been on those nights when she came with me and Daddy while we sang. She used to call it her "mother of the singer" look, but her body-defining jeans and bright pink blouse were also what she called date clothes, so basically, it was all the same. Whether it was as my cheerleader or some man's date, she was getting all gussied up and preening.

"I just need to get ready and then we'll go." I smiled at her, relaxing more now that I was home. At least I *was* relaxing until a stray thought hit me. "Have there been any odd guests or strangers around lately?"

Mama had started toward the kitchen as I ascended the stairs, but she stopped and looked back at me. Her hands landed on her hips and her gaze narrowed. "Why do you ask?"

I bit back my frustration and tried to sound calm. "Have there?"

She paused, and I could all but see her thinking over the faces she'd seen and the events of her days. She had that same faraway look when she was paging through recipes in her mind or surveying the fridge to see what we had and what she could create with it. I hated seeing that look because of the question I'd asked, but I needed to know.

After a few moments, Mama shook her head. "No one." Then she looked me straight in the eye and repeated, "Why?"

I shrugged and half answered, "I saw a couple of strangers on campus, but I usually recognize everyone. I don't want to make a thing of it, but it seemed odd."

All of that was true. I had just omitted the part about their stalking me and discussing me.

Mama nodded. "I'll keep an eye out. If anything seems worrisome, we'll let Echo know."

And there was nothing more to say: for her, Echo was the answer.

I made a noise of agreement and headed up to get dressed. It was a party for one of my friends, as well as my first time singing for the club in years. Plus, of course, Alamo would be there, and I wanted to look good for him. I wasn't foolish enough to think that Alamo I were . . . *something.* We'd had a couple of good nights, and we seemed like we could have more of them. I wasn't ready to start thinking of commitments—or maybe I was simply rationalizing because I was gun-shy after things with Noah had become so supremely fucked up. If I was to be completely honest with myself, I might admit that Alamo seemed like a fantasy come to life. I wasn't ready for that kind of admission, not anywhere other than in one quiet corner of my mind where I could ignore it.

That didn't mean I was prepared to see him with two girls when he walked into Wolves & Whiskey a few hours later. It was foolish for it to matter, but it did. My heart fell.

Noah—who had been watching me with his kicked-puppy expression since he'd seen me walk into the bar—followed my gaze to Alamo and started across the room. I wanted to follow, but I was still singing. I'd promised Echo himself that I'd stay up there for at least twenty minutes but "preferably longer."

Noah's date stood to follow him, but one of the women stopped her. I couldn't say I was sorry that she did, but I wasn't particularly pleased that Noah was acting all protective *now*. There was a time I would've loved it, but that was in the past.

On the other hand, I didn't love seeing Alamo with two women hanging off his arms. I'd rarely ever seen him bring girls to the bar, and I'd certainly never seen him bring two of them. Tonight he had one on each arm. Maybe I'd misunderstood what happened between us. Maybe it wasn't as explosive for him—or maybe this was his way of proving that we were as strings free as I'd said initially.

I bit back a sigh, looked back at the band, and said, "Etta James' 'It's a Man's Man's Man's World.' "

Chapter 26

ALAMO LET GO OF BOTH GIRLS' ARMS WHEN HE SAW DASH heading his way. "Just stay out of it," he told Zoe.

"Stay out of—"

"I mean it," he cut her off. "Ana? Everything is fine. You're safe here, okay? You know that, right?"

She nodded, but she also stepped a little closer to Zoe.

All Alamo got out was "Dash, this is my" before a fist came at his face.

If it wasn't so irritating, Alamo would be amused. He'd wanted a chance to punch Noah Dash for months, and here it was. He'd rather not do it in front of the girls, but by the time a second fist came at his face, any hesitation was gone.

He reacted on instinct at that point. He dodged the

second punch and threw two of his own, a nice one-two combination.

"You had no business touching her," Dash said.

"That's *Ellen's* decision, not yours." Alamo's fist shot out at Dash again, but he didn't make contact this time.

"Alejandro Roberto Díaz!" Zoe's voice snapped out. "Do not break that boy."

Dash was distracted enough to glance at her, and Alamo landed his next punch.

"Enough!" Killer was there, and he looked about as pissed off as Alamo felt. He grabbed Dash. "What the hell, cuz?"

Dash shook his head. "Ask him."

Killer looked at Alamo. "Well?"

Alamo shrugged. "Ellen and I went riding."

"And?" Killer looked between them, clearly expecting more.

"And then he shows up here with two whores and—" Dash's words were cut off by a slap across his face.

Zoe crossed her arms and glared up at him. "Whatever your problem is with my brother, it doesn't give you the right to disrespect us."

"Your brother?" Dash echoed. He looked at Alamo. "You bring your sister on your dates?"

This time Zoe sighed. "*Pendejo!*"

"Watch your language," Alamo muttered.

"Seriously?" His sister's hands went to her hips. "You know better than to get in a fight, Alejandro, and you expect me to let him"—she gestured at Dash—"speak to *me* like that?"

"I don't. He was wrong, and you can yell all you want. Hell, hit him if you want. Just . . . that's not a word you need to be using," he said, feeling vaguely embarrassed that she had picked up his cussing. He knew she was a grown woman, but it still stung that his own colorful language was something his very sweet, smart, and fierce little sister had adopted.

"Ana and I are getting a drink." Zoe grabbed Ana's arm and half dragged her past Killer and Dash. She waved behind her. "Sort *that* out."

"Sorry I'm late for the party," he told Killer. "I had to pick up my sister and her roommate."

"I didn't know she was due to visit," Killer said, completely ignoring Dash. Most of the club didn't know about Zoe, but obviously, Killer knew pretty much whatever Echo had thought necessary. That meant he knew about the trouble back in North Carolina and about Alamo's sister.

"Someone care to fill me in?" Dash asked, his voice calmer now.

"My sister and her roommate surprised me. I'm late. You jumped to conclusions. Zoe's worried because I have a temper, and she thinks I shouldn't be punching people. Ellen's looking at all of us like she's going to kill us or at least never speak to us again."

"Not me," Killer quipped. He waved at Ellen, who after a brief warble when the fists were flying had continued on. A woman who ran with bikers wasn't the sort to flinch over a little brawl.

Ellen was singing Nina Simone's version of "Feeling Good," and maybe it was a little bit of bias because he was finally able to touch her and talk to her without worry, but he thought she sounded even better than when he'd heard her before—and that was saying something.

Alamo had no idea she was going to sing here. He supposed that meant that keeping their trips to Memphis quiet was unnecessary. He wondered briefly if her singing here would also mean that she would have other Wolves offering to take her to clubs. On the one hand, hearing her belt out the blues was a treat. From the moment he'd heard her, he'd thought she had a *voice*, one that should be recorded, but that wasn't his place. At the same time, he hated that everyone else in the bar was hearing her, and he hated the idea of her making an album. He felt a surge of possessiveness over hearing her.

He stared at her, smiling even though she looked away as soon as he did so. He wasn't sure how to tell her he *hadn't* messed up. All he'd done was walk in the door.

"She's good," Killer said. "If I didn't like her voice so much, I'd feel guilty that my father somehow conned her into singing tonight. I never understood her clothes thing, but the girl's got a set of pipes."

"She's better than most of the bands I've heard up in here," Alamo said, still watching Ellen, who was now pointedly not looking at him.

"Echo knew about the party?" Dash asked. "I thought it was a secret."

Killer shrugged. "I don't know how he knows most of what he does, but whatever it is he does, I'm guessing he's responsible for Ellie being up on that stage tonight. She doesn't ever tell the old man no, and he's been waiting for her to be willing to sing again for a while."

"I didn't know she was your sister," Dash interjected half apologetically to Alamo. It wasn't an actual apology, but it was phrased in such a way that it felt like Dash was expecting him to say that it was "okay" or "not a big deal."

"My family is none of your business." Alamo glared at him. "Neither is what Ellen and I do. She's not yours."

"She's still under my protection when it comes to keeping her safe," Dash started.

"Bullshit. You're looking for a fucking excuse in case you decide you want her back," Alamo pointed out baldly. He wasn't spoiling for a fight, but he wasn't going to ignore one if it came his way—even if it was with the biker who would be club president. There was only so much disrespect a man could tolerate before he was nothing more than a pup playing at being a man. Alamo wasn't interested in taking that leap backward. He looked at Dash and warned, "Don't push me again. Next time, Killer might not be here to step between us."

Before Dash could reply, Killer slung an arm around his cousin. It wasn't restraining yet, but it would become so if necessary. It was a tried-and-true move that was useful with drunks and others who were at risk of becoming unruly.

"Come on. Your date's going to be sore if you don't get back to her."

Alamo shook his head and concentrated on continuing to hold his temper. Maybe it was stupid to have come here, especially with the girls, but he hadn't expected it to be an issue. Ellen had been the one who insisted that there were no strings, and he figured he'd introduce her to his sister and Ana when he got to the bar. He certainly hadn't expected Dash to come out swinging.

Earlier, he'd thought about staying home. He was admittedly a bit overprotective about the girls, and he didn't want any confusion as to whether or not any of the guys could look at his sister like . . . well, like guys looked at women. He couldn't even think the words. Zoe might tease him that she was going to go out and "get some," but he knew that so far she wasn't actually interested in acting on that. Taking his baby sister into the Wolves' den wasn't something he'd considered seriously before. He tended to keep her separate from most of them. There were those who knew her back home, but they'd known her since she was a kid. They knew not to provoke her or, worse yet, to look at her the way men looked at women. Zoe mocked him mercilessly about it, but he still saw her as a child.

Tonight, however, was a party for Killer's going away, and Alamo called him a friend more than he did with any other biker. The two of them didn't have all the bullshit or politics between them. That was rare.

Plus, admittedly, it wasn't just being a friend to Killer that made Alamo come to the bar tonight. He knew Ellen would be there. Now that he was finally able to be around her, he wanted to see her. It wasn't just sex. He wasn't sure it ever *could* be just sex with her. He was willing to try if that was the only thing she wanted, but he was hoping that she'd change her mind in time.

Chapter 27

I LOOKED ACROSS THE BAR TO SEE IF ECHO WAS CONTENT with my singing. It wasn't *just* because he was the president of the club. I wanted him to be happy with my performance, not because I'd been ordered to do it, but because I liked and respected him. I wouldn't go so far as to call him a father figure, but he was the closest thing I had to it—as he had been with Noah and Killer.

Growing up, I'd thought of him as a mix of scary uncle and God Himself. What Echo said was law. What Echo ordered was done. What Echo wanted was what everyone else accepted. Those were facts as clear as addition or spelling. As I got older, I realized exactly what that meant, how far he would go to keep us safe. The men who had killed my father were dead because Echo had declared it good that they die. I remembered hearing him telling Mama that, and hearing her sob and thank him.

"I always protect my family, Ellen," he said when he found me sitting on the steps. "You and your mama need anything, you let me know."

I nodded.

"And if you can't reach me, you tell any of the Wolves . . . or Miz Evans over at the school. They'll let me know." He met my gaze and talked to me like a grown-up, and I was grateful to him for it. "Wolves protect their pack. Your dad is still a part of my pack."

"Yes, sir."

"You look after your mama, you hear? She's not used to being on her own. Your father . . ." Echo's words trailed off, as if he was suddenly realizing that I wasn't an adult after all.

I hated it.

"Daddy made all the decisions. Mama's job was to be happy," I supplied for him.

"Exactly," Echo said quietly. "So you need to be strong for her, and let me know if you two need anything."

"Yes, sir."

"And if Noah or Zion need anything, you tell me that too," he added. "Sometimes boys forget to ask for help. So you keep an eye on them."

I don't think Echo meant for me to end up in either boy's bed, but maybe he did. There was something about the way his mind worked that I still didn't understand. He had machinations even within his plans. Sometimes I think he thought of the Wolves as his own little dukedom, and he wasn't far off. He was our ruler, and my life so far had been shaped by what he wanted.

Tonight he wanted me to sing for his son. So I sang. It was that simple.

"Do you have any requests?" I asked after I finished my song. I didn't need to direct the question. Everyone there knew to wait until he spoke. Echo was an older version of Killer, more weathered, rougher around the edges, hair still raven-dark; he moved with a predatory grace that his son lacked. That and the complete self-assurance he exuded would mark him as the man in charge. The fact that he was watched obediently by every other biker there didn't hurt either.

"Joan Jett," he said.

"Anything particular?" I asked.

When he shook his head, I grinned and decided to do Joan Jett covering AC/DC. I looked at the band and said, "Dirty Deeds."

Then I met Echo's gaze and said, "Being a part of this *pack* in any way is an honor, and I'm awfully glad your son's smart enough to realize it, even if he's going off to play toy soldier." There were laughs. Echo grinned and raised his glass at me. When the laughter died down, I glanced at Killer and Aubrey then. "And you two better not forget that *Killers'* not the only Wolf, or Wolf's daughter, in town who can get things done. I've got Aubrey's back, and I'm not the only one. Family"—I looked back at Echo—"protects family. Always has. Always will."

The Wolves let out a boisterous sound that was somewhere between a howl and a yell. Echo simply smiled at me. Killer nodded at me. A few of the Wolves called out their agreement.

"You tell 'em, Ellie!"

"You heard the lady!"

Echo nodded at me, and the drummer started. I started clapping my hands, and the Wolves and their old ladies joined me. By the time the guitar came in, the women were on the floor dancing. By the chorus, most everyone in the bar was singing "Dirty Deeds Done Dirt Cheap" along with me. It wasn't a Joan Jett song *originally*, but she'd covered it.

Aubrey pulled Killer onto the floor to dance, and once I got past the shock of his agreeing to dance in public, I was impressed. We'd danced as kids, but he and Noah both had always refused to dance in public.

"Get your ass out here, Dash," I said into the mic. "If Killer can do it, you better too."

People pushed him toward the floor, and Aubrey took his hand and pulled him to them as soon as he was in reach. It stung briefly that she was standing where I once had been with them when we were younger, but it passed in a blink. She was the one for Killer, and she was Noah's friend. She had every right to be there, and I was happy to see the boys both smiling at her.

Killer called, "Hey, *old man!*"

He motioned Echo forward with a sweeping gesture.

Echo shook his head, but Mrs. Evans said something, and when Echo didn't stand, she shrugged and joined her granddaughter on the floor. No one else was ballsy enough to try to convince Echo to go to the floor, and he couldn't very well come up unless he was sure it wouldn't look foolish. Power requires respect.

When the song ended, I said, "One more song . . . just for the lovebirds who prefer something a little slower." I met Echo's gaze again. "Or want an excuse to dance with their ladies."

I turned to the band and said, "Etta James' 'At Last.'"

As the song started, Echo stood and flashed a smile that made him look a lot younger than he was. Mrs. Evans turned to look for him, as if she knew that he'd come to the floor this time. There was something a little heartbreaking at seeing them together. She'd been one of my favorite teachers, and although she'd always paid a little extra attention to Killer, she was a fair teacher, a good one, one who treated her students with respect. I was glad to see her happy, but I was even happier to see Echo smile the way he was as he took her into his arms.

Killer and Aubrey were dancing, and Noah's date was flouncing across the bar even as he was leaving the dance floor. He said something that made her cross her arms over the excessive cleavage she was flashing. I almost felt bad for her. Even though I didn't really want to talk to him, I didn't wish him ill. We were friends before we'd been anything else, and I knew I'd forgive him sooner or later.

I chanced a look at Alamo, whose gaze was fastened on me like he was a starving man. I shivered visibly, and he smiled. Whoever those two girls with him were, they weren't looking at him the way he was looking at me. Maybe they were friends or something. I had never been a jealous or possessive woman, and the flash of it that I'd felt at seeing him burned away in the intensity of how he was looking at me.

Plus, if the girls were here as Alamo's dates, Killer wouldn't have stepped in between Alamo and Noah. Killer might not be all showy about it, but we had been close friends as kids. Now we were rediscovering our old friendship. I wasn't sure who they were or what the deal was with those two, but I knew that Killer wouldn't have walked away if Alamo had disrespected me that way.

Alamo watched me as I sang, and all I could think about was the way we'd kissed after the last time I'd been onstage. I wasn't sure how he'd feel about that sort of thing here in front of the Wolves, and I didn't want to risk rejection in front of them. The safe thing, the wisest thing, was to not do or say anything. I should treat him exactly as I had before. That was the smart plan.

But by the time I finished the song, he was standing in front of the stage. I knew where we were, knew that more eyes were on me now than a moment ago when I was singing.

He held his hand up to me.

I stared at him, frozen as if with stage fright.

"Zoe is my sister," he said softly. "I brought her here because I couldn't *not* see you."

"That isn't . . ." I shook my head. "You don't owe me explanations about who you spend time with."

"What if I want to owe them?"

There was a lot more to that question than I was ready to answer, but I knew what I wanted to say. I couldn't. Knowing everything I did about him, all I wanted was to leap into his arms and say yes to whatever he wanted. I wasn't sure I was ready to risk my heart yet.

I also wasn't sure it was even a choice anymore. I'd realized it when I felt that surge of possessiveness earlier. I might not be ready to admit it aloud, but my heart was already his. It had been before my body was.

Silently I took his hand and stepped down.

"What's it going to be?" he prompted. "Give this a chance, Ellen."

"You're sure?"

"I was sure months ago. I'm *still* sure." He didn't pull me closer, but he wasn't keeping me at arm's length the way Noah always had. It was all but spoken that he wanted to stake a claim . . . Here at Wolves & Whiskey. In front of all and everyone who knew me best.

Unlike when we'd gone to bars for me to sing or when we went riding, this was more than just us. It wasn't like he was declaring me his old lady, but it was a step toward being something other than a secret fling.

I kept his hand in mine as I stepped closer and looked up at him. "I think you ought to kiss me."

He smiled like he'd just been offered a prize, and then he pulled me even closer and kissed me in the middle of the dance floor.

That was it, a statement. It was terrifying to me to do so, but the touch of his lips made me forget that in the next heartbeat. I was his and he was mine. It was that clear . . . to everyone.

When he pulled back, I said, "If we're going to date, I should meet your sister."

Alamo draped his arm around my shoulders and led me to the two girls he'd walked in with.

And I pretended not to see the numerous assessing gazes. It was all manageable. Noah was carefully smiling at us, as if it pained him to do so, but he was determined. Alamo's sister was studying me as we approached, but not with hostility.

All told, it looked like things were going to be better than I could've hoped.

Chapter 28

On Monday I decided to make use of one of the two unexcused absences allowed in my accounting class. As much as it pained me to admit it in public, I was good at accounting, so the absence wouldn't hurt me. It seemed like a contradiction for someone who preferred design and music to excel in accounting, but I'd always had a head for numbers. It was the most practical thing I could do with my life, so I took business classes as a backup plan.

I tucked a few essentials in my bag in preparation, and then I drove to campus like normal.

After I parked, I acted like I had on Friday, ignoring my khaki-clad stalkers and proceeding toward the campus buildings where my classes were held. Today I whispered a silent prayer that I wouldn't run into Noah, Aubrey, or any of my professors—especially the Payroll Accounting one.

I ducked into my building, grateful to have avoided anyone I knew, and then slipped out the side door and headed back to the lot to wait for my stalkers. I figured that once they realized that I'd ducked away they'd come back to the lot to watch my car.

Then I could ask why they were watching me. Admittedly, confrontation wasn't *always* the wisest plan. Perhaps it was a bad plan today too, but it was the easiest way to be sure I got the answers I wanted. Depending on what they had to say, I could go to the Wolves or—hopefully—I could resolve it here on my own without doing that.

I walked toward their car once I hit the lot.

They weren't anywhere in sight, but I had time and patience enough for this part. I figured they had an alarm, though, so I was hoping that my next action would yield results. I found their car, which stood out in the community college lot, and hip-checked it. As far as plans went, it was pretty basic, but "sound an alarm to summon idiots" seemed just about complex enough for the jackasses who'd been following me.

I slung my bag over my shoulder, hopped up on the hood of their car—and waited. It wasn't uncomfortable, and I liked that I could watch for their approach. Once I was comfortable, aside from wincing at the car alarm, I settled my open-topped bag in my lap for easy access.

It didn't take even five minutes for them to come into the lot.

Shorter Khaki was talking to Khaki in Charge, hands gesturing broadly as he spoke. I could tell the exact moment that they spotted me because those wildly waving hands stilled, right hand mid-gesture.

They silenced the alarm.

I waved at them with one hand. My other hand was half in the top of my bag so I could hold my phone. It was subtle enough with the way I was seated that it could look like I was just resting my hand there, not that I was poised to send a text for help.

For several moments, they simply stared at me. There was no readable expression, no words, nothing that gave a clue as to what they'd do next. Then Khaki in Charge smiled in a way that made me think this might have been a very bad idea.

He walked confidently toward me. Shorter Khaki hung back. It was the sort of natural routine that spoke of a history of a predator and a vulture. Khaki in Charge would take down the prey, and Shorter Khaki would wait for the leavings. I wasn't sure if that meant actual threat of injury or if their routine was more of a "collect one-nighters" sort of bad behavior. Either way, they triggered the primal alarms that almost every woman has when faced with these sort of men. They didn't mean to do well by me; that much was increasingly clear.

It wasn't the answer I'd been hoping to find, but my

recon experiment had already told me that this was a situation that required backup. I might want to handle things on my own, but I wasn't going to do so if it caused *more* problems for my Wolf family. The question was whether I should call for help or run. I slid my hand farther into my bag, feeling for the right place to press to hit SEND.

"I saw you," I said as he approached, trying to make him look at my face instead of my hands.

"Saw me?" Khaki in Charge echoed.

"Watching me." I looked past him to be sure that I could track Shorter Khaki too. He hadn't moved, standing back half awkwardly like he wasn't sure whether to stay or go.

Khaki in Charge smiled. "You're a pretty girl. Men must watch you all the time."

Appealing to vanity wasn't a bad strategy, but I wasn't as stupid as he was obviously assuming. Honestly, I'd guess that *most* women weren't so foolish as to fall for empty praise from a guy who set off warnings. My guess was that if he got anywhere, it was by way of his wealth. Maybe that and dulled senses from a couple of drinks would make a woman ignore that tickle that had already started to cue that flight was a wise choice.

I said nothing.

"Do you have class today?" Khaki in Charge asked, although we both knew that answer.

"I do, but there was this nicely dressed man watching me pretty seriously on Friday, so I thought I'd pause here and ask why." I was still keeping my voice light enough that it could be mistaken for flirtatious. I didn't know if he was buying it, but straight-out confrontational—which had been my preferred plan—seemed unwise now that I'd met him.

"I'm Jason Worthington, by the way."

"Angel," I lied.

"Really?" Jason said.

"You doubt me?" I smiled lightly.

Jason's companion snorted and muttered something I didn't hear. I doubted it was anything I *wanted* to hear though. They were slime. That much was obvious by the way they looked at me, and that was after the host of facts already lined up against them.

"You think he'll be more willing to face just two of us?" Jason's cohort asked. "He thought he was so smart coming up here, but it only took a few incentives for us to find people willing to watch for him. Those patches on his coat made it pretty obvious where he'd run. Narrow in on the 'chapters' of that gang."

"They're not a gang," I snapped at Shorter Sleaze.

Jason laughed. "So you're not so sold on him that you can keep your mouth shut about him, but not about the thugs."

Shorter Sleaze nudged Jason. "You know that whores with bikers are passed around like a bowl of chips."

I pushed SEND on my prewritten text message, wishing I could amend it with the few things I'd learned. Whoever these guys were, they were here to find Alamo. I hated summoning him to trouble, but I was feeling increasingly cornered.

"Maybe I should go." I started to slide off the car, but Shorter Sleaze lunged and grabbed my arm.

I struggled, stomping on his foot and then kicking back at his shins. I jabbed my elbow into his gut as hard as I could. He let out a grunt and released me.

Before I made it more than a few steps, my knee gave as Jason kicked me from behind.

"Now now, *Angel*," he said as he stomped on my ankle. "The spic seemed awfully protective of you, so I'd rather you don't go just yet."

The pain in my ankle was a fairly good indicator that I wasn't likely to be able to run if I managed to get to my feet, but being on the ground wasn't a safe plan either. On the other hand, I was in the school lot. Screaming seemed pretty girlie, but better to resort to the girlie ploys than to end up in a bad way.

I opened my mouth, and Shorter Sleaze kicked me hard enough that I gasped for air, choking my scream until it was more of an abbreviated yelp. He jerked me to my feet by one arm, and I discovered that putting any weight on my ankle was not a good plan.

"Your mutt put me in the hospital," Jason said as he stepped closer to me. "Some little bit of trash went whining because she changed her mind, and he showed up and beat me. I could've put him in jail."

The temper that threatened to boil over was vying with

the increasing urge to vomit from the pain in my throbbing ankle. Jason shook me, and I put my foot down hard. That was it. The puke won. I turned my head and vomited all over Shorter Sleaze.

For a moment, Jason stared at me, and then he laughed.

Shorter Sleaze looked like his whole lifetime's tempers erupted in one instant. He balled up his fist and raised it, but it wasn't his laughing friend he hit. He punched me in the face—which made Jason laugh harder.

After a moment, he looked at his friend. "You can't get in my car like that. Call a cab."

Then he dragged me to his back passenger car door, opened it, and shoved me inside. "Don't spew in my car," he said, and then he slammed the door and walked around to the front.

My purse was still on the ground outside the car, and I felt like my face and leg were both thumping in time with my racing heart. I had severely overestimated myself, and underestimated the uptown asshole who was apparently kidnapping me.

He climbed in the front seat.

"You need to let me out and just drive away," I warned him.

"Or what?"

"I was raised by bikers. Do you honestly think this is a good idea?" I blinked against the new tide of nausea.

"He put me in the hospital, and I couldn't press charges because of the little whore who got cold feet," Jason snapped. "Díaz owes me."

"The Wolves protect their own," I said, both trying to buy time and trying to head off the shit storm that would come if he hurt me any further. It might already be too late to stop retribution, but I wasn't interested in any of my family seeing jail time over this.

Jason said nothing else. He simply started the car and pulled out of the lot, leaving his friend behind and taking me God only knew where.

Chapter 29

ALAMO WAS TRYING TO FIX THE HEAP OF A CAR THAT Killer's woman had bought, but when he got Ellen's text, he thought he was going to snap his phone in his bare hands. He dropped the wrench in his hand.

"Killer!"

"What the . . ." Killer's words faded as he glanced at his own phone. "She's an idiot."

Alamo was already snatching his keys up.

"I'll call Dad, and—" Killer's words died as his phone rang. He answered, "Yeah, I saw it. Where are you? . . . Meet you there."

There were times when planning wasn't Alamo's strong suit, not a lot of them, but that happened. Zoe and Ana came to the door. “Stay in the goddamn house. There’s a gun in the top drawer. No one in unless it’s Ellen or a Wolf. Got it?”

“What’s . . .” The rest of Zoe’s words faded as she looked at Killer. “Fine.”

Killer pulled out his gun, checked the clip, and stalked toward his bike. He threw a leg over it as he spoke into the phone he now had at his ear. “Echo, yeah. It’s Ellie. School lot. That’s all I know. She sent the guy’s plate number. Dash sent it to Mike, so everyone should have it. We’re moving.”

“Stay in the house, Zoe.” Alamo repeated as he went to his Harley.

Then he was on his bike and moving. He hated to snap at her, and he hated scaring her, but now wasn’t the time to deal with that.

As they rode, he saw more and more Wolves on the road. They all knew who they were looking for, and Alamo had never been so grateful that Ellen was a part of the Wolves family as he was today. He had no idea why anyone would give her shit, but he didn’t care. Whoever they were, they were done. It was that simple.

The next twenty minutes felt like a lifetime, but he wasn’t allowing the thought of what could be happening even to form. Ellen would be safe—and then he’d lock her in the house or at the least send a fucking guard with her if she needed to leave the house.

They were at a light when he felt another text. It wasn't a *red* light, but he didn't care. He stopped. Killer did the same.

"Douche called Jason. Took Ellie to motel out by the old gym."

Before he finished reading the first text from Dash, a second came in: "Beef with Alamo. Bastard limping along the road explained. Meet there."

Dash's text was worse than a fist. Ellen was in danger because of Alamo. He had brought this here, and it was Ellen who was hurt.

"Jason raped Ana, my sister's friend. I put him in the hospital," Alamo said tersely.

All Killer said in reply was "We're closer than Dash is."

And they were off again.

Alamo didn't let thoughts of what could be happening into his mind. Ana had sworn that Jason hadn't been violent, that he'd just gotten her too drunk to move. That awful truth was the only comfort Alamo had. The asshole wasn't violent.

He couldn't let any other thought into his mind.

They were headed toward the motel in question when Killer swerved. Alamo looked to the edge of the road to see Ellen there and Jason Worthington trying to drag her to her feet as she kicked at him with one leg.

The car was on the edge of the road with the rear passenger door and the driver's door both wide open. Seeing the asshole he'd put in the hospital at the start of the year wasn't going to put Alamo in the best of moods whenever it happened, but seeing him touch Ellen was a sure recipe for explosion.

It was a toss-up to see whether Killer or Alamo was off his bike and headed toward them first.

Worthington let go of her, and Ellen pushed to her feet unsteadily.

"Back the fuck up." Alamo glanced at her.

She was limping as she headed toward him. Her clothes looked intact too. He wasn't some caveman who believed a woman was "ruined" if she was assaulted, and he sure as hell didn't think it was ever even a remote possibility that it was a woman's fault if someone hurt her. That didn't take away the fear. He'd seen Ana after Jason raped her. He saw how she still flinched, how she needed to know where the door was, how she scanned crowds and parking lots. It made him livid to even set eyes on the piece of dirt who'd done that to Ana. Knowing that same man had touched Ellen even for a second . . . it did nothing for his self-control.

The roar of several bikes came toward them, but this wasn't Wolf business. This was about Alamo's unfinished business, and it had hurt Ellen.

Worthington opened his mouth to speak, but Alamo's fist was shutting it before a word was said. He honestly didn't know how many times he punched him. He hit and waited to see if Worthington got back up. If he did, Alamo punched him again. If he didn't, he kicked him and ordered, "Stand."

"Alamo!" It was Dash, not Killer, who caught his wrist.

Alamo spun on him.

"Ellen needs a doctor," Dash said carefully, gesturing toward her. She was in Killer's arms.

"Miss Bitty's meeting you at the hospital," Echo said from behind him.

The club president motioned toward a boat of a car, the one Mrs. Evans drove. The older woman was at the wheel now.

"There was an accident," Killer said. "Ellen was hit walking along the road. The driver wasn't here. Just the car."

"Alamo?" Ellen said, pulling him the rest of the way into the moment. "I can't walk to the car."

Carefully he took her from Killer's arms. "I'm so sorry."

"It's fine," she said. "I should've told you that there were people following me."

At that, Echo sighed. "We're going to have a talk when you're healed up, Ellen."

"Yes, sir. I didn't mean to cause trouble and—"

"Losing you would be trouble," Echo said firmly. "Go on with Maureen. I need to see if the boys and I can find the driver of the car that hit you. You didn't see him, did you?"

Ellen glanced at Jason, where he was being pinned to the ground with a boot to his throat. "No, I didn't. I fell and was right there until you all arrived."

Echo nodded. "I expected as much."

A rusted-out truck pulled up, and Jason Worthington yelped something.

"Boys," Echo said.

And then he walked away, leaving several Wolves with one sobbing man. He'd raped and beaten at least one woman and now he'd beat up Ellen. It wasn't a great loss that he'd apparently vanished.

Alamo carried Ellen to the car, and once she was settled in the backseat, Echo rode off in one direction and his old lady drove toward the hospital.

There was a muffled shot a moment later.

"I can check your car, Mrs. Evans. I think it has a backfire problem," Alamo said mildly, offering her an explanation in case she needed one.

Through the rearview mirror, the older woman's gaze fell on Ellen and then she lifted it to meet his eyes. "I guess my hearing's not as good as it once was. I didn't hear a thing."

Chapter 30

Waking up in a hospital bed, even though it was not unexpected after I'd drifted in and out the past few hours, was startling. Mama and Alamo were both there.

"You're going to break my hand, Mama," I said lightly.

She looked down at me. "You're lucky you're too old to take a switch to."

"I love you too," I told her.

"Go call the boys, Alejandro," she ordered. "*Both* of them."

"Yes, ma'am." He leaned down and kissed my forehead. "Do you want me to come back or—"

"Of course I do!" I stared up at him in confusion. "Unless you don't want—"

"Oh, for goodness sake!" Mama snapped. "You, go make those calls and get your ass back in here. You, he wants to be here, but the boy's got a case of the guilt."

I realized what she meant as Alamo's gaze found mine. "It wasn't you that hurt me. Let them know I'm okay and come back? Please?"

He nodded once and slipped out of the room.

The door clicked shut softly, and my mother sighed. "You scared everyone. Echo and the boys were all upset. Big Eddie has been calling like you were his little chickadee."

"He loves you," I told her. "You do know that, right?"

Mama sighed again. "He's too damn young to love me."

I laughed, and then winced because it hurt. "Maybe he was when I was a kid, but he got older."

"So did I." She stroked my face. "Your daddy wouldn't mind me being happy, would he?"

I sniffled. "No, he wouldn't."

"You're grown now," she said. "I wasn't going to have some man around like he was your father, but you're all grown and snagged yourself a Wolf of your own. Maybe I ought to let Big Eddie stay over to keep an eye on me while you're healing up."

"How long am I staying in the hospital?"

She shook her head and said lightly, "You'll be out tomorrow, but Alejandro tells me that he has a nice soft bed on the ground floor and that ankle of yours is busted up."

I laughed despite everything. "You're kicking me out to

shack up with Big Eddie? You *do* realize I knew he was sneaking in since I was a kid."

Mama smacked my shoulder gently. "Don't be silly. I'm kicking you out so you can convince Alejandro not to let guilt make him run."

Tears filled my eyes. I wasn't sure whether they were from amusement or worry or both. Whatever pain medicine they had given me probably wasn't helping matters. "You really are a terribly meddling woman, Mama."

"Meddling would be telling you that I wouldn't let Echo tell you that there was some music manager been pestering me for weeks after hearing you sing," she said primly. "Meddling would be stepping up to the man himself and telling him that if he pressured you to do something you weren't ready to do, I'd sell the damn house and pay him back."

I blinked at her. "What did you say?"

"It's your choice, baby," she murmured. "I didn't know he'd been pulling strings or trying to push you."

There were no words. My mother had tried to push *Echo*. It had to be the pain medicine. Maybe I was sleeping. Subtly I pinched my wrist.

Mama rolled her eyes. "If you want to talk to them, you can, but it needs to be your choice."

I took her hand again and squeezed. "Thank you. I just thought . . ." I didn't know how to say that I thought she wanted me to use my voice for money without sounding rude. So I kept my silence on that. She obviously knew anyhow.

"You're my baby, Ellen. Sing or don't. I just want you to be happy."

"And with Alamo?" I teased.

The door opened and Alamo stepped inside. Mama looked at him, the sort of look that said she was weighing and measuring him like he was a holiday turkey. Then she smiled and said, "He's a fine-looking man, and you watch him like he's a big dessert after a long diet." She shrugged. "Plus, he loves you. He might not know it yet, but he does."

I felt my mouth drop open, but no words came.

Mama stood. "I'll be back in the morning when they release you." She walked up to Alamo and took his arm. She tugged and he leaned down. She kissed his cheek. "You hurt her, and you'll be shy a few parts all men seem to be proud of." Then her gaze dropped to his crotch for several moments too long. She looked back at me. "No nooky till the doctors give the okay, and I'll be asking."

After she walked out, I extended my hand to Alamo. He came to the bed and took my hand. Then he stood there. It wasn't the same sort of comfortable silence we'd shared before.

"It's not your fault," I said.

"He came here to get revenge on me."

"I didn't tell anyone there were strangers watching me."

Alamo frowned. "I didn't tell you why I left Carolina."

"I tried to handle it alone," I added.

He met my gaze, and I stared back at him. After a moment

he sighed, and I said, "How about we agree that we both made a few mistakes and call it done?"

He tensed. "Call what done?"

"The guilt?" I frowned, trying to figure out what I'd missed. I hated pain medicine. It made my thinking slower than I liked. I replayed the words in my head until I realized what he thought. "I'm not done with you, Alamo."

He smiled.

"Plus I can't go home because Mama's finally letting Big Eddie out of the closet," I said bluntly.

"What?"

I half shrugged. "Club secret. He's in love with my mother. She's been pretending they don't end up in bed all the time." My eyes drifted closed. "Now that I'm apparently all settled, possibly with a music manager and a hot Wolf from North Carolina, Mama's letting him out of her closet."

Alamo laughed softly. "Do I know your 'hot Wolf'?"

I smiled but kept my eyes closed. "Shush, I'm dreaming about you."

He laughed again. "I'm not staying in a closet."

I meant to reply, to tell him about the time Mama literally made Eddie go into her closet when she heard me come up the stairs. It was sort of funny. At least it had been when I was a teenager. I laughed every time I saw him for weeks after that, picturing him standing there in the middle of her skirts and purses. We never discussed it. Maybe I'd mention it now that they were about to be official.

"Official," I muttered.

"That's the plan," Alamo said.

I smiled again. That hadn't been what I meant, but I liked the thought of being his old lady. I liked the thought of anything to do with him really.

OF COURSE, THE next day when I was surly from the pain of being jostled on the ride to his house, I was a lot less smiley.

"You're sure you're okay?" Alamo asked for the fourth time. He kept sweeping his gaze over me as if I were going to suddenly manifest new injuries. The line between sweet concern and anxiety-ridden was seeming to blur.

"I'm *fine*."

He brushed my hair back, carefully not touching the swelling around my eye. "I could kill them for touching you."

I caught his hand. "Murder requires Echo's sign-off."

Alamo made a noise that was more growl than word. "Like he wouldn't. You know he was almost as angry as Killer . . . and Dash."

The delay before he could force himself to add Noah's name was to be expected. They hadn't exactly buried the hatchet. I wasn't sure if they would, but I had hopes.

A knock on the door had Alamo tensing.

"Got it," Zoe called out as she sailed through the room. She was a curious mix of temper and tenderness. I wouldn't say that we were done sizing each other up, but right now she seemed to see me as a wounded animal—or more important, a wounded animal that her big brother wanted to protect—so I was seeing the tender side.

"No," she snapped from the doorway. "You cannot come in."

Alamo was up and across the room in a blink.

"Ask Alamo" was the reply from the door. *Noah.*

"It's my home too," Zoe snapped. "I say you're not welcome."

For a moment Alamo paused. Obviously he'd heard enough to know who it was too. He stood out of sight from the door, arms folded, wide smile on his lips. Honestly, it was the most cheerful he'd looked since he'd brought me home. It almost made me want to pretend I didn't realize it was Noah.

"Zoe," I called out.

"Yes?" Her voice was light and chirpy. "Nothing to worry about, just a street peddler. No thank you. No one here needs what you're selling."

I sighed.

"I said I was sorry," Noah snapped. "Ellie? Tell the harpy at the door to let me in."

Alamo rounded the corner. His voice came back. "*What* did you say?"

"I'm not here to start trouble, man. I just wanted to check on Ellie. She's been my best friend for twenty fucking years, and I'm not going to have some jumped-up—"

Slap.

"Noah, please shut your mouth," I called. I pushed myself

off the sofa and started hopping toward the door. It was easier than bending down and grabbing crutches.

At least I thought it was until all three of them came into the room.

"Sit your ass down," Noah said.

Alamo didn't bother with words. He scooped me up carefully and carried me to the sofa.

Zoe smacked Noah's arm again. "You see what you did? She could've fallen." She pulled back to hit him again, and this time he caught her hand in his.

"Do it again, and I'll put you over my knee like the brat you're being," Noah said quietly.

Alamo paused and looked back at them.

"Hey," I whispered, "can you not fight with him? Please?"

Alamo's gaze came to settle on my face.

"I'm yours, but he's still my friend. *Platonic*." I kissed Alamo softly and added, "And she can handle him."

Alamo settled me on the sofa again. He seemed to have let it go, but then he glanced at Noah and Zoe. The frown Alamo got as he looked back at them was not encouraging.

"She's my baby sister," he muttered. Then, louder, he said, "Zoe, can you grab the frozen peas for Ellen. Her eye is swelling again."

Zoe broke off her glaring match with Noah and stomped out of the room. Once she was gone, Alamo leveled a glare at him. "You touch my sister, and I'll break every part of you that even thought of brushing against even *one stray hair* of hers. You hear me?"

"What?" Noah looked thoroughly gobsmacked. "Why would I . . ."

I gestured frantically behind Alamo's back.

Noah amended, "Not that's she not, er, a lovely . . . person."

"She's a fucking angel," Alamo snapped. A cold smile came over him and he added, "And she's off-limits. Under my protection. As in you aren't ever to be alone with her or think about touching her."

Noah laughed. Idiot that he was, he laughed. He was still grinning as Zoe walked back in. His gaze fell on her for a brief moment, and he said, "Not a problem, man. Not a problem at all."

Zoe looked from him to Alamo and back. "I don't even want to know, do I?"

She handed me the peas and walked out of the room without another word. Noah watched her go, and Alamo watched him stare at Zoe. And all I could think was that I was damn glad that she was headed back to North Carolina soon.

GET BETWEEN THE COVERS WITH THE HOTTEST NEW ADULT BOOKS

JENNIFER L. ARMENTROUT

WITH YOU SAGA
Wait for You
Trust in Me
Be with Me
Stay with Me
Fall With Me
Forever with You

NOELLE AUGUST

THE BOOMERANG SERIES
Boomerang
Rebound
Bounce

TESSA BAILEY

BROKE AND BEAUTIFUL SERIES
Chase Me
Need Me
Make Me

CORA CARMACK

Losing It
Keeping Her: A Losing It Novella
Faking It
Finding It
Seeking Her: A Finding It Novella

THE RUSK UNIVERSITY SERIES
All Lined Up
All Broke Down
All Played Out

JAY CROWNOVER

THE MARKED MEN SERIES
Rule
Rome
Rowdy
Jet
Nash
Asa

WELCOME TO THE POINT SERIES
Better When He's Bad
Better When He's Bold
Better When He's Brave

THE SAINTS OF DENVER
Built

RONNIE DOUGLAS

Undaunted
Unruly

SOPHIE JORDAN

THE IVY CHRONICLES
Foreplay
Tease
Wild

MOLLY MCADAMS

From Ashes
Needing Her: A From Ashes Novella

TAKING CHANCES SERIES
Taking Chances
Stealing Harper: A Taking Chances Novella
Trusting Liam

FORGIVING LIES SERIES
Forgiving Lies
Deceiving Lies
Changing Everything

SHARING YOU SERIES
Capturing Peace
Sharing You

THATCH SERIES
Letting Go
To the Stars

CAISEY QUINN

THE NEON DREAMS SERIES
Leaving Amarillo
Loving Dallas
Missing Dixie

JAMIE SHAW

MAYHEM SERIES
Mayhem
Riot
Chaos

Available in Paperback and eBook Wherever Books are Sold
Visit Facebook.com/NewAdultBooks
Twitter.com/BtwnCoversWM

Discover great authors, exclusive offers, and more at hc.com.